White Rose

of

Promise

Chrissy Garwood/Chrisolite Books
29 Weston Hill Road,
Sorell, Tasmania, Australia, 7172
www.chrissygarwood.com

Direct quotations from Scripture are taken from the World Wide Bible (WEB) and are available in the public domain. Other verses are written from memory and are marked CG paraphrase.

Book Layout ©2017 BookDesignTemplates.com

Cover Design: Belinda Pollard

White Rose of Promise/ Chrissy Garwood —1st ed.

ISBN 978-0-6485434-0-4

White Rose
of
Promise

A River Wild Romantic Suspense Novel

Chrissy Garwood

Chrisolite Books
Sorell, Tasmania, Australia

I dedicate this book to my mother and father for fostering in their eldest child the ability to dream. Your guidance and prayers have helped make me the person I am today.

ಔ ✿ ೞ

Contents

CHAPTER 1
(Friday 30th June)

Anticipation –
A Promise Given

❦ ☼ ❧

❦ ☼ ❧

"You're dreaming. Nothing is real."

Even in Ria's dreams, there was no escaping the harsh voice of self-reproach. As she woke, people and places faded, leaving only a certainty she had belonged there. All she could recall was a single long-stemmed white rose, given with a promise. The identity of both promise and giver eluded her now, and remorse tore at her.

A little longer in the dream might have brought Ria enough joy and peace to strengthen her for this new day. She yearned for God to reveal more clues about the fulfilment of His promises. Disappointing days and nights of broken sleep were diminishing her faith.

She heard in her heart the familiar whisper.

Come unto me all who are weary and heavy-laden, and I will give you rest.

I'm sorry Lord. I know You're here with me and this day will be filled with Your presence, but right now I'm not very thankful. Please make me obedient to Your will, and help me find You in the quiet places of my heart. Teach me to be patient, faithful and true to Your calling—

"Ria!" The shrill cry shattered her moment of peace. Ria reluctantly opened her brown eyes to find her niece standing too close to her bed. "Mum said you're driving me to school. I'm going to be late!"

Matilda stood with her hands on her hips, a look of disapproval on her pretty face. She flipped her long blonde hair over her shoulder. The mannerism took Ria back to her childhood mornings. Her sister Sofia had woken her just like this.

But there the similarities ended. Sofia had been dark, curvaceous and easy-to-please. Sofia's daughter was slender and fair with an impatient, unforgiving temper. The dusting of freckles across Matilda's light skin complemented her flashing blue eyes. She must resemble her Scandinavian father, whom Ria had never met.

Enduring the teenager's hostile scrutiny, Ria rummaged through her suitcase. She was tired from the unfamiliar schedule. Late nights at the family restaurant had broken her habit of rising easily with good grace. She mumbled an apology.

"You're not going to wear that!" Matilda snorted with disgust at the unfashionable grey-checked skirt Ria chose. The teenager hurried away as Ria tucked in the equally unflattering shirt. Ria heard her complain to Sofia about the injustice of going out in public with her aunt.

Ria was transported two decades back in time. Then it had been her maiden aunt who disapproved the same suitcase. Zietta Maria had sorted through her clothes, removing anything 'inappropriate'. The list of what was missing afterwards was longer than what remained: no shorts, no trousers, nothing frilly or flirtatious, no colour, nothing that revealed too much skin or accentuated her developing curves. She had been free from her aunt for six months, yet there was still nothing to wear that might brighten her spirit.

Her aunt had even forced her to change her name, mortified that her namesake had brought shame to the family. Under her supervision, the carefree child Maria became the censured and tormented Ria.

When Ria had returned to Melbourne from her twenty-year exile in Sydney, Sofia's gracious offer of hospitality was welcome. But sharing a bedroom with sixteen-year-old Matilda was more complicated than anyone expected.

Have patience. Trust Me. Have I not brought you through the wilderness years and returned you home, as I promised?

Lord, home is nothing like I imagined it would be. I got used to the wilderness, and now I feel as if I'm lost all over again.

I will never leave you nor forsake you. Trust me. Where I am, there is your home. Do you believe this?

You know I do, Lord. But it's so hard! Help me to trust You more. Please forgive my selfishness and my pride, and make it possible for me to serve You.

Fifteen minutes later, Ria drove through the early morning traffic. Matilda sat in petulant silence beside her. Did Matilda know Ria had once been like her – young and confident, certain the life ahead of her was filled with potential? Arriving at their destination, Matilda escaped without a word of thanks.

Grateful for a few minutes of solitude before she returned to Sofia, Ria drove to a nearby park. This place was familiar from her childhood. She took out her well-worn Bible and re-read the passages that had guided her decision to come home. Today a passage from Isaiah 40 captured her heart. Ria claimed the promises, whispering aloud, "Proclaim to her that her hard service has been completed, that her sin has been paid for, that she has received from the Lord's hand double for all her sins."

Surely her years in exile were an adequate penance? She had been faithful and obedient to her older relatives. Forgetful Nonna and her mother's unforgiving sister, Zietta Maria, had reformed her. Father Finnegan, her old parish priest, had told her so and her new Christian friends had agreed. How she hoped it was true that her exile had served a higher purpose, the testing of her heart! She desperately wanted to believe God's compassion had brought her here, not His judgement. Ria prayed to be made worthy to receive His promised blessings.

Of all the Scriptures, Ria identified most with the story of Joseph from Genesis. Betrayed by his family, he was taken far from home. God transformed Joseph's tragedy into a story of victory, complete with a reunion and a family of his own. One verse drew her attention often: "Genesis chapter 50 verse 20: As for you, you meant evil against me, but God meant it for good, to bring to pass, as it is today, to save many people alive".

What had God planned for her future?

Ria acknowledged her loneliness. How often must she push away the thought that God was promising her more?

Ask, and you will receive. Seek and you will find. Knock and the door will be opened to you.

Help me to ask the right questions, to seek the right things. Give me the courage to wait until You open the right door. I want to be patient and obedient. Search my heart and find the hidden things.

I thought I was content with the life You gave me, but now I yearn for something more. Where did this longing come from? If it hasn't come from You, then turn my heart back to Your purpose. Lord, keep me safe and steadfast until You reveal Your plan. I don't want history to repeat itself. You've forgiven my sin and seen my faithful service. Have mercy on me.

In the final moments of solitude, the vision of the white rose came again, and Ria's hope awakened.

Returning to Sofia's home, she found her sister impatient to leave. "There you are, Maria! Papa is expecting us at ten. You know Fridays are our busiest days."

Quickly, Ria readied herself. As Sofia drove, Ria recalled her childhood adoration for her beautiful sister. Three years her elder, Sofia had always been strong-willed and rebellious. Determined to make her own decisions in life and her own choices in love. Ria imagined the family restaurant as Sofia's sanctuary from the storms of life. While Ria was away, her sister had married and divorced twice and was now raising three teenagers on her own. Ria wondered what role Sofia had played in Papa's decision to exile her. This reminded her of the unfulfilled promise of visits from home.

Sofia heard Ria sigh and glanced towards her. "You're not happy."

Lord, I don't want to talk about this with Sofia.

"Maria, you've changed so much," Sofia tried again. "You used to laugh all the time, amusing us with your stories and games. It worries Mama and Papa to see you so sad and withdrawn. You startle at the slightest thing and keep disappearing."

"I'm sorry, Sofia. It's taking me longer to settle than I imagined. Once I have a job and a place of my own, things will be better."

"You don't need a job! There'll always be a place for our Maria in the restaurant. We can get you a little flat, so you don't have to share with Matilda. I know putting up with an emotional teenager is difficult."

Ria tried to explain. "We both know I'm a liability in the restaurant. Your Maria disappeared a long time ago. For twenty years I've been serious, sensible Ria, and I can't find Maria again. I understand Matilda's annoyance about sharing her room, having her life disrupted by a stranger."

"It was hard for you living with Nonna and Zietta Maria all those years?" Sofia asked.

"I learned to think about other people's expectations, and to be more considerate. That makes me a good secretary. I can be efficient and professional in an office, yet in the restaurant..." Ria's voice faded. She had lost her sense of connection with her family. At the restaurant last night she had seen regret in Papa's eyes. Ria had been so confident that the past no longer had any hold over her. How could she have been so wrong?

Ria was immensely relieved when they arrived. Now she could escape her sister's close scrutiny. After greeting her parents she began her assigned tasks. As she carried a tray of glasses from the kitchen, Papa approached her.

"Maria," Benito began, "Father Finnegan phoned from Sydney this morning."

Ria stopped, dreading what might follow. The old priest would only have contacted her family about Zietta Maria.

Her father continued, "He said *Saint Anthony's Retirement Home* want to discuss the extra fees you've been paying for your aunt."

Ria lost her grip on the tray. She gave a desperate cry and fell to her knees. The crash of shattering glass on the unforgiving tiles echoed her anguish. She focused her distress on the broken shards. Had there been a further increase in expenses at her aunt's retirement home? Ria's savings were gone. Despite working every day in the restaurant, she could afford no more.

"Maria! Stop worrying about broken glass and tell me what this phone call is about. Wasn't the sale of Nonna's house enough to pay for *Saint Anthony's*?"

Ria remained on her knees. "It was, but then Zietta Maria decided she needed other things."

"Why didn't you tell us?"

"Six months ago my salary was enough to cover everything. The extra payments have only been a problem since I lost my job."

"You must love your aunt very much."

She couldn't look at him. No-one knew that following Nonna's death her mother's sister had cast Ria out of the house – telling her she was a 'wayward, selfish girl' who had always been an impossible burden.

"Let me clean up!" Sofia muttered, pushing Ria aside. "You've broken a dozen wine glasses. Papa's right. You're a terrible waitress."

Ria's face burned with shame. Her father came to her rescue, inviting her to follow him upstairs to prepare the private function room. Behind her, she heard her mother remonstrating with Sofia for her bluntness.

For Ria, this incident reinforced the urgency of finding more suitable work. Life would be better for everyone.

Count your blessings.

Yes, Lord. Thank You that I have a place to stay, work to keep my hands busy, and all the promises that You will be with me in every situation...

Believing –
A Promise Guarded

ॐ ☼ ঙ

Philippians 4:6-7
Be anxious for nothing, but in everything, by prayer and petition
with thanksgiving, make your requests to God
and the peace of God which surpasses all understanding
will guard your hearts and your thoughts in Christ Jesus.

ॐ ☼ ঙ

Ria accompanied Papa up unfamiliar stairs. So much at *Ristorante di Fontana* had changed, although the decor was the same – red plastered walls hung with Papa's favourite gold-framed Mediterranean scenes. The ground-floor dining room had been enlarged to extend into the neighbouring building. Above the new section, a mezzanine had been built to create this private dining room.

Ria helped Papa push smaller tables together to arrange one long table.

"You didn't ask any questions about Father Finnegan's call," Papa began.

"It could only be bad news."

"Zietta Maria has moved into the High Dependency Unit. The doctors think she has many years ahead of her, but she no longer leaves her room. You should cancel the extra payments you've been making."

"Father Finnegan was very kind to let us know."

Benito seemed to hesitate. This was an awkward conversation – they were still strangers to each other.

He said, "Father Finnegan hoped you would keep in touch after you moved back to Melbourne."

"I will phone him on Sunday afternoon," she promised, turning towards the sideboard. She took out white table linen and silverware.

"Are you going to tell him you've stopped attending Mass? Your Mama's upset because you won't come with the rest of the family."

Ria paused and looked at him. Would he listen to her explanation this time? Benito waited.

"Father Finnegan will understand. Zietta Maria insisted I attend Mass, but I was never welcome. Even though I was part of that congregation for twenty years, no-one came to find out what happened to me after Nonna died. I was on my own for six months, and only Father Finnegan showed any interest. He came despite Zietta Maria's constant litany of my weaknesses and failings. It was Father Finnegan who encouraged me to look for fellowship elsewhere, so he knew that I was attending a contemporary church in Sydney. Finally, I had found a place where people accepted me without prejudice. That's why I searched for a similar church as soon as I arrived here in Melbourne."

Benito seemed surprised by the intensity of her words. Ria bowed her head and practised the quiet humility that Zietta Maria had preferred. Had she revealed too much about her tormented sojourn in Sydney? The awkward silence lengthened.

He glanced at his watch. "I'll go downstairs to fetch the candles and fresh flowers so you can continue here."

Lord, I don't want to upset my parents. Finding this little congregation seems like the only thing I've done right since I came home. If only the new church wasn't so far away, and I could go to Mass first.

Benito returned with renewed determination evident on his face. He smiled at the progress she had made while he was gone.

"We're booked out for the evening. The downstairs restaurant will be very busy. I've decided to give you full responsibility for this dining room tonight."

"But Papa..." she protested, but he would not listen. He launched into an enthusiastic explanation of her assignment.

"We are preparing for a regular booking we have on the final Friday of each month. Sebastian Romano invites his employees to our restaurant for dinner. He's the son of an old friend and a valuable patron. His praise for your Mama's cooking is generous. Indeed, he has not missed a monthly dinner in the past five years. What better way to show appreciation for his loyalty than to have my daughter in charge?"

"Sofia would be much better than me."

"I need her in the main dining room," Papa insisted, his face clouding over. "You'll have your niece to help you. She'll be able to advise you – but that shouldn't be necessary."

Ria was perplexed by Papa's blindness to Matilda's hostility. How would the guests respond if there was an argument between them?

He continued. "Leonardo will be here too, but as one of the guests. He has only good things to say about his new employer."

Why did Papa think another hostile teenager would make the experience easier? She held her tongue. More puzzling was the impression that Papa had heard uncomplimentary comments about Romano. What was her father not telling her?

Papa took her silence as acquiescence. Ria finished the table decorations on her own. Her hands adjusted the short-stemmed blooms in their shallow bowls, while she prayed.

Lord, You know how important this is to Papa, but all I can see is potential for disaster and disappointment.

A sharp pain ripped through her fingers. The white rose centrepiece held hidden thorns and blood dripped onto the tablecloth. A call from below reminded her there was no time to re-dress the table. Lunch guests were arriving. Ria nudged the flower bowl sideways to conceal the stain. This bowl was at the head of the table. The change ruined the aesthetic perfection she had achieved. She frowned at the offending rose. How could a sign of encouragement become another bitter regret?

She hurried downstairs. Sofia demanded an explanation for Ria's need for the first-aid kit. "Did you cut yourself when you broke those glasses?"

"I pricked my finger on a rose thorn," Ria murmured, unsure why her sister was still angry. She had seemed compassionate and caring before they arrived at the restaurant. Was the broken glass one mishap too many?

"You should be more careful. Papa said you're going to be in charge of the upstairs dining room tonight, and you mustn't disappoint him."

An unbidden question came. Was her sister worried about Papa's disappointment? Or was she more concerned about Romano's opinion? Ria assured her sister she would do her best. She longed for her lost delight in the restaurant to return. As a teenager, Ria could transcribe orders with great care. Delivering those precious slips of paper to the kitchen had brought her joy. Under the watchful gaze of her Papa, she had carried laden plates to diners with grace and confidence. Remembering how easy it had been made the present awkwardness more difficult to bear.

The busy lunchtime hours passed with Ria avoiding any further mistakes. Finally, the restaurant closed to allow preparations for the evening ahead. Ria was free to escape to the small office upstairs to finalise the new menus. She was comfortable and self-assured with this task. She had worked in a corporate office from the time she finished school. The documents were printing when her youngest nephew Marco rushed in. Everyone was waiting downstairs for her to join them for a substantial meal. It was customary for staff to eat together before the restaurant opened again for dinner.

Reluctantly, Ria followed Marco downstairs. She smiled when she found herself seated beside him at the crowded table nearest the kitchen. Though only thirteen, he was becoming her best ally, and she took comfort from his presence.

Almost immediately after Papa recited the blessing, Mama turned to Ria. "Maria Evangelina, you must eat more," Mama Rosa insisted, placing a slab of lasagne before her. "You're far too thin. People are talking about you. If only you would take more interest in your appearance. Sofia, why don't you take charge of your sister?"

This would be the last opportunity to eat before closing time, but Ria was not hungry. Moving food around her plate pretending to eat, she reviewed other things Mama had said recently: too serious, too quiet, too timid, too clumsy. The conversation went on around her while Ria's thoughts turned inward. She smiled wryly. How ugly and awkward she felt working alongside her confident, beautiful sister. If only she could hide in the kitchen.

The frantic activity in the kitchen mesmerised her. She felt drawn by the noise, eager to watch Mama Rosa's passionate cooking. All the staff adored her Mama. The years had added weight to her comfortable frame, and a little grey to her black hair. But nothing had diminished her zest for life. She seemed blessed with bountiful energy. She still bustled from one workbench to another, sampling dishes and shouting encouragement. No-one in the kitchen seemed to mind her severe reprimands. There was always a shower of praise when she finally declared their dishes complete.

From an early age, Ria had claimed a food preparation workbench. She still enjoyed helping with simple tasks in the kitchen, but quickly surrendered her place to Marco when he hurried in after school each day. She could not risk jeopardising their developing friendship.

Marco – already tall for thirteen and darkly handsome like Papa – nudged her secretly with his elbow. Papa was talking to her about the coming evening.

"I used to know Romano's father a long time ago," Benito was saying. "We lost contact, but I met Paulo again a few months before he died. He'd seen one of our television advertisements, and believed God wanted him to come and see us. He came to dinner a few times with his sister. Your Mama Rosa didn't like Paulo's sister; she criticised everyone and everything. The sister has just died, so Paulo's son is alone now, with his business and his employees as his adopted family. So it is important we Fontanas always make him welcome."

"Yes, Papa," Ria murmured and looked up to find Matilda glaring at her across the table. Glancing to Sofia, she found another who did not seem pleased.

She looked down at her plate to discover Marco had swapped with her while no-one was looking, and this one was empty. She thanked her nephew with a small smile. Excusing herself from the table, she escaped upstairs to collate the menus.

The familiar task restored her composure. More at peace, Ria picked up the menus. She glanced around the room to make sure nothing was forgotten. Then she caught a glimpse of her reflection in the wall mirror, still where it had been in her childhood. The office/storeroom had once been the bedroom she had shared with Sofia.

Tears pricked her eyes. She was confronted by the woman she had become, so much older in appearance than her thirty-five years. Gone was the smiling dark-haired girl just beginning to blossom. Instead, there stood a thin, austere woman with dark hair pulled back severely from her face. Her critical gaze noted the unflattering white shirt and shapeless knee-length black skirt. These might have been passable in the boardroom but were out of place here. No wonder her Mama kept commenting about her appearance.

The hands on the clock were moving closer to 6 pm. The increasing weight of Papa's expectations fell heavily upon her.

What am I doing here, Lord?

She was certain God would never leave her. He had been a constant source of strength and encouragement while she was in Sydney. So why was she finding it so difficult to trust Him now?

Her sister was calling from below. "Maria Evangelina! Where are the menus?"

Ria visualised Sofia standing at the bottom of the stairs, hands on hips. A thin smile appeared on the reflected face in the mirror. How easily everyone else knew their place in this household. Ria hurried to the narrow stairs.

Laughter floated up to meet her. She could hear her father's booming greeting for old friends who dined with them often. She wasn't sure which unsettled her more – the way the familiar routines had continued without her, or that everyone expected her to step back into her old life?

The restaurant held tightly to tradition. Papa would be taking familiar faces to their usual tables in the older part of the restaurant. He would return to share in their storytelling later in the evening. From her watchful position behind the bar, Sofia would reign over the new dining room.

Her sister's bright, easy laughter often drew admiring glances. Sofia stood with her back to the large mirror, reflected light crowning her dark beauty. Tonight her sister was wearing a colourful off-the-shoulder top which accentuated her curves. Sofia was secure and confident in her role. Papa was always open about his admiration for his gregarious older daughter.

After delivering the new menus to Papa, Ria paused to exchange greetings with his old friends. Then she collected her apron and order book. Sofia was waiting, scanning the dining room. The other waitresses were already circulating among the tables. Each one was wearing a short skirt and bright floral top, with the same small black apron around their waist.

"I've sent Matilda upstairs to check nothing is missing from the table," Sofia began. She directed her critical gaze towards her younger sister. A momentary frown was quickly replaced by a practised smile. Ria was sure this was meant to bestow confidence.

"Now, remember all Papa has told you. No-one is to be kept waiting for their drinks. The guests come separately, so start taking drink orders as each one arrives. Matilda is only assisting, so remember you're in charge. There are twenty-one booked for this evening, which should be manageable, even for you. Papa will bring Romano up. Immediately after Papa finishes introductions, come down. I will have Romano's drink ready for you to collect. After that, Romano will signal you when it's time to order meals." Ria noticed a hardness to her sister's [1]countenance at the mention of Romano's name. But she kept her questions to herself.

Sofia paused as if she had something important she wanted to add. It was unusual for her sister to be reticent. The unspoken message hung ominously in the air between them. Ria grew even more uncomfortable. What other warnings had her sister kept to herself?

"I'd better go then." She broke the lengthening silence, hoping her sister missed the tremor in her voice.

"Don't forget to smile," her sister called after her.

Lord, I feel like I'm walking into the lion's den. Please help me avoid any serious mistakes, and keep me from disappointing Papa.

I am with you always. Rest in Me, and let Me be your confidence. Stay in the peace that I am giving you.

Confidence –
A Promise Hoped For

ஐ ☼ CB

Romans 5:1-4
Being justified by faith, we have peace with God
through Jesus Christ... We rejoice in hope of the glory of God.
Not only this but we also rejoice in our sufferings,
knowing that suffering produces perseverance;
and perseverance, proven character; and proven character, hope.

ஐ ☼ CB

The extended table in the mezzanine dining room was almost full. Surprisingly, Ria kept up with the drink orders. Matilda had vanished, but Ria managed the frequent trips to the bar without mishap. Her sense of accomplishment evaporated when she saw Papa appear in the doorway.

Her father was tall and of generous build. But the man who accompanied him was a head taller and much broader at the shoulders. Sebastian Romano was wearing a black leather jacket and blue denim jeans. His red T-shirt accentuated his bulging muscles. He was heavily tattooed except on his face. A scar on the left side of his forehead drew attention to his dark, hooded eyes. His air of authority stilled all conversation. Even her father seemed under his thrall.

Papa waited while Romano greeted each person before seating himself. Only the man at his right addressed him as anything other than Boss. There were no women at the table, although there were still three empty seats at the far end. One of those must be where her nephew Leonardo would be sitting. Silence fell, and those dark eyes turned towards her.

"Romano, may I introduce my youngest daughter, Maria. She will be taking care of you this evening."

The giant acknowledged her with a nod. Though his mouth formed a small smile, Ria noticed it did not make it to his eyes. There was a cold dismissal in the way he took in her appearance. With a gracious farewell, Papa departed, leaving her standing alone. Ria blinked. Romano must have spoken to her, and her face flushed with embarrassment. Remembering Sofia's instructions, Ria retreated, tripping on the first stair. Regaining her balance, she heard laughter as she fled.

"Another woman who can't wait to escape from you!"

Catching her breath, Ria waited at the side counter. There was a small hatch in the adjacent wall, where she would later leave the meal orders. Sofia was preoccupied, passing her the laden tray and making no comment. Too quickly, Ria found herself ascending the stairs. Her hands were trembling more than usual. With extreme care, she placed the tall glass of beer on the table in front of Romano before retreating to stand against the wall. She devoted all her attention on watching for his next signal.

Voices on the stairs startled her. Leonardo and a red-haired man appeared.

"Thanks for the ride," the man said.

"Anytime, Freddie," Leonardo replied.

They were closely followed by her niece Matilda and the final guest. The latter pair kissed passionately, oblivious to anyone else in the room. Ria wasn't sure what to say or do.

"I've missed you so much!" Matilda exclaimed, and they kissed again.

No-one had warned Ria that Matilda had a boyfriend among the guests. Had that topic been avoided because of Ria's history? Could this be what Sofia had wanted to mention? Did Ria's parents know about Matilda's relationship and did they approve? She blinked and looked away, trying to push these thoughts from her mind.

From the comments around the table, Ria discovered this relationship was not new. She glanced towards Romano. He raised one eyebrow as if to remind her she was in charge, and Ria stepped closer to Matilda and spoke quietly. "Matilda. Could you take the final drink orders for me?"

The hostile look Matilda threw her almost broke Ria's resolve. She forced herself to stand her ground. There was no way she could manage service for this many guests on her own and she had to find a way to make this work. Leonardo came to stand beside Matilda and remonstrated with her. "Remember where you are. Do you want to make a scene and upset your grandfather? You promised Mama!"

Matilda kissed her boyfriend again, and he joined Leonardo at the table. She stepped closer to Ria and hissed: "I'm sick of you. I don't want your approval. I don't care what you think. For all our sakes, go back to the convent you escaped from! You don't belong here, and I want my life back!"

Oh, God! Keep my mouth closed. Don't let me answer her from my own wounded emotions. Be my peace.

My peace is always with you.

Matilda's voice had risen, and all eyes turned towards this unexpected drama. The room quietened in anticipation. The two women stood facing each other, the tension between them obvious. They were the same height, but there was no family resemblance. Matilda's youthful appearance and enthusiasm accentuated the austere darkness of her older relative.

"I'm sorry," Ria apologised before retreating. She looked towards Romano. "I'll go and tell Papa you would like me replaced with another waitress." Without waiting for his reply, Ria turned with a sense of relief.

But the giant at the head of the table called her back. "Maria! We'll order now."

He took command, directing Matilda to the far end of the table. He brought Ria's attention to those closest to him. Ordering progressed quickly. Either everyone was very hungry or the evening would be lengthy. When she had taken all the orders, Romano chose red wine for the table and dismissed her. She visited the small kitchen service hatch, and then, to avoid Matilda, she hid in the hallway leading to the restrooms. When Ria heard Matilda's footsteps heading back up the stairs, she re-emerged to collect the wine from Sofia.

Leonardo and Matilda stood in quiet conversation, their backs turned to the stairs. They were unaware of her return. Ria placed the bottles on the table and began to fill the diners' glasses. Behind her, she could hear Matilda's voice rising again. "All our lives, Mama has been telling us if we didn't behave, she would send us away like Papa Benito did with Maria Evangelina. It was the ultimate punishment, and now here she is! What did I do to deserve this? I'm sick of being told to be quiet, and I don't want to be good! See what being quiet and good has done to her? I would rather be dead than a shrunken old hag like her!"

Looking down, Ria was dismayed at the red stain slowly creeping across the white cloth. She hastily removed her apron to mop up the flow. It felt as if every eye was fixed on her mistake. Seizing the sodden apron, she grabbed her tray and fled.

Sofia heard her running feet. "What have you done now?"

"Why is it always MY fault!" Ria threw her tray and spoiled apron on the counter, and bolted for the rear exit.

"Maria Evangelina! Come back here! Maria! Oh, I don't have time for this."

℘ ✪ ℭ

Romano drained his beer glass and slammed it against the table harder than he intended. An ominous silence fell over the dining room as he pushed back his chair. He needed solitude and strode towards the stairs, cigarettes in his hand.

His employees understood he only smoked when he was angry. It was either that or destroy something in his rage. He had already been stressed over his problems at the workshop. He didn't need to be surrounded by troublesome women. While he was gone, Dave would make sure the mess was cleared away, and Matilda removed.

He stood unnoticed on the stairs, considering his options. All he wanted was to go outside and smoke in peace. If he moved now he could pass by before Sofia saw him. That woman had heard the rumours regarding his criminal connections, and made it clear she thought him unworthy of her father's loyalty. If he was to continue enjoying Benito's hospitality, it was essential to avoid another confrontation with his daughter. Sebastian was not in a suitable mood to control his tongue. He hurried in the same direction that strange waitress had gone, hoping she wasn't outside.

Unfortunately, he found Ria pacing the small courtyard talking to herself. "Please God, don't let me cry. Don't let me cry. Don't let me cry..."

Leaning against the lamppost, he watched her in silence. She looked as if she was in greater need of a cigarette than he was. At the click of his lighter, she turned towards him in alarm. Inhaling deeply, Romano offered her the cigarette packet. She stepped back in horror, sprawling onto the bench near the wall. He laughed at this unexplainable reaction. A small curiosity began to grow. This stranger seemed so out of place in the restaurant. He inhaled again, waiting to see how she would respond.

Had Benito said this awkward little woman was his 'younger' daughter? She looked many years older than Sofia who he knew to be in her late thirties. This new daughter's timidity starkly contrasted with her outspoken, opinionated sibling. Then he remembered the comment Matilda had made about the convent. She must be one of those devout women dedicated to religious piety. That would explain why she was staring at him as if he represented the devil. He had experienced enough of that kind of disapproval from his aunt, and his resentment started to rise. "Of course!" he said into the silence. "You don't smoke."

ℬ ☼ ℭ

Ria didn't hear him. Her mutinous mind transported her back two decades to a meeting with another man. He had worn chef's whites – young and handsome, laughing at her for another reason. She had come outside to take rubbish to the bins hidden behind a screen and hadn't noticed him standing there.

He had a lit cigarette in his hand, and held it out towards her. The younger-self hesitated before approaching him. He brought the offered cigarette to her lips. She had been flattered at his attention and didn't want him to think she was only a child. But the coughing that ensued after one small puff betrayed her. He had reached out, patted her back, then kept his arm around her. Raising the cigarette to his own lips, he inhaled and then kissed her.

This was her first kiss, and she felt the thrill while tasting the bitterness of the smoke. The arm around her tightened, drawing her hard against him, and she pulled back with alarm. Now he was laughing at her shyness. There was something in the way he laughed that made her like him less than she had a moment before.

"Not here, and not now, but soon, little Maria, you're going to be mine. I'm going to awaken the woman in you, and take what I want from you. We both know you will be powerless to resist."

Her tormenter had described his intentions eloquently before he let her go. She had escaped back into the restaurant, her mind filled with turmoil. She trembled at his threatened violence, but he had warned her to keep silent. He was Mama Rosa's favourite apprentice, and everyone thought he was wonderful. The other waitresses daydreamed about him. Had she given him encouragement? He seemed so certain she was powerless to resist him. She felt ashamed at her foolishness.

She never saw him again. Next morning, she awoke to discover Papa had decreed her exile for 'behaving like a prostitute'.

As suddenly as the memories came, Ria dropped back into the present. Romano stood watching her. A single tear trickling down her cheek was the only evidence her heart was breaking all over again. She looked away, embarrassed and ashamed.

Into the tense silence, the pager at her waist buzzed. Brushing her hands down her skirt as if to smooth away the past, Ria stood up. She replaced vulnerable openness with the practised mask of concealment.

"The entrees are ready," she said, turning towards the restaurant.

He watched her go and finished his cigarette. He wasn't sure what he had witnessed. He was slow to realise he wanted answers about this quiet, conflicted woman. His discomfort grew. Circumstances had again conspired to put him in the wrong place at the wrong time. Just once, he would like to be in the right place at the right time.

Declaration –

A Promise Questioned

ଔ ☼ ଔ

Isaiah 61:1b-3
The Lord has sent me to bind up the broken hearted,
to proclaim liberty to captives, and release to those who are bound;
to proclaim the year of the Lord's favour...
to give them beauty for ashes, the oil of joy for mourning,
and the garment of praise for the spirit of heaviness

ଔ ☼ ଔ

Ria believed the worst was over. They had enjoyed their meals, and ordered many more drinks. The mood lightened, making some of the diners more talkative. Romano kept silent watch over the table. He seldom responded to the conversation unless directly addressed. Yet he seemed to be aware of everything that was happening.

As Ria served coffee, an unexpected question was asked.

"Are you really a nun?"

Turning to the questioner, she remembered hearing his name. Dave was seated closest to Romano, and he was fiddling with the floral table arrangement. There was a golden wedding band on his hand. She wondered if he was genuinely interested. He didn't have the same hardness to his expression as his employer. He was waiting for an answer.

"What?" The word was out before she could silence it.

"Matilda said 'go back to your convent', so you're a nun?"

"No," she replied cautiously, remembering she was supposed to be more hospitable. "I'm not a nun. I thought I wanted to be one, but God had another plan."

This topic was so personal she almost forgot where she was and who was watching. How grateful she had been when she first discovered God's acceptance and forgiveness. She had promised to serve God always. Even Zietta Maria had approved of her plan to become a nun, but Father Finnegan had intervened. Instead, she was sent to work for a respectable company.

"What kind of plan?" Dave asked, trying to draw her back from her reverie.

"I'm still waiting to find out," she conceded.

Ria had thought working for that Sydney company was God's ultimate plan. Enrolling in evening classes had brought her a portfolio of excellent qualifications. Finally, she had become personal assistant to one of the company directors. All that had ended suddenly a month ago, and now she was adrift with her future uncertain. This realisation brought her fully back into the room.

"So how long will you have to wait?"

How was she to answer? Dave's persistence was beginning to alarm her. His questions challenged her silence.

"What are you doing here? Where does working in a restaurant come into *God's plan*?"

Hearing her own thoughts spoken aloud by a stranger hurt more than she thought possible. Ria responded with unexpected sarcasm. "What does it look like I'm doing? I'm making a spectacular mess of everything. I used to work in an office, but those skills are redundant here."

"So why did you want to be a nun?" persisted Dave, returning to his original question. She frowned at him, the white rose still in his hand. Why was his persistence making her irritable?

"Why do you think I wanted to be a nun?" she threw back at him, aware that others were listening. She wanted to tell these men to mind their own business.

"Give Dave a proper answer."

Ria wasn't sure who was more surprised at Romano's unexpected interruption. The room fell silent at his stern reprimand. She glared at him, and she saw him acknowledge the sudden heat of her anger. To bring the emotional fire under control, she looked away.

O Lord, I lost my temper, and I'm sorry. Help me to know how to answer this question.

Isaiah 61.

Ria deliberately turned away from Romano. She hoped to lessen her awareness of that man's glaring intensity. She directed her attention to Dave, her heart aching over the white rose in his hand.

"I believed God was calling me to a life of sacrifice. I thought He would send me out into the world to heal the brokenhearted and set the captives free."

"So why didn't you?"

"I was too broken to help anyone else."

"So what happened to break you?" Dave asked.

Ria choked back the tears. She shook her head to indicate she would say no more and started clearing the table.

"What if you had to know you were broken before you were ready to help someone else?" Romano's unexpected words tortured her.

Turning to look at him she cried, "If you know anyone who wants help from a hated old maid let me know! My family will be most relieved to be rid of me!"

Ria snatched up her heavy tray and headed for the stairs.

"Touched a nerve there, Boss," a voice said.

Laughter seemed to follow her as she hurried away. How dare they laugh at her discomfort? Was it not enough that she was upset with her own behaviour? What was it about these men that inspired her uncharacteristic rudeness?

Ria narrowly avoided a collision with Papa on the stairs. He had the bill in his hand.

"Everything went well?" Papa asked and she mumbled a reply, pretending the tray was heavier than it was and hurrying past. Sofia was watching from behind the bar where she served customers their final drinks. Most of the downstairs diners had departed, and the lights had been turned down low. Ria took Papa's arrival as permission to surrender her responsibility.

In the kitchen, all was relatively quiet. Mama Rosa was sitting at a corner workbench sharing coffee with the other chefs. They were discussing tomorrow's schedule. Marco and the younger kitchen hands were energetically loading and unloading the dishwasher. Ria carried her tray over there and started to help. She would hide here until the upstairs guests had departed.

"Maria Evangelina! What are you doing in here?" Sofia stormed across the kitchen, grabbed Ria by the arm and propelled her across the room. Everyone turned towards her, and the colour drained from her face.

"Romano isn't leaving until he talks to you," her sister hissed. "Papa's embarrassed. What have you done? I told you to be careful. Romano isn't someone to cross!"

Lord, I can't seem to do anything right. Please forgive my selfishness and help me to make amends.

Sofia continued to scold Ria all the way to where Papa and Romano were talking near the bar.

"Ah, there you are Maria Evangelina," Papa exclaimed.

"I'll talk to her alone," Romano commanded. He gestured for her to come with him into the shadows.

"Maria Evangelina is a name that comes with great expectations," he growled. She couldn't tell if he had taken offence or was making fun of her. His use of her full name made her even more uneasy. "Were you avoiding me? Your Papa has asked me to give you a chance to redeem yourself."

She started to apologise. Romano impatiently silenced her with the wave of his hand. "Shut up and listen. Do you have office skills? I'm looking for a new office manager. The agency sends silly girls who are too easily intimidated. Come for an interview tomorrow and bring your resumé. Here's the address."

Cautiously, Ria accepted his business card. "Your father has already given his consent." Before she could respond, he walked away. "Don't be late," he called back over his shoulder, and she watched him leave.

"What was that about?" Sofia demanded, drawing Ria back into the light. Her sister's expression changed from anger to dismay, perhaps because of the hope on Ria's face.

"I think he offered me a job."

CHAPTER 5
(Saturday 1st July)

Examination –
A Promise Tested

଼ ☼ ଽ

Psalm 25:12b-15

Who fears the Lord? He shall instruct him in the way that he shall choose. His soul shall dwell at ease. His offspring shall inherit the land. The friendship of the Lord is with those who fear him. He will show them his covenant. My eyes are ever on the Lord, for he will pluck my feet out of the net.

଼ ☼ ଽ

Ria had arrived forty-five minutes early and already walked up and down both sides of the street. Now she stood on the opposite footpath, outside the multi-level shopping complex. Between her and her destiny was a four-lane thoroughfare. Pacing to and fro, indecision tortured her. Should she wait until noon or try the door again? As she paced, the nearby traffic lights synchronised with her mood, alternating between 'Go' and 'No'.

The *Romano* building was more impressive than she had expected. The distinctive double-storey brick complex had a black facade. It looked more industrial than anywhere she might be comfortable working. Six double roller doors, side by side, stretched halfway down the city block. Each displayed the red sports car logo with *Romano* text. The towering concrete walls, topped with wire-reinforced glass panels, appeared impregnable. The only disruption at street level was a single window. An intimidating security grill obscured the interior. Beside the window, painted directly onto the surface of a metal door, was the declaration: 'Reception. 8:30 am – 5:30 pm. Monday – Friday'. The upper section of the building was constructed of smoky glass – small square panels covered with reinforced mesh.

Adjacent to the black building was a private car park and a petrol station with a tow truck parked beside it. Each bore the *Romano* legend. Earlier, Ria had gone to the petrol station to purchase a bottle of water, and recognised the man behind the counter from last night's dinner. He greeted her by name. His nametag read 'Freddie'. He wore a red polo shirt embroidered with the *Romano* logo. She contemplated whether he felt branded wearing that uniform. Would Romano expect to have propriety rights over his employees? Did he direct them to come and go at his bidding? This train of thought troubled her.

Looking at her watch, Ria realised she must wait another fifteen minutes. Retrieving the business card from her bag, she studied it carefully. The reverse side bore a handwritten message: 'Noon Saturday', a phone number and a large letter 'S'. Ria confirmed the number she had programmed into her phone, then pressed the call button.

ᘒ ☼ ᘓ

Romano watched her from his upstairs' vantage point but didn't respond to the ringing phone in his pocket. This morning, he realised he shouldn't have invited her here while he was alone in the building, but he always found it hard to admit an error.

The simple tests he had devised for the agency girls should suffice. First, he wanted to see whether she resumed her pacing. Her nervousness was plain. What would it take to make her flee?

🕮 ☼ ꥠ

Ten minutes later, the phone in her hand buzzed with an incoming call. Ria glanced at the screen and then across at the building. "Hello?" she asked tentatively. Did he know she was already here?

"I have released the door locks, so come in now. Do you have a problem with dogs?"

"No-o." Could he detect her uncertainty?

"Good." That single word terminated the call, leaving her staring at the silent phone.

Lord, why is he asking about dogs? Something isn't right. I don't feel safe.

Even when you stand in the Valley of Shadows, fear no evil.

Stand, Lord? Stand in the Valley? Shouldn't it be 'walk in the Valley'? Why do I need to stand?

Stand firm and put your trust in Me.

Lord, I'm afraid. Please help me stand firm. Thank You for promising You'll never leave me nor forsake me. Thank You for going with me into this Valley of Shadows.

I am always with you. Stand firm and trust Me.

Carefully crossing the street at the lights, Ria found the heavy door opened effortlessly. She took a deep breath and stepped inside. A loud buzzer sounded. With a definitive click, the door relocked behind her. She fought the urge to test whether she could open it again. Instead, she scanned the bright space before her, immediately noticing a security camera. Was he watching her, taking note of her hesitation?

An imposing wooden counter set in a white wall divided the reception area. Two glass-topped doors, side by side, were labelled "Staff Only". A third door led to a visitor's restroom. On the other side of the counter were two large desks. One had a book spread open on the polished surface beside a multi-line phone console. The crowded second desk sat at right angles to the first. She identified several computer monitors, keyboards and other electronic equipment. A large bank of filing cabinets lined the rear wall.

Should she go further in, or wait? Beneath the window behind her were two black leather couches. But the instruction to stand firm kept her on her feet.

Her nervousness increased as the delay in his coming unravelled her fragile composure. Then frenzied barking disrupted the silence. More than one dog was approaching! Two of the largest black dogs she had ever seen appeared on the other side of the counter. Tan markings on their faces accentuated their fierceness. Their barking intensified when they saw her. Ria quaked at the sight of their bulging eyes, sharp white teeth and snapping jaws. Both of them were jumping so high she expected them to leap over the counter at any moment. She tore her eyes from the ferocious dogs and a cold chill washed over her. Romano stood scrutinizing her and she longed for somewhere to hide.

Stand firm. Don't back down or turn away.

"This is Tiny," he said seizing a red collar, drawing one excited dog to him. He made a big show of grabbing for the other animal. "And this is Fifi." Ria stared at the way this powerful man struggled to control both dogs. If they were so dangerous, why would he bring them to meet her? This must be a test! Noting the dogs' diminutive names, Ria decided this man had a wicked sense of humour.

"Hello, Tiny," she said and forced herself to greet the other one. "Hello, Fifi."

He laughed before shouting, "Friend! Play!"

Without further warning, Romano released Tiny. With a clatter of claws, the huge dog leapt over the expansive counter. Ria screamed. Tiny sniffed and nuzzled at the hands she put up to defend herself. The animal leapt up, placing both front paws on Ria's shoulders and licked her face with its coarse tongue. Fifi was quick to join in the fun, and Ria found herself battling to stay upright in the crowded space. The energetic pair forced her retreat until she leaned against the entrance door. Determined not to give in to panic, she crossed her arms over her chest and pushed forward. As she extended her arms, both dogs backed away. Their unexpected obedience surprised her. How easily the powerful animals retreated! Instinctively, Ria patted each of them to show her gratitude. "Good dogs. Down, Tiny. Down, Fifi. Stop licking me. I've had enough!"

Turning her eyes back to their master, she declared, "Mr Romano, that was mean."

"Dogs are a very good judge of character." Ria's eyes widened. He laughed again, opening the door so she could enter the office. "No-one calls me Mister. I prefer Boss."

"I'm not comfortable calling you Boss when I don't work for you."

"Then call me Sebastian," he challenged her. She held her breath. Not even her father dared address him by his Christian name.

Romano reached into a jar on the counter and tossed dog treats to the excited animals. Ria watched in fascination as they snatched the biscuits from the air. The dogs devoured them with a snap of their fierce jaws. "Don't let their greeting fool you. If I hadn't identified you as Friend, you would have been in trouble."

She looked down at the dogs, now on either side of her. They nudged her closer to him. "I'm not in trouble now?"

Her discomfort amused him. Now she was more afraid of him than of the dogs.

"Perfectly safe," he mocked her, sitting down behind the first wooden desk.

He leaned over and pulled across a wheeled chair from the other desk. Cautiously sitting, she found her feet couldn't touch the floor. Without a word, he forcefully adjusted the chair. The seat lurched down into a lower position. Tiny came to lie at her feet, while Fifi took up a watchful position between Ria and the door. Now it was impossible for her to move without his permission. This was not going to be an ordinary interview! Tiny sensed her disquiet and snarled.

"Good dog," she murmured, leaning forward and scratching the animal behind the ear. Tiny settled down again contentedly. Fifi snuffled forward, not wanting to miss out, and Ria had to scratch the second dog as well.

"You brought your resumé?"

She took the folded two-page document from her well-worn handbag. He silently read the typed information. This provided her with an opportunity to study him.

He seemed even larger and more muscular than he had the evening before. This time he wore a plain black T-shirt and blue jeans with black leather work boots. She studied the intricate patterns tattooed on the arm closest to her. A tombstone design captured her attention. It included a six-digit number and two dates, twenty years apart. The latter date was six years ago, and she did some mental calculations. For the earlier date, she would have been a carefree nine-year-old. Had he ever been carefree?

"What are you doing here?" his angry voice broke into her thoughts and her face reddened at his disapproval. Tiny growled again.

"I need a job."

He waved her resumé in her face. "With these qualifications, you should be working in the city centre."

"This is my first interview in three weeks," she explained, fighting back tears. "I've put my name down with four agencies and sent off applications for dozens of jobs. The last agency said I was overqualified and should ask people I know to recommend me. Apart from the restaurant, I don't know anyone here." Somehow the recent excitement made it impossible for her to conceal her emotions. These past few weeks had been difficult. To her embarrassment, this stranger could evoke a response she had managed to hide from her family. What would he think of her tearful reaction?

"Why didn't you stay where you were?"

Again the accusation stung. "God told me it was time to come home."

He inhaled, and the muscles in his arms tightened as he clenched his fists, her resumé crumpling in his hands. "Do you always do what God says?" he demanded, and both Tiny and Fifi raised their heads and became alert.

"I find it's the easiest way forward." She was careful to meet his intense gaze while trying to stay calm.

He studied her intently, before turning his attention back to her resumé. With her heart pounding, she waited for his response. Her palms began to perspire, and she rubbed her hands on her clothes. Now she began to doubt the prudence of wearing the same skirt and a similar shirt to the one she had worn last night. Mama had wanted her to borrow something more casual from Sofia. Ria didn't want her physical appearance to have any impact on his decision. She even wore her hair in the usual unflattering style. He had already seen her like this.

Her choice was also practical. She would return to the restaurant when the interview was over. She had taken the train instead of borrowing her sister's car, saying she wanted to know the travel time. Glancing at her watch, she tried to calculate how long she had before the next train. The station was two blocks away.

"It says here you've only worked for one company. For the last ten years, you were personal assistant to a company director."

"I've listed Mr Williams as one of my referees. He was the second person I worked for. Each time he was promoted, he took me with him. I have a written reference if you'd like to see it?"

He eyed her with suspicion, taking the second document. "How old were you when you started working for him?"

"I'd just turned nineteen."

"Were you sleeping with him?"

"No!" she cried in alarm.

"You can see how it looks," he remarked sceptically.

"And you can see how I look!" she retaliated, the flash of temper lighting up her eyes and animating her face. "My relatives wouldn't let me out of the house if there was any hint of that!"

Romano turned towards a row of framed photos on the wall beside him. He took one down and handed it to her. "This is my father when he bought this building. The woman standing beside him is his sister. Apart from Dad, she's the only family I had. She sat at this desk for twenty-six years, running the business and making life miserable for everyone. Aunt Constance blamed me for everything. From my father's decision to move to Melbourne to her remaining single all her life. She especially blamed me for my father's premature death eight years ago. She said I'd brought only trouble and disgrace to the family."

Ria examined the photo and saw a striking resemblance between his aunt and her own. She waited. Her personal pain stirred within her in unanticipated empathy, and she looked up at him. Unexpectedly, he banged his fist on the desk. Both dogs jumped up and barked. He signalled to them with his hand to regain control and they lay down. There was bitterness in his revelation. "I'm finally free of her constant criticism only to discover I can't manage without her!"

"Which is why I'm here, Sebastian," Ria suggested hopefully. His name felt strange on her tongue. She was uncomfortable with the familiarity but couldn't bring herself to call him 'Boss'. Now she had begun, she forced herself to continue before her boldness evaporated. "You can replace your old aunt with someone else's old aunt, and solve everyone's problems. I won't have any reason to criticise you, and you can get me out of my family's restaurant so I won't be there to annoy them."

He laughed harshly at her frankness. Instead of taking offence a new determination awakened in her heart. It became essential to show him she was suitable for the job.

CHAPTER 6
(Saturday 1st July)

Faithful –
A Promise of Provision

ঠ ✡ ଓ

Psalm 23:1-3
The Lord is my shepherd: I shall lack nothing.
He makes me lie down in green pastures.
He leads me beside still waters. He restores my soul.
He guides me in the paths of righteousness for His name's sake.

ঠ ✡ ଓ

"What do you know about running an automotive business?"

"Absolutely nothing," Ria admitted, "but I'm willing to learn."

"Come into the workshop."

Clearly, Sebastian wasn't finished testing her yet. The dogs went ahead through a connecting door into a large space open to the roof. Immediately, Ria's senses were assaulted by unfamiliar sights and smells. She had stepped from the familiar office into a foreign and expansive land. Ria stood and stared around her, trying to make sense of it all. He was in no hurry to lead her further in.

Sunlight streamed into the massive workshop through a series of skylights. Huge electric lights hung from the heavy metal girders. These massive beams formed the supportive skeleton for the roof. Metal chains and other unrecognisable gear hung everywhere, creating a labyrinth of obstacles. An enclosed structure formed the ground and upper floors, on the office side. These rooms continued across the distant rear wall. Tracing the outline of the upper windows was an impossibly-high metal walkway.

Closest to the office, there was a white internal wall with more doors. He pointed to those doors. "Those are the staff facilities: the break room, locker and shower room, a weights gym, plus the industrial laundry and clean-up room. We will look at those later."

Sebastian turned to a metal staircase closest to the office door. He signalled silently to the dogs and Ria watched them hurry away into the maze. Tiny gave a bark, and the pair wove in and out of the shadowy distance until they disappeared. "Hunting rats."

She wasn't sure if Sebastian was trying to frighten her, but she was determined not to ask him. He signalled her toward the stairs in the same manner. This confirmed her fear that he expected her to exhibit a similar kind of obedience.

The stairs were wide enough for two people to walk side-by-side. Yet this intimidating man had her pressed close against the narrow handrail. This allowed her a good view of the precipitous drop. Another test? She held onto the rail tightly, baffled by a strange, lightheaded sensation. Height had never been unsettling. Was she afflicted by his threatening presence?

At the top of the stairs, the walkway turned to follow the outline of the building. Directly above the office, there was an open doorway. Sebastian stepped inside. One light after another came on to reveal a massive storage room. The deep shelves overflowed with boxes. The facing wall was bright with natural light from the windows. At regular intervals, clipboards were suspended from metal hooks at shoulder height. He reached for the closest one, passing it to her. The top sheet had a descriptive heading that matched the handwritten shelf label. The sheet was filled with unfamiliar names. All handwritten, with sizes and quantities in different columns. There were spaces for comments as items were used and replaced. The completed sheets underneath were stained with dark oily finger marks.

"Do you think you can keep track of all this?" he asked.

Looking again at the clipboard and then along the shelves to the distant end, she hesitated. "Is this information also in a database, or is this a manual system?"

"Manual, as in everything on paper?" he laughed sarcastically. "Aunt Constance didn't trust computers. I had to do the online ordering myself. Those filing cabinets in the office are full of paper. Boxes of previous years' records are stashed on the top shelves in every storeroom. Are you sure you want this job?"

She looked directly at him and took a deep breath. Ria knew she was qualified for this. Now she must show him she wasn't intimidated by the immensity of the task.

"Will you prioritise what you want, and leave me to work out the best way to achieve it? It's going to take months to introduce the kind of change you need. Do you have a portable scanner with Bluetooth connectivity?"

"No, but if that's what it takes to make Maria Evangelina happy, then I'll get one."

"Don't call me that. Please call me Ria."

"I'll call you whatever I want."

She looked intently at him trying to determine whether he was serious. How could she work for such a dictator? Afraid she might say something she would later regret, Ria turned away. Carefully placing the clipboard on the hook, she walked to the doorway and stepped out.

Lord, this man makes me so angry. Please forgive my wounded pride and my selfishness. Please help me to make amends, and keep me humble.

Blessed are the peacemakers...

Pausing on the walkway, she placed both hands on the rail and looked down over the workshop. She marvelled at the immensity of his domain. From this new vantage point, she had a clearer view of the paired workstations. Each one was matched to large shelves filled with heavy metal boxes and other equipment. Banks of electronics and racks of tools were neatly arranged at intervals behind the workstations in parallel to the doors. Towards the rear, she could see another roller door set in the side wall that might lead out to the car park.

At his approach, the metal beneath her feet shook. Too soon, he was standing beside her. Waves of dizziness washed over her, and she fought to stay calm. "I'm sorry," she said, her white knuckles gripping the rail. "That was impolite, and I apologise. Did your father build all this?"

"Dad sent me regular updates while I was in prison. He knew it was going to be difficult for me to rebuild my life when I got out."

"He must have loved you very much," Ria said, waiting to see if he would say more. This was the first mention of prison, and she was shaken by the revelation. Was this what Sofia had wanted to tell her last evening? Was Sebastian Romano even more dangerous than he appeared?

ॐ ☼ ☪

He was astonished by how easy it was to talk to her. His usual reticence had vanished. "When Dad arrived, he bought a large allotment, knowing the land would go up in value as the city expanded. Selling some to the shopping centre developers allowed him to pay off all his loans. Dad invested the surplus money well. After he died, Aunt Constance kept the business running in his memory.

"If Dad did everything for love, then she resented me even more because of it. Aunt Constance was convinced I'd squander his millions, so I set out to prove her wrong. I extended the car park, built the petrol station, and upgraded the workshop. The car park and the petrol station are very profitable. But Aunt Constance refused to acknowledge my success."

He led her along the walkway, passing other staircases. He pointed out the different workstations, detailing their purposes. She continued to surprise him with her intelligent comments and insightful questions.

He pointed out the door towards the rear on the ground floor which led out to the dogs' exercise yard and kennels. It was next to the storeroom where the tyres were efficiently sorted into tall towers. A separate area was set aside for the auto electricians. *Romano* also offered bodywork repairs and customised specialty services. If she came to work for him, she would be kept busy. From their vantage point, they could see eight courtesy cars parked near the side roller door. There were other parked cars. He pointed out one draped with heavy canvas.

"When I got out of prison that was the first thing Dave showed me. You said my Dad loved me. The car under that canvas is better evidence than all of this. When I was a boy I wanted to own a Maserati. Dad bought a 1962 model, an insurance write-off. He sourced the parts needed to repair it. They were stored for my arrival, so I had a project to occupy my time. After six years, it's finally ready to be inspected. I should have it on the road next week. That car is worth more than a million dollars. That's one reason I have security cameras around the workshop, and why the dogs are here. No-one can enter the workshop without triggering a notification to my phone. I can access the live feed from the cameras no matter where I am."

He directed her attention to the strategic cameras located within the workshop. "There is a monitor in the office, and the live feed is saved to a hard drive. I learned in prison to always watch my back, to expect trouble. I can never be too careful." He looked pointedly at her. "I have a security firm on permanent standby. So far I've been lucky, but all the tools and equipment are worth a lot of money. So I do what is necessary to keep everything safe."

"You said Dave was here when you came out of prison. It must have helped to have someone who knew your Dad well?"

"Dave and I went to school together, and our fathers were work colleagues. When Dad talked about the move and what he had planned, Dave asked if he could come with him.

"Dave has four brothers, so there was no real prospect for him in his own family business. He says he has no regrets. I've offered him shares in *Romano*, on top of the generous salary he negotiated with Dad. But Dave said he preferred to have a cash payment so he could buy his wife a big house. I also pay his three children's private school fees."

They continued along the walkway, arriving at the extensive second-floor structure above the rear storerooms. The long white wall had curtained windows and only one door. Outside the door, the walkway widened to create a platform and the practical handrail became an intricately patterned mesh enclosure.

"Another storeroom?" she asked.

He reached out to open the door. Inviting her into his private domain had never been his intention, but he still knew nothing about her. Perhaps this unexpected opportunity would help him decide whether he wanted her to stay or go.

"This is where I live," he said ushering her inside. "Can I get you something to drink? I can offer you a beer, red wine or whisky? Oh, that's right, you don't drink."

"Who told you I don't drink?"

Again he heard the hint of confusion in her voice. She was standing inside the threshold of the still-open door. They were in his large modern kitchen, with the lounge room visible through a wide archway. He strode to the refrigerator. Turning back towards her, he raised an eyebrow and held out a bottle of beer.

"I'm going to say no anyway. I shouldn't be here. I'm supposed to be back at the restaurant soon." She looked at her watch again. "There's a train in fifteen minutes. Do you think this interview will be over before then?"

Her response irritated him. "You came by train? You don't drive?"

She smiled hesitantly. "The company I worked for paid for me to learn, and I sometimes borrowed a company car. I couldn't afford my own."

"Why couldn't you afford your own car? You worked for a big company. What did you do with your money?"

He was annoyed to hear a hint of Aunt Constance's criticism in his hasty remark. Was he worried about what he might discover? Until now he had been sure the hard years in prison had made him master over all emotions, except his anger.

"All my money went to Nonna. I had a small allowance. Zietta Maria thought money would only lead to more wickedness."

Turning his back to conceal his curiosity, he took both bottles through the archway. Sebastian sat down on a black leather couch, placing one bottle on a coffee table while he drank from the other. He wanted to find out more about her wickedness. "Money worried Aunt Constance too. She believed I would waste Dad's money on drugs and whores. Her choice of words, not mine, in case I've offended you." He studied her to see if she was offended but couldn't tell. "So I made certain she had no cause for complaint. I drink in moderation, and have the occasional cigarette, but have avoided women. I wonder what she'd say about you? You're the first woman to come here, and I can't even persuade you to have a drink."

Draining the first bottle, he placed it on the table and picked up the other one. Usually, he was careful about how much he drank, but something about her response fuelled his thirst. "Come in and sit down. Don't you trust me?"

"I don't even know you."

"It's hard to get to know me from over there."

"God warned me to stand firm, so I'm staying here."

Rising from the couch, he drank deeply from the second bottle. He was unaccustomed to having anyone disobey him. "Aunt Constance talked about God all the time too, about how there would be punishment for the wicked. I know I was on her list. She was big on retribution and justice."

"I believe God is more interested in mercy and compassion. God offers forgiveness and love to anyone who wants it. All you have to do is ask."

He looked at her critically. She talked about forgiveness and love, yet she acted as if she didn't have either. If it was so easy, why didn't she ask for herself? "My Dad had a favourite saying from the Bible. I have it tattooed on my arm." He walked closer to show her the tattoos, a door design with the words 'Ask', 'Seek' and 'Knock' written in red ink.

"I know that verse too," she responded, with an unexpected smile. "I have changed the words a bit to help me understand it better. Ask and keep on asking, seek and keep on seeking, knock and keep on knocking. And everyone who asks will receive, everyone who seeks will find. Everyone who knocks will have the door of opportunity opened to them."

While she spoke she closed her eyes, and by the time she reopened them, he had moved much closer. A strange determination to see how far he could take this conversation made him reckless. There was nothing in her appearance or behaviour that could be mistaken as an invitation. Yet he wanted to unwrap her disguise and know her intimately. "There's something I'm going to ask," Sebastian said bluntly. "But I'm already certain your answer will be no."

"Then don't ask."

"I won't know for sure until I do."

He took another step closer, expecting her to run, for alarm was evident on her face. One of his hands reached out and traced the outline of her jaw. He moved his hand lightly along the curve of her neck, across her shoulder, and down her arm until he took hold of her hand. She was trembling at his touch, so he leaned closer. "Come to bed with me?"

ಬಿ ✿ ಛ

Horrified at his suggestion, Ria was certain she had given him no encouragement. Hastily she pulled her hand free. This job had seemed perfect, but if this was the price to pay, she would have to let it go. Taking a deep breath she replied. "I promised God I would wait for the man He'd chosen for me."

"How do you know He hasn't chosen me?" he retaliated.

"You wouldn't be talking to me like this if you were the one. I'm waiting for someone who loves me."

"There are different kinds of love," he suggested, and she blushed.

"God wants me to wait until I'm married for your kind of love."

Tell him about my love.

How, Lord?

Love is patient...

"God teaches me love is patient, love is kind, love keeps no..." She hesitated, her own heart listening to the words as if for the first time. "Love keeps no record of wrongs." Immediately, Ria realised she'd allowed her past to keep her from experiencing God's love. As she acknowledged this revelation, her eyes were opened. She reached out her hand and placed it over the tombstone tattoo on his arm. "What did you do that sent you to prison?"

࿔ ✿ ࿔

He recoiled as if she had struck him. What was happening? How did she know this tattoo was a permanent reminder of the crimes he had committed and the price he had paid? He took another step further away. He rejected the sensations awakened by her touch, refusing to acknowledge this new weakness.

"I killed someone," he declared. "I was sixteen, drunk and angry. I only hit him once, but he went down hard, and he didn't get up."

"What did he do to make you angry?"

"He challenged me to a fight. He said I was looking at his girlfriend, which I wasn't. Even then Aunt Constance's poison made me cautious around women. But he wouldn't leave me alone. So I hit him."

The signs of his growing anger must have been easy for her to read. Her gaze softened towards him, which annoyed him further. He didn't want her pity. He needed another drink. He went to get one.

"God offers forgiveness. He's the God of Second Chances. All you have to do is ask..."

He stood at the refrigerator and drained his third bottle of beer, then laughed bitterly as he strode back to confront her. "You talk about God's forgiveness, yet you carry around your own wrongdoing like a shroud! What did *you* do that was so wicked your father sent you away?"

She gasped. Looking down towards the floor, her voice faltered.

"Th-there was a man... a chef from the restaurant. One night in the courtyard he caught me and kissed me. He threatened me and said it was my fault for tempting him, and I believed him. I was too afraid to tell anyone. By keeping quiet, I condemned myself. I didn't know Sofia had seen me with him and told Papa. The next morning, Papa said terrible things and sent me away to Sydney. Much later, Zietta Maria informed me my attacker had said I'd shamelessly pursued him. Your aunt isn't the only one to use the word 'whore'. My aunt also told me Papa thought I behaved like a prostitute."

To see her obvious shame and humiliation roused his emotions in a new way. He recognised her vulnerability. How naive was she to think she was to blame? It was unjust she should be punished for someone else's offence!

"A stolen kiss doesn't make you a whore!" She held her breath as if his words pierced her heart. "You're not a whore," he repeated, raising her chin to make her look at him.

He watched closely – something was happening. She looked directly into his eyes and her fear was gone. Her eyes were bright, and she looked twenty years younger, radiant and alive. His body responded with an irresistible hunger as a new temptation entered his mind. He knew he was strong enough to force her to surrender...

Immediately this realisation was followed by a wave of self-hatred and disgust. How could he think he was beginning to care for her when he intended to ruin her? Pushing past Ria, he strode angrily along the walkway. He could hear her light steps hurrying after him, so he leapt for the closest metal stairs, and ran down them two steps at a time. The sound of his heavy boots rang out in the open space.

"Sebastian!" she cried. Hearing her speak his name tormented him. "Sebastian, please wait! Tell me what I've done to upset you. Sebastian!"

"Stop following me and go back," he shouted, but she continued to come after him. Both dogs appeared, alert and barking in response to the shouting.

He swore loudly. "It's not safe. You're not safe. You have to go back!"

"I'm not leaving you alone with your anger."

Swearing again, he went back up the stairs and seized her arm, dragging her roughly downwards. He had to get her out of the building, but the dogs were excited. Was he calm enough to control them?

At the bottom of the stairs, he saw a familiar cardboard box. Rummaging around, his hand grasped a tennis ball. Tiny and Fifi stopped barking and eagerly watched him. He hurled the ball with all his strength. The dogs launched themselves after the yellow missile. It could be heard rebounding off distant surfaces.

"Their favourite game," he informed her and hauled Ria in the direction of the office. He moved with ease but her street shoes slipped on the concrete floor. The sound of running claws warned him of the dogs' rapid return. Tiny had the ball in his jaws, but Fifi was in hot pursuit. Sebastian pushed Ria behind him, and held out his hand for the ball intending to throw it again.

Tiny dodged past him, dropping the ball at Ria's feet. Now both dogs were dancing expectantly around her.

"Even my own dogs like you better than me," he growled. He retrieved the ball and handed it to her, recognising his error too late. Both dogs leapt at Ria and she was smashed to the ground. In their excitement, the dogs knocked over a bucket of oily water, and the floor was awash.

"Tiny! Fifi! Outside!" He yelled the well-practised command. Reluctantly the excited animals turned to him. He repeated the command. Only then did they trot across the workshop towards their outside yard.

"For someone so small, you cause a lot of trouble," he grumbled, pulling Ria upright.

Dirty water dripped from her hair, now loose and hanging down below her waist. She stood shivering, silent and unresponsive. He studied her closely. The crumpled once-white shirt clung to her slender frame. Through tears in the fabric, red marks on her arms and torso revealed where the dogs had scratched her skin. They meant no harm; her injuries were his fault. He had forgotten the ballgame often turned into a wrestling match. His employees understood the risk. Their heavy overalls provided some protection, and they were much stronger. Better able to stand their ground. Even if Ria had been expecting the attack, she was too lightly built and her shoes too slippery for her to stand a chance.

She pressed one of her hands against the left side of her head, then tried to push wet hair from her eyes with the other hand. She seemed to have forgotten he was there. As if she had gone to some other place where he could not reach her. Ria took a tentative step only to lose her footing again. He swore and caught hold of her. Her fragility distressed him. Now, his resolve to be rid of her wavered as he gathered her into his arms.

CHAPTER 7
(Saturday 1st July)

Guidance - A Promise of Deliverance

ॐ ☼ ಜ

Psalm 23:4-5
Even though I walk through the valley of the shadow of death,
I will fear no evil, for You are with me. Your rod and Your staff
comfort me. You prepare a table for me in the presence of my
enemies. You anoint my head with oil and my cup overflows.

ॐ ☼ ಜ

Ria was certain she was dreaming. All around her, swirling rainbows of light flashed in harmony with waves of pain. This breaking surf was drawing her down into a blue whirlpool. She tried to open her eyes, and the world exploded in a galaxy of iridescent stars. A strange darkness enveloped her like a raging torrent, then the pain faded to a distant memory.

Nothing remained but the heavy darkness. Now she floated, a soothing river bearing her gently towards a distant light. The glimmer turned into a glow. This grew until it burned like holy fire and consumed everything else. Her heart responded to the light, and she knew she was in the presence of God. Now on her feet, she was surrounded by crystal purity, overcome by a peace beyond description.

Is this Heaven?

No, merely a place to watch and pray during the coming battle. The destiny of this lost lamb will be decided this day.

Lost lamb? Sebastian? I'd never describe him as a lamb.

All around her, the light oscillated in response, and she turned towards the One who was the Source. Instantly, she was standing in an unfamiliar room. Sebastian sat beside a low table cluttered with bottles. His phone was lying beside him on a black couch, and a shredded cigarette packet lay at his feet. Gone was the confident self-assurance she both feared and admired. His head was in his hands.

Lord, what's happened to him? He looks so lost and alone. Please speak to him about Your love and show him Your presence.

The lingering silence was disrupted by a loud noise. Surely that was the entrance door buzzer? She waited. Through a door, three men cautiously entered. The first she recognised as Sebastian's friend, Dave. Two uniformed police officers accompanied him. One of them was talking on his mobile phone.

"Officer McCormick and I have now entered the building. An associate of Romano, Dave Henderson, has provided us with access to the building. He said he received a request for assistance. When we arrived, the premises were locked. We have located Romano but have yet to determine whether the guard dogs are loose in the building. Henderson assures us they cannot access this room."

"Romano hasn't responded to our presence. I'm searching the room now while McCormick watches him... I've found a possible casualty."

Officer Vitali moved purposefully to a couch opposite Sebastian. There someone lay motionless, wrapped in black, a bloodied bandage around their head. Ria moved forward to peer at the pale face framed by dark, wet hair. She was shocked to recognise herself. Sebastian spoke and she turned towards him. He continued staring at the floor, his whole body sagging with the weight of his revelation. "She's dead. I killed her."

Is he talking about me? How did he kill me? Why don't I remember?

Watch and pray.

Lord, he seems so broken. You came to heal the broken-hearted. Help him understand. Show him Your forgiveness.

He is slow in recognising his own need.

The two police officers became more alert. The one using the phone checked for signs of life. Meanwhile, the second officer cautiously approached the giant who had spoken.

80 ☼ ೞ

Dave couldn't believe what was happening. His oldest friend was falling apart before him. Dave had been present on the fateful night when Seb had killed someone else. Nothing about this situation made any sense. He should have been safe here. Seb reached for one of the bottles on the table, found it empty and rose to his feet. Dave stepped closer and cautiously put out his hand to dissuade him from getting another drink.

"That's not going to help, Seb. You need a clear head to explain what's happened here." Seb folded onto the couch, and Dave reeled – Seb never listened to advice. "I came as soon as I got your message, and the police were waiting outside the building. They said you called them."

While Dave waited for a reply, Officer Vitali's brutal monologue continued. "One deceased female; Caucasian; late twenties; head trauma. Scratch marks, probably canine, on arms and upper torso. The body is naked but wrapped in damp towels, in a secure location. The suspect Romano is present and has been drinking heavily. Yes, he is known to us – unarmed but dangerous. Immediate backup requested."

"How much have you had to drink?" Officer McCormick asked.

"Three beers before she fell, and then..." Seb gestured to the empty bottles. Officer McCormick nodded. "You said she fell? Can you tell me more?"

There was no response. Dave stared at the dead woman. There was something familiar about her dark beauty. Where had Seb met her? Since coming out of prison, he had quickly discouraged any who paid him attention – his wealth added to his dangerous appeal. Seb had been determined to prove Aunt Constance wrong about his wickedness. He had lived the celibate life of a monk...

Inspiration struck him as Dave remembered the waitress who had wanted to be a nun. She had been dark like her sister Sofia, but he wouldn't have thought her beautiful. He looked again.

"What's *she* doing here?" Dave gasped in recognition. "It's that waitress from the restaurant!"

"You know her?" Officer McCormick turned towards Dave.

"I think so. Her name is Maria Evangelina, but sometimes they call her Ria. Her surname is Fontana. Do you know the *Ristorante di Fontana*?"

"The Italian place owned by Benito and Mama Rosa? My family eat there all the time," Officer Vitali called from across the room. "She works there?"

"She's their youngest daughter, but last night was the first time I'd seen her. We have a work dinner at the *Ristorante di Fontana* once a month, and last night she was our waitress.

Benito was very keen to introduce her to Seb." Dave turned puzzled eyes towards his friend. "Seb, what's she doing here? You hardly looked at her all evening."

"She was in the courtyard when I went out for a smoke."

"Did you bring her home with you?"

"No, she came today. I interviewed her for the office job."

"What office job?" Officer McCormick asked, and when Seb didn't respond, Dave answered for him.

"Aunt Constance, Seb's only relative, died five weeks ago. He's been trying to find a suitable replacement. There have been a few applicants, but the women don't stay long."

"Why not?"

"He doesn't trust women. His aunt mercilessly persecuted him, and there was a witness at his trial who lied about what happened. So he makes the working conditions seem more dangerous and demanding than they are. Usually, they take one look at him, and then he introduces them to the dogs. That makes them nervous enough to leave."

"So is that what he did when she arrived? He 'introduced' her to the dogs?"

Seb stirred. "Ria knew straight away they were friendly and she thought trying to frighten her was a mean trick." Now he had started the story poured forth. "I asked her to come at noon. Ria was early, but I kept her waiting."

"How do you know she was early?" Dave asked.

"I watched her from the upstairs window. She looked nervous, but I'd made her promise her father she'd come. I let her into the building and she met the dogs. She tried to be braver than she was. I showed her the workshop from the upstairs walkway.

"Ria had potential. I teased her, and she didn't hesitate to let me know when I annoyed her, but then she calmed down again. We talked about my Dad, and she said he must have loved me very much. Later we argued about God and forgiveness. That happened in my flat."

"You took her to *your flat*?" Dave couldn't believe what he was hearing.

"It's not what you think! I went in, but she stood in the doorway. She wouldn't come in, saying God told her not to. I offered her a drink, but she said no to that too. I started to get angry then. We talked about my problem with anger and why I went to prison, and then I asked her to tell me her secret."

"What secret?"

"When she was a kid, she was attacked and falsely accused. Her family believed her attacker and sent her away. When I saw how innocent and vulnerable she was, I realised how easy it would be..." he let that sentence trail away unfinished. Then he shook his head. "I turned my anger on myself because I knew I was no better than the man who ruined her life. I told her to leave, but she didn't understand, so I tried to make her go. If I hadn't been angry she wouldn't have fallen."

"You say she fell. Where did this happen?"

"She fell twice. The first time we were crossing the workshop. Near Station 12 you will find an overturned bucket. The dogs knocked her down, but I thought she was alright, just wet and upset. Then she fell a second time on her own. She didn't want me anywhere near while she was in the shower. I didn't trust myself either, so I went away for about fifteen minutes.

"I started to worry when she didn't answer after I asked if she needed more towels. I could hear the water still running so I went in. Ria was lying in the bottom of the shower, and there was blood everywhere. I wrapped her in towels, brought her out here and tried to stop the bleeding. She wouldn't wake up. Her eyelids fluttered, then there was this terrible noise and she stopped breathing. I couldn't bring her back. It's not the first time I've watched someone die."

The officer looked up from his notes. "The dogs, are they secure?"

Seb nodded, and Dave reluctantly left the room with Officer Vitali to make sure. They would also visit Station 12 and the flat. Thankfully there were enough cameras to confirm whether his story was true. Surely this was just an unfortunate accident, not something more sinister.

ಬು ☼ ೞ

Ria followed Officer McCormick as he searched for further evidence. A trail of bloody footprints went through the locker room to the showers. Her clothes were rolled up on a bench with those treacherous shoes tucked underneath. The water was no longer running, but the glass screen was smeared with blood. There was a dark stain on the shower base. The policeman took photos with his phone camera and wrote notes. He reported his findings to his colleagues.

"It looks as if his story is true," Vitali said, "the dogs are in the yard, and there is a watery trail all the way from where Romano said the first fall happened to here. There is no blood at that location and no sign of a struggle or blood in the flat. No evidence he assaulted her there, either in the lounge room or any of the bedrooms."

"The shower matches his account too," McCormick added, "but there are no surveillance cameras there, so we will have to wait for Forensics to examine the scene."

"So why does he insist he killed her if it was an accident?"

Why Lord? Why is he taking the blame for my death?

Because he knows his heart is capable of evil and he understands no other way but to take responsibility and pay the penalty.

But You've made another way, Lord. That's why Jesus came and died for sinners. If they ask for forgiveness, they don't have to pay the penalty. How is he to know that? Will he have to take the punishment for my death? Will he go back to prison?

It isn't long since you were set free from the same chains that bind him now. You believed the lies of the enemy. Those subtle untruths became strong chains binding each of you to a future that was never My plan. My plan is to give you both a hope and a future. Watch and see what I will do.

The silence in the room was broken by insistent ringing from the phone beside Sebastian. Officer McCormick looked at the screen. "Leonardo Fontana?"

Sebastian's phone fell silent, and then Dave swore as his phone started ringing. Dave pressed the speaker button. "Dave!" Leonardo's voice intruded into the room. "Do you know how I can contact the Boss? I tried his number. My aunt Ria, you know, from dinner last night, well the Boss asked her to go to the workshop today. She hasn't come back, and she's not answering her phone."

Rising in the air, Ria went through the ceiling, the upper storeroom and then out through the roof itself. The workshop diminished beneath her. Soaring over the city, she marvelled at the detail she could see. She descended again. Down through another roof, her parents' bedroom and the dining room ceiling – into the family restaurant. The table was set for the customary afternoon staff gathering, food laid out ready to serve. Mama and Sofia were waiting near Leonardo. He too had the speaker activated on his phone.

Papa sat in his customary place at the table, with Marco to his left. Matilda was scowling. Ria saw the text message she was sending to her boyfriend. She was complaining about her annoying aunt again. The remaining staff waited patiently, concerned for their beloved employers. There was an uneasy hush to their usually spirited conversation.

"Dave?" Leonardo asked again, "Dave, has something happened?"

"Is your grandfather there?"

Leonardo frowned, before passing the phone to Papa Benito. The nineteen-year-old turned to look at his mother standing beside Mama Rosa. The older woman was wringing her hands in her apron.

"Benito Fontana."

One of the policemen must have picked up Dave's phone. "This is Officer Ricardo Vitali, Benito. I regret to inform you there has been an accident involving a young woman. Preliminary investigations have identified the victim as Maria Fontana."

Mama Rosa began to wail. Sofia drew her further away while Papa continued to talk with the policeman. "An accident?"

"I understand she had an appointment to meet Sebastian Romano earlier today? Can you confirm any details about that appointment?"

"I'm sorry, you said an accident? Which hospital has she been taken to?"

"I regret to inform you the victim sustained critical injuries and she didn't survive."

Ria watched each person absorb that information. Her mother and sister were weeping. Papa now stood, his familiar cheerfulness evaporating. Matilda put down her phone, consternation on her young face. Her nephews both

65

moved nearer their mother. The others looked stunned by the unexpected news.

> Lord, please help them with their grief. Please help them understand that you are the Resurrection and the Life. Though I'm dead, I'm more alive than I ever was before. Bring them comfort.
>
> *Blessed are those who mourn.*

Papa raised his voice. "How did she die? And why are you asking about her meeting with Romano? Did he hurt my daughter?"

"You must understand, Benito, our investigations have only begun. I can tell you Romano is helping us with our enquiries. The accident happened at his premises, and he was with her when she died. After we have corroborated his account, we will be able to give you more details."

"I want to see her! Tell me where to go!"

"Her body will remain at the scene. She won't be moved until the forensic investigators have collected all the evidence."

"Then I'm coming there!" Papa disconnected the call, throwing the phone onto the table. He turned to his grandson and shouted, "Leonardo, drive me to *Romano*. Sofia, give him the keys! You'll have to look after Mama. I have to see Maria Evangelina for myself before I believe she is dead!"

Papa hugged his wife, before leading his grandson out to the car park.

As Ria watched them leave, she rose again, and from a great height followed Sofia's car through city traffic.

☙ ☼ ೞ

Leonardo parked and led the way to the front entrance. There was a police car parked at the door, yet no-one tried to stop them. Usually, Leonardo came to the workshop with confidence and enthusiasm. Today he was overwhelmed by a terrible dread. He idolised the Boss and was fearful of what he would discover. Could Romano really be responsible for the death of his aunt?

The nineteen-year-old thought back to the previous evening. Leonardo doubted the Boss would have given the newcomer a second glance, except for the fuss Matilda made. Yet there was that conversation at the end about whether Ria was a nun. Perhaps that had something to do with the unexpected job offer? He was still puzzling over this when he heard more vehicles arriving. A convoy of vehicles, lights flashing, pulled up and blocked two lanes. Police officers hurried to redirect traffic. Already there were spectators gathering outside the shopping centre across the road.

Taking a deep breath, Leonardo pressed his hand to the sensor. He waited for the handprint recognition software to grant him access. It was fortunate there was no password to remember. Leading his grandfather into the reception area, he let the external door lock behind them. This should buy them time before someone challenged their presence. Leonardo stood contemplating how to locate the Boss when the police officer found them. Leonardo recognised him as one of the regular restaurant patrons. How strange to have a familiar face meeting them here!

"Benito, you shouldn't have come," Ricardo Vitali said. "You have to promise you'll stand where I tell you and keep quiet, or you'll find yourselves outside. Do you understand?"

"The forensic team is here," Officer McCormick was saying to Dave and Romano. "Detectives Murray and Kirby will be in charge of the investigation. I expect they will take you both down to the station to formally interview you."

"Can I say goodbye to her before I go?" Sebastian asked. McCormick looked at him as if calculating an advantage for granting this request.

꙰ ✪ ꙰

Reverently, Sebastian approached the body. He knelt down, gently lifting her fallen hair from her face. "I'm so sorry, Ria," he said quietly and silent tears fell.

He couldn't remember the last time he had cried. He was overwhelmed by a sense of great loss. While he'd waited, his heart had persuaded him that here lay a woman he could have fallen in love with. The one his Dad had in mind when he built the three-bedroom flat. His Dad had hoped there was a loving and faithful wife with the possibility of children somewhere in his future.

What would he give to go back and undo the unfortunate series of events that led to this catastrophe?

꙰ ✪ ꙰

Ria saw her father and nephew enter the room. Officer Vitali silently cautioned them to stand still. The first of the forensic team, two men wearing white jumpsuits, pushed through the door and paused as well.

Sebastian spoke again. "Ria, you said forgiveness was mine for the asking. You told me your God was merciful and compassionate, and love kept no record of wrongs. I want that kind of love. But there's no way to undo my mistakes. I don't know if you can hear me, but I'm asking you to forgive me. God, if you're listening, she said you're a God of Second Chances. If only you could give me another chance? I want another chance!"

He laid his head on her chest and sobbed.

Hanging in the air over him, Ria was grieved because Sebastian could not see her. As he spoke the light became blindingly bright. The air vibrated, resonating with the Holy Presence. She turned towards the One who had been her Comforter through the wilderness years. A new understanding awakened within her.

You asked me to watch and pray. This isn't Heaven, but a place to wait for the lost lamb to be saved. I asked how this could happen if there was no-one to show him the way? You have a plan and a future for both of us...

She paused as the wonder of what was about to happen dawned in her.

Love always trusts, always hopes, love perseveres. Love never fails. Whoever loses their life for me will find it. I AM the Resurrection and the Life!

The light around her exploded. Her whole being convulsed as she plummeted into the velvety blue darkness. As she slammed back into her body, there was an audible sound like thunder. Sebastian was thrown violently backwards by the force of her return. Wave upon wave of pain flooded her consciousness, and she moaned before opening her eyes. A galaxy of iridescent stars flashed before her.

"O, God! I'm going to be sick," she moaned, and she was.

Stunned silence greeted Ria's resurrection. Then Officer McCormick rushed towards her, rolling her onto her side. He held her while she vomited.

"My head hurts," she moaned softly.

ॐ ✿ ॐ

Leonardo leaned down in concern as his grandfather fell to his knees in disbelief. Officer Vitali turned to assist. Benito had tears streaming down his face. "My daughter is alive!"

The two Forensic Officers rushed forward. They began to ask questions and bark orders. "Where's that ambulance?"

Benito struggled to his feet and rushed forward. The policeman held him back, out of the way as others burst into the room with renewed urgency. "Let them do their job."

"You said she was dead," Leonardo declared accusingly.

"I can't explain it," Vitali responded with a shake of his head. "There's been no sign of life for over an hour. She wasn't breathing and there was no heartbeat."

"God has given us a miracle," Benito proclaimed. "He listened to Romano's prayer, and He gave Maria back to us."

Leonardo didn't know how to respond to this impossibility.

"Phone Sofia and let her know Maria Evangelina has come back to us. Wait, give me your phone, and I'll call her myself."

Handing over his phone, Leonardo was thankful he'd retrieved it from the table at the restaurant. He watched his grandfather go through the door, talking rapidly.

Leonardo looked at Ria and was shocked to see the towel had slipped again. Moving quickly, he went into the uniform store and found a red polo shirt. He brought it back, handing it to the first person who noticed him. Turning to see what the Boss was making of all this drama, Leonardo felt confused and uncertain.

He doubted the man he admired could be responsible for whatever had befallen his aunt. Yet his mind rejected any alternate possibility. The Boss was sitting beside Dave on the other couch. They were the strongest, most confident men he knew yet both of them sat in stunned silence. Leonardo stood near them and waited, wrestling with his own thoughts. What did this mean?

"Dave," Romano finally spoke, his eyes fixed on Ria. "What happened?"

"I don't know. I heard you ask God for a second chance, and then bang! I think you got an answer."

"But she was dead."

"I know."

"And she's not dead now? She's alive?"

"Yes."

"So God is real?"

"That's one explanation..."

"Why would God listen to me?"

"I don't know."

"What do I do now?"

"I think you have to sit here and see how this plays out."

CHAPTER 8
(Saturday 1st July)

Honoured –
A Promise of Importance

ॐ ☼ ☾

Revelation 21:5
He who sits on the throne said,
"Behold I am making all things new."
He said, "Write, for these words of God are faithful and true."

ॐ ☼ ☾

The curtains at the large window were open. Ria impatiently watched the setting sun disappear over the city. As she reclined against the raised bed head, the crisp hospital sheets confined her. Plump pillows supported her upper body and cradled her bandaged head. The nurse assigned to her care was checking the digital monitor and writing notes on the chart. Ria was still wearing the red polo shirt. Her hands smoothed the *Romano* logo as she pondered what she would say when Sebastian came to see her.

It had been over an hour since the last doctor examined her. Her parents were waiting down the hallway, but she had asked the nurse to tell them she was resting. She wanted to talk to Sebastian first. The nurse, Nancy, had commented on her growing agitation.

"Do you want me to get the ward clerk to call him again?" the nurse asked.

Shaking her head brought immediate regret, intensifying the pain. At least she could be thankful the flashing stars no longer accompanied her every move.

It had been fifty minutes since the ward clerk had phoned Sebastian to ask him to visit. Ria's admission to this private hospital in the city centre had flustered her. Her concern about the expense was met with reassurance. Sebastian Romano was paying for her treatment. He had asked to be personally contacted if there was anything else she needed.

What she needed most was to see him. She had to speak to him to make sure he understood he was forgiven.

Lord, why doesn't he come?

Put on my peace, and put off your anxiety. You have journeyed where few have travelled. Be still and know that I am God.

Lord, I thought when I opened my eyes I would be completely healed. I didn't expect so much pain and all this medical drama. Please help me be patient and obedient, and teach me how to rest in Your peace.

She sighed again. There would be more intrusive tests in the coming days, more questions to answer, more explanations to give. Two detectives had questioned her briefly in the ambulance. She didn't tell them why her explanation was a repetition of Sebastian's story. Arriving at the hospital, she had repeated again and again her account.

Her wound had been neatly stitched and a white bandage wrapped around her head. Strong pain medication was prescribed and administered. She had been shaken to learn she was not to be left unattended. There were whispered conversations about how long her heart had stopped. The list of possible long-term side effects was extensive and terrifying. A discussion continued about her dramatic reanimation. Because more than one person had mistakenly confirmed her death, her body must have been in a deep coma.

No-one would listen to her protests that she was in no danger. She did not want to be confined to her bed, hooked up to electronic monitors. This did not match her expectation of what would happen after her resuscitation. Yet she kept to herself the details of her conversation with God and the visions she had experienced.

There came a knock at the door. Ria became giddy with excitement, so great was her relief that he had come. Hopefully, she could compose herself once she saw he was alright. Looking self-conscious, Sebastian entered the room, holding a large bunch of red roses. At the sight of him, her heart began to race, and she was emotionally overwhelmed. He stood looking at her, apparently taking in the bandage crowning her long dark hair. She still wore the red *Romano* polo shirt. Her bright eyes and animated smile reassured him of his welcome.

Neither of them said anything.

Nancy stepped forward to take the roses from him. "I'll get a vase for these. You can have ten minutes alone with her," Nancy said to him, closing the door behind her.

"Hey Boss," Ria said softly, deciding to make light of their situation. If she had not been so intoxicated by the newness of her feelings for him, she might have been more careful.

"Hello, Ria."

"I can call you Boss now," she continued, gesturing with her hand for him to come closer.

"You have to give me the job now. I already have the uniform."

"I didn't think you would want to work for me now." He sounded uncertain.

75

ഔ ☼ ౨

Sebastian was puzzled. He had been receiving updates on her condition. Could her head injury be responsible for her changed demeanour? She had a fractured skull and a serious concussion. Or was it the pain medication? Her behaviour seemed childlike.

Before the accident, she had kept her distance, both emotionally and physically. Now she was calling him closer. Was she having fun at his expense? How did that match with their earlier conversation?

"The hospital said you were going to be okay?" There was an unasked question behind his words.

"Lots more tests on Monday, but I'm feeling more alive than I have ever been. I'm so happy to see you." She sounded breathless.

"Why are you talking so quietly?"

"So you have to come closer to me," she laughed, taking hold of his hand and pulling him nearer. He couldn't reply, only gaze into her dark eyes in bewilderment.

"Boss, do you remember I asked you not to call me Maria Evangelina? You said you would call me whatever you liked because you were the Boss. Well, Boss, I need a new name. The old me, the one called Ria, died in your arms today, and the new me wants to know what name you have chosen?"

Before he could respond, the door burst open. In rushed her parents, with an apologetic nurse close on their heels. Nancy took a cautious position inside the room.

"Maria Evangelina!" her Mama cried, rushing across the room to wrap her daughter in a generous embrace. Her father held back, staring at Sebastian.

"Mama!" she replied. "I'm sorry for all the worry I've caused you today."

"Papa?" she said, releasing Sebastian's hand and reaching out to her hesitant father.

Benito embraced her, then stepped back to stand beside Mama Rosa. They both looked at Sebastian.

There had been a difficult conversation at the workshop after Ria had left in the ambulance. Sebastian had given a censored account of the accident to her relatives. He had been careful in the details. Yet even as he'd spoken to her father, his mind had rebelled. His imagination taunted him with graphic visions of what might have happened. As if she were able to see where his mind was taking him, Ria reached out and took his hand again.

"Mama and Papa," she began, "I won't be working in the restaurant anymore."

"Maria Evangelina..." her father began, but she raised her hand to stop him.

"Please don't call me Maria Evangelina. It hurt so much when you sent me away. Whenever I hear that name, I'm reminded how much disappointment I have brought you."

"All right, then I'll call you Ria..."

She interrupted him again, speaking hurriedly. "Ria was a name given to remind me of my shame because I was no longer worthy of the name I was born with. The woman who bore that shame died this afternoon, and now I'm someone new. Sebastian is going to give me a new name, one that comes with a promise and a future."

She looked expectantly at him. Sebastian hesitated, unsure whether she was serious or not. He decided he'd play along with whatever game she presented to him. Everyone waited.

Remembering her strong faith took him back to the afternoon. When he was finally alone, he'd gone upstairs to his flat. There he had hunted for his father's leather-bound

Bible. He found it stuffed in a cardboard box in a spare bedroom. He'd sat there on the floor, opening the Bible to the beginning. The early stories in Genesis were familiar. He was shaken to discover God created Eve to remedy Adam's loneliness. He had hardened his heart in prison, but now he acknowledged a deep yearning to be loved. A few hours alone with Ria had demolished all his defences.

One of Adam's duties was to assign names. Ria's request for a new name felt like his own personal experience of the same opportunity. The belief that God was real and was showing him what he needed to do was alien to him, yet he gave her his answer.

"Eve," he began and then paused because it didn't sound right. "Evie. Your new name is Evie."

ᏸ ✿ Ꮣ

Benito watched this exchange with growing concern. Had his daughter just called the younger man Sebastian?

"What do you think, Papa? Will you be able to call me Evie?" Her excitement at having a new name reminded Benito of watching a little bird about to take flight.

"Evie Fontana is a good name to go with a new beginning," her father replied cautiously. He looked at her mother, and they exchanged worried looks. What had happened to the solemn, cautious woman who had left the restaurant that morning? She was nothing like this restless girl in the hospital bed. Their daughter had been demure and quiet, strictly avoiding anything suggesting impropriety. Yet now she seemed oblivious to either her appearance or her behaviour. The borrowed polo shirt accentuated rather than hid her feminine curves. With her hair loose she was almost unrecognisable.

Unexpectedly, she giggled and winked at Benito. He remembered her often doing this many years ago. Childish laughter had characterised her early years. She had kept them wondering what mischief would entertain her next. She especially enjoyed playing clever tricks on her sister. Romano seemed disconcerted over the way she clung to his hand. Had she chosen him as the new target of her tricks? Benito's growing apprehension made him wish there was some way he could warn Romano.

"But Papa, I'm thinking Sebastian owes me more than just a new first name. Look, he has already written his surname across my heart." She gestured dramatically to the logo spread across the front of her red polo shirt. "What would you say if I became Evie Romano?"

Romano looked uncertainly from the laughing girl to Benito.

"You know, Papa, when the police found me I was wearing nothing but a towel. Surely you will demand he marry me? If he doesn't, I'll be lonely for the rest of my days."

Benito was unable to look at Romano. He remembered another awkward situation with a different man. How angry he'd been when Sofia told him she had seen Maria kissing Nicholas. The hasty questions he'd put to the chef had brought scandalous answers. He recalled the shocking words he'd used when telling Maria of her fate.

To his shame, there followed a second memory – a tearful Sofia coming to him a few months later. Nicholas was the father of her unborn child, now his eldest grandson Leonardo. He had insisted the pair marry immediately. Maria was not invited to the wedding. He didn't want the past affair reignited, one sister preferred over another. Sofia's marriage failed. Nicholas had multiple affairs and refused to accept any responsibility for his infidelity. Benito's pride had stopped him from questioning whether he'd been wrong about Maria.

Benito looking directly at his youngest daughter's open face. He saw no bitterness about what had happened. She seemed unaware she was bringing the painful past into the present. Was she also unaware the impact her marriage proposal would have for Romano? What if this worldly man thought she was offering herself to him without reservation?

This afternoon, when he realised she was naked, Benito had been outraged. He had imagined the worst betrayal by Romano, whom he'd welcomed as an honoured guest. Sofia had constantly cautioned him because of Romano's criminal connections. Yet the younger man had carefully explained that her honour was intact. Was this how Romano was to be repaid for trying to protect her?

Into the silence, Romano spoke cautiously. "Evie is right. I have dishonoured your family and will agree to marry her to make amends."

Clapping her hands, Evie laughed with delight. "I'm glad that's settled! Mama, look! I've found a husband, so you can stop worrying about me."

ಐ ✪ ೞ

Sebastian watched her carefully. Did she really expect him to marry her? She'd declared earlier that he wasn't the one God had chosen for her. Did she understand this agreement meant he would expect her in his bed?

He pondered how he could find out. He leaned close, taking her chin in his hand. She smiled as if waiting for him to kiss her. Their lips touched briefly, and then he pulled away. Showing her how much he wanted her would reveal nothing about her own intentions. It might also drive her further away.

Her eyes widened in surprise, then she drew him towards her and gave him a lingering kiss. His body responded and he kissed her passionately in return. Then he remembered where they were, and how she came to be in the hospital. He took a determined step away. He mustn't let his physical desires lead him into further trouble.

"I don't think you're very well," he suggested gently. "Earlier today you wouldn't have kissed me, nor made light of marriage. We'll talk about this tomorrow." Abruptly he left without looking back.

ଅୁ ✿ ୡ

As suddenly as her emotions had lifted her to an unknown ecstasy, Evie – she refused to think of herself as Ria anymore – was thrust down into the depths of despair. Her cheerfulness dissolved and she was inconsolable. Nancy ushered her worried parents from the room. Through the open door, Evie heard every word. The nurse delivered a clinical explanation. Extreme mood swings and uncharacteristic behaviours were indicative of their daughter's serious condition.

"Don't tell anyone what happened tonight. She may see things in a new light in the morning, and have a change of heart."

Lord, are they right? Am I feeling like this because of my injuries? Am I going to regret this in the morning?

Have I made a fool of myself again?

Evie waited for the familiar response.

Lord, why are You silent?

More tears spilled from her eyes, and her body shook as she sobbed. Nancy re-entered the room and tried unsuccessfully to settle her. Then she fetched two white tablets in a plastic cup.

"Shh," Nancy said. Evie swallowed the bitter tablets. The nurse placed the water glass on the cabinet beside her bed. Evie's eyes went from the glass to the vase filled with red roses. Nancy had placed them on the same cabinet so Evie would be able to look at them from her bed. More tears flowed, and Nancy went to get a cloth to wash her face.

"It will all seem much better in the morning," Nancy reassured her.

Impossible –
A Surprising Promise

꙰ ☼ ꙰

Mark 10:27
Jesus said, "With men it is impossible,
but not for God,
for all things are possible with God."

꙰ ☼ ꙰

Morning came far sooner than Evie expected. Despite the medication, her night had been restless, haunted by exploding stars and crashing waves. In her dream, she had plummeted into a blue river, wild and terrifying. She awoke thirsty and opened her eyes to look for the glass beside her bed.

To her disappointment, the glass was empty. Her eyes wandered to the red roses, reminding her of the terrible trick she had played on Sebastian. He had left so suddenly. Now she was fighting against the tears.

A different nurse approached the bed. She was wearing the same navy blue uniform but looked older, with her red hair carefully pinned behind her head. This nurse was holding Evie's patient notes.

"What time is it?" Evie said.

"6 am. I didn't realise you were awake. My name is Gaylene. How is the pain?"

"I'm very thirsty."

Gaylene poured water into the glass. She watched closely as Evie gingerly raised herself to drink.

"Oh!" Evie cried, dismayed at her clumsiness.

Gaylene retrieved the glass from her trembling hand.

"I was hoping I could get out of bed today..." Evie whimpered.

"What you need now is more rest, so lie still while I get you something for the pain."

Evie sighed deeply, looking at the red roses. She didn't like this feeling of helplessness. What would he think of her lying here like an invalid? The prospect of lonely pain-filled hours drained away her joy.

I'm sorry, Lord. So quickly I forget how I walked with You. I thought I would never lose the joy of being in Your presence. But now my body feels so weak and tired, and I fear I'm losing my way.

When you are at your weakest My strength shines through.
Evie's heart was relieved that God had answered her. She sighed.

The nurse returned with more pills. Gaylene raised Evie's head and held the water glass. She ensured Evie swallowed the pain medication while ministering to her thirst.

"Did you sleep well?"

"I had the same dream over and over."

"Was it a good dream?"

"It should have been, but no. It is good to be awake." She sighed again.

ဆင္ ✿ ၢ

Gaylene looked at her patient closely. Dark shadows had developed under her eyes. A colourful bruise was emerging from the white bandage. Both bore testimony to yesterday's trauma. Evie was stoically attempting to conceal her true condition.

A growing curiosity reminded Gaylene of the gossip at the morning briefing. The notice above the bed confirmed Evie's name change. The afternoon nurse had recounted the developing drama to the next shift. In turn, they had eagerly passed on her story. Those red roses beside her bed added to the speculation. Was Evie involved in a dangerous love affair? Her patron was a wealthy businessman.

Last night, there had been a confrontation between her parents and her alleged attacker. Yet the police seemed satisfied her injuries had been due to an unfortunate accident. Everyone was speculating about whether he would make an appearance today. Gaylene had been told to keep watch for a tattooed giant.

She heard the breakfast trolley clatter along the hallway then a knock came at the door. Expecting it to be the attendant Gaylene moved the trolley-table closer to the bed. Evie gasped. Turning, Gaylene recognised Romano from his description.

Indeed he looked dangerous, and she thought about calling Security. This intimidating man barely acknowledged Gaylene's presence. He came to stand on the opposite side of the bed. He reached into a pocket of his black leather jacket. Taking out a white phone and charger, he placed them beside Evie on the bed. "I thought you might want your phone," he said quietly, leaning close. He appeared troubled by her appearance.

଼୦ ☼ ୭୪

He reached for Evie's trembling hand and folded her fingers around the long stem of a single white rose. At the sight of the rose, she held her breath. It was identical to her vision. Why was Sebastian giving her a white rose, when he had already presented her with a bouquet of red ones?

God, what is happening here? Is this a coincidence?

They were interrupted by the attendant placing breakfast before her. Sebastian lifted the lid to show her what was on offer.

"Are you hungry?" he asked, looking as if he might offer to feed her. A wave of humiliation washed over her. Evie shook her head, before closing her eyes as the pain intensified. His hand gently brushed away an errant tear. She attempted a small smile as she forced herself to look at him again.

He spoke softly. "You must know how sorry I am?"

Her heart fluttered in her chest in response to the intensity of his presence.

He continued speaking. "It is hard for me to see you in pain, knowing I caused your suffering. I promised you I would keep you safe."

"It was an accident."

Lifting the hand clasping the white rose Sebastian kissed it. "So you forgive me?" he asked.

"Of course I forgive you!"

He stared at her for a moment and seemed satisfied with her answer. He smiled and turned as if to leave. "Eat your breakfast, then. You need to regain your strength. I'm off to meet Pastor Edwards to talk about the wedding. He said he could see me before the 10 am Sunday Service."

"Pastor Edwards?" she squeaked, and he laughed at her surprise.

He pointed to her phone. "You don't have many contacts in your phone, which made it easy to track down where you go to church."

She stared at him.

"I needed to be sure you weren't hiding any old boyfriends from me. My Dad said every good marriage should be built on truth and honesty." He paused. "I have also spoken with Father Finnegan, and he said to tell you he'll be praying for your swift recovery. He is rejoicing that the news of your death was quickly surpassed by your return from the dead. He looks forward to receiving his invitation to the wedding. He hopes you don't keep me waiting too long. He said he has grown old waiting for you to find someone who could see through your disguise."

He paused at the threshold to her room, and he laughed. "You play a good game, Evie Fontana. You won that white rose for your honesty, but from the look on your face, I think this round goes to me."

Breakfast was growing cold, but Evie had no appetite. She picked up her phone to check who he had called. Sebastian had spoken to Father Finnegan for over an hour last night, not long after he left the hospital. There were two calls to her new pastor. Each lasted little more than thirty seconds. Then there was an incoming call from Pastor Edwards lasting half an hour. She wondered what they had talked about, as she had only met her new pastor a few times.

Lord, please guide the conversation between Sebastian and Pastor Edwards. I'm thankful Sebastian talked to Father Finnegan. Please bless the old priest. You know he encouraged me to seek You with all my heart. Without his gentle redirection, I would never have been able to accept Your forgiveness. Thank You for seeking me out, calling me to You, and setting me free. Now I'm asking You to pursue Sebastian with the same patience and compassion, so he too can come to know You as his Redeemer. If You have brought Sebastian and I together, please clear away the obstacles and make it all work out. Your plan is perfect...

Now her mind focused on her heartfelt prayers. Evie drifted back to sleep and didn't wake again until mid-afternoon.

$$\text{ʬ ☼ ʬ}$$

Sofia was upset. Sunday was the only day the family restaurant closed. This made the midday family gathering a special occasion, the one constant that sustained her in the midst of so much change. Mama Rosa always prepared her favourite recipes. Everyone knew they could relax and enjoy her bountiful feast. No-one left before Papa declared the meal complete. Even the rebellious teenagers accepted this restriction because the remainder of the day was free. But today everything was rushed and Papa insisted the whole family must visit her sister.

When they arrived at the hospital, they walked past an empty ward station. No-one challenged them. With his arm around Mama, Papa led the way to Maria's room. Sofia followed a few steps behind with Marco and Leonardo. Matilda dawdled, walking while texting her boyfriend.

Sofia was concerned about this visit. Her parents seemed troubled when they returned to the restaurant last evening. Today she had walked in on an intense conversation that ceased when they saw her. Papa wouldn't talk about what happened at the *Romano* workshop. He only gave a brief description of his own reaction when Maria Evangelina woke up.

Accustomed to having Papa's confidence, Sofia was sure he was hiding something. She also worried about how withdrawn Leonardo had become. He had barely uttered a word since yesterday afternoon. She was certain her prediction that no good would come from his job with Romano was being fulfilled.

In contrast, Marco was chattering incessantly. Her youngest child was eager for details. He anticipated telling his friends the fantastic story. His aunt had been dead and came back to life! It sounded like a fairytale.

They arrived to find a 'No Visitors' notice on the door. When her parents held back from entering, Sofia felt uneasy. Matilda impatiently pushed past them and opened the door. She stepped into the room, and everyone followed her. The curtains at the large window were closed, darkening the room. Silence fell. Briskly opening the curtains, Sofia let in the afternoon sunshine. Only then did she look at the sleeping figure. She gasped in amazement. Was this really Maria?

Sofia directed Matilda to the two remaining chairs on the opposite side of the bed. Meanwhile, Marco impatiently stalked the room. The room was spacious, decorated with pale blue walls and bright floral prints. It was more like a small holiday apartment than a hospital room.

A nurse walked in, startled to discover so many visitors. She introduced herself as Nancy, then retrieved the redundant notice from the door. Nancy approached the patient and spoke quietly to her. "Your family are here."

The sleeper opened her eyes. Nancy gently raised the upper section of the bed so she was reclining comfortably. Then she brought the glass of water to Maria's dry lips so she could drink. A few minutes later, Nancy left the room to get more chairs.

After her parents had finished with their tearful hugs, Sofia stood up. She delivered the small overnight bag she had prepared. "Here are some things I thought you would need."

"Thank you, Sofia. I'm sorry for all the trouble I've caused."

Sofia was about to respond when the door opened again. In walked Romano carrying shopping bags. Sofia needed all her strength to keep quiet. She had told Papa this beast was a violent criminal, but he wouldn't listen.

The object of Sofia's anger ignored her hostile welcome. He met her fierce glare with cold eyes. He turned to greet the other members of her family, before approaching the foot of the bed.

"How are you this afternoon, Evie?" Romano asked, placing the shopping bags at his feet. There were gasps and exclamations of surprise.

"Papa," Sofia demanded, "why is he calling Maria 'Evie'?"

Romano turned to Papa in amusement. "You didn't tell them?"

Papa shook his head cautiously. "She was asleep when we arrived. An announcement of this importance is hers to make."

Maria interjected quietly. "Sofia, please call me Evie from now on. I hope you can understand my need to make this change? I want to leave the past behind. Let the old me go so I can be happy again."

Sofia opened her mouth to protest, but a cautioning word from Benito silenced her.

"What's in the bags?" Marco demanded impatiently, and Romano laughed again.

"Did your grandfather tell you Evie slipped and fell? She needs some safety gear..." He handed a bag to Marco who pushed Sofia aside so he could place it in Maria's lap. When her trembling hands struggled to release the contents, Marco eagerly helped. Inside the bag was a box containing a bright pink safety helmet. Tucked inside the box was a card bearing the message 'Love from Tiny and Fifi'.

A second bag contained a large shoebox. Inside was a pair of black leather workboots, a smaller version of the ones Romano wore. Maria smiled tentatively at Romano. Marco took the boxes and card and carried them around to show everyone.

"I threw away what you were wearing yesterday," Romano said. He delivered the next parcel himself, forcing an outraged Sofia to step out of the way.

Cautiously, her sister took the bag from him and looked inside. She brought out a small black T-shirt with a scooped neckline and a sports car image on the front.

"Something for you to wear when I drive you home in my Maserati."

The next item was a pair of skinny black pants. They were followed by a red-and-black tartan miniskirt. Both would be scandalous on Matilda. How dare he give these to her sister?

"The shop assistant said the pants will fit like a second skin. I told her you would want something to wear over the top to protect your modesty."

The stricken look on her sister's pale face infuriated Sofia. She wanted to take up the outrageous clothes and throw them back in his face.

But he wasn't finished. "I told you I threw away *all* your clothes..."

Sofia gasped when she saw the brand name on the remaining bags. They were from an expensive lingerie boutique. Her sister hesitantly took the smaller bag from his hand and peeked inside. Now her face blushed red with embarrassment, and she didn't seem to know where to look. Matilda darted forward to grab the bag. She revealed a handful of flimsy red and black lace before Sofia could snatch it from her.

The final gift lay unopened on the bed. Romano reached into the bag to reveal a long red nightdress. The luxurious silk garment had narrow straps. White ribbon roses decorated the sweetheart neckline. Her sister's eyes widened. Draping it over her, he reached into the bag again for an identical one except it was black. Finally, he tipped the bag upside down. A shimmering robe featuring a white rose pattern on a red background fell into her sister's hands.

"Something to remind you of my promise," that evil man said, as he leaned over Maria and kissed her. His victim fainted.

CHAPTER 10
(Sunday 2nd July)

Jeopardy -
A Promise at Risk

☙ ✿ ❧

Psalm 25:16-19
Turn to me, and have mercy on me, for I am desolate and afflicted.
The troubles of my heart are enlarged. Oh bring me out of distress.
Consider my affliction. Forgive all my sins. My enemies are many.
They hate me with cruel hatred.

☙ ✿ ❧

Sebastian sensed Evie's collapse and stepped back with concern. A shrill alarm erupted from the digital monitor.

"Clear the room!" Nurse Nancy shouted, rushing forward to push buttons and check monitor readings, but no-one moved. Sebastian was reassured to see Evie's chest rise and fall. He wanted to be there when she regained consciousness, but the angry nurse pointed sternly toward the door.

Her family followed him from the room.

"What just happened there?" Sofia hissed, stepping up to Sebastian and glaring at him. "What did you do to my sister?"

He chose to ignore her, so Sofia turned to Benito, her voice rising to match her growing frustration. "Why are you letting him treat your daughter like this?"

"Your sister is a grown woman..."

The disapproving nurse stepped out into the hall, firmly closing the door behind her. "Take this argument to the waiting room. Evie is very distressed. Your shouting isn't helping. The doctor is on his way. He will determine whether she is well enough to see any of you." Nancy looked pointedly at Sebastian, making it clear she thought him responsible. "Use this time to work out your differences, or I won't let any of you back in to see her."

In the waiting room, they sat in uncomfortable silence. Sebastian faced the open doorway leading back to the ward so he would be first to know when there was any news.

Mama Rosa gave her husband a nudge and Benito broke the silence. "Perhaps you went a little too far?" he suggested awkwardly.

"Went too far?" Sofia interjected, looking even angrier. "What are you talking about? This isn't some child's game."

Last evening, Benito had called Sebastian to discuss Evie's provocative behaviour and its similarity to some of her childhood pranks. Sebastian had said he intended to play her game to its natural conclusion, and now he waited while Benito attempted to explain.

"Do you remember when your sister was young? We were never sure what cunning plan she'd come up with next. Sofia, you were always annoyed when she drew you into her fantastic schemes. Do you remember when she convinced you that the butcher was sending us crocodile meat? Or that time she persuaded you that our dining room was being used by international spies to pass coded messages?"

Sofia went pale, as if there might be more to those incidents than her father knew. Her children were paying close attention.

"Perhaps the traumatic accident sent her back to childhood," Benito continued. "Whatever the reason, when we visited last night your sister was behaving strangely. She set Romano a challenge to match her in a new game."

"What kind of game?"

"A complicated one. The difference between winning and losing is unclear," was the oblique reply. "Evie sought a promise from Romano, and unless she changes her mind and releases him, he has agreed to marry her."

"She can't marry him!" Leonardo exclaimed at the same time as Sofia screamed, "Papa, you can't let her marry him!"

Sebastian laughed at the irony. He knew they objected for opposite reasons. He was well aware that Leonardo idolised him, but Sofia barely tolerated his patronage at the restaurant out of respect for her father, and the fact that his wealth made him a valuable customer. She seemed unable to forgive him for past differences.

"Whether I marry or not is for Evie to decide. Perhaps I win whichever way the game goes?"

"When Evie played at her best, she never lost. Despite her cleverness, Sofia never won," Benito warned him.

ଛ ☼ ଔ

Sofia's indignation loosened her tongue. She declared recklessly, "I won the final game!"

All eyes turned towards her, even Romano leaning forward.

"What?" Papa exclaimed.

"I won the final game! I don't know if Maria understood I'd beaten her, but she never played again."

"When did you play this final game?" Papa asked.

"The last night she was with us before you sent her away. The night I told you I'd seen her with Nicholas."

"Nicholas? Leonardo's father?" Marco asked. He had been so quiet Sofia had forgotten he was there.

Frowning, Sofia looked towards Leonardo, who responded by reaching across to Matilda. He handed her some folded money. "Take Marco out."

Matilda looked from Leonardo to Sofia and scowled before standing up.

"Come on Marco," she insisted, dragging her reluctant little brother from the room. "If you stop complaining, we'll spend Leonardo's money on those video games you like."

Everyone waited until the sound of the departing teenagers faded. Leonardo spoke first. "What about my father? What has he to do with your sister?"

Sofia tried to ignore the pain in her son's voice. She fixed her eyes on her father's face to avoid looking at Romano. It was time she let this secret go; it had tormented her long enough. "I loved Nicholas, from the moment he walked into the restaurant, but he said he wasn't interested in me. That made me even more determined to win him. I watched for any excuse to be close to him. The other girls were all flirting with him too, except for Maria but she was just a child. She said she couldn't understand why everyone was making such a fuss over him. I dated other men but only to try and make him jealous, so he would see what he was missing.

"That night, I saw him go out to the courtyard, and I followed him. He didn't see me there in the shadows. Then Maria came out with the kitchen bin. He called her over and when he kissed her I was furious. Why would he want *her* when he could have *me*?

"She was struggling, trying to get away from him, and then I heard what he said. He told her what he intended to do to her when she turned sixteen. He assured her he was strong enough to make her do everything he wanted. Those were the kind of things I thought I wanted him to do with me, and I was desperate to let him know how willing I would be.

"He said she had been teasing him by pretending she wasn't interested. I remembered all the times she'd played tricks on me, and I half-believed him. How could she do this to me? How could she steal away the man I loved? Then he warned her not to say anything to anyone about his plan. He reminded her he was Mama Rosa's favourite, and I knew that was true. The restaurant needed him. I needed him.

"While I stood there in the dark I came up with my own plan. I was jealous. I decided to use what I'd witnessed to blackmail him. But first I had to make sure he couldn't have Maria. So I lied to you about what I'd seen and you were so outraged you sent her away."

Sofia was crying now. "By the time I realised Nicholas was heartless and cruel it was too late. I was already pregnant with Leonardo. I wanted to tell you what Nicholas was really like, and what I had done to Maria, but I was too ashamed. You said we should get married, and I knew it wouldn't last, but I didn't know what else to do. I'm so sorry Papa. Can you ever forgive me?"

Her parents were standing now, and Sofia stepped into their embrace. Tears were falling. It had been so long ago. The emotions were painfully raw because no-one had dared to speak about what had happened.

"Why didn't Maria Evangelina say anything?" Mama Rosa asked sorrowfully. "She let us think she was to blame."

"She stayed silent because her father called her a prostitute," Romano interjected scornfully. "Then her aunt labelled her a whore."

Sofia looked at him in horror. She had never seen him so furious.

"She told you?" Sofia whispered, her face ashen.

"What must you think of us?" Benito cried.

Romano laughed bitterly. "You have my sympathy. I already know what you think of me, the latest in a long line of abusers. You abandoned her to a life of shame, while my actions led to her death."

"But she isn't dead," Benito reminded him. "You asked God for a second chance, and He sent her back. Now, I know the doctors say she isn't well, but I can't forget that miracle." He turned back to Sofia. "We all have concerns about this situation. I'm not going to pretend it's going to be easy for any of us, especially Romano. Perhaps she has no intention of marrying him, but Romano has decided to play the game and take his chances. No priest would agree to perform the ceremony while she's unwell so we have time on our side.

"Last night, for a few moments, the Maria I remember was with us. I realised then how much I've missed her, and I'd do anything to have her return. She talks of a new beginning. I've decided it must start with us. If that includes playing this little game, then that's what we will do."

Matilda and Marco had just returned from their walk when Nancy came into the waiting room. "The doctor wants to know when Evie last ate. She has slept through all her mealtimes here. That may explain why she fainted, although the emotional stress didn't help. He has asked if she's ever been diagnosed with an eating disorder."

"We don't know anything about her medical history," Benito confessed. "Our daughter has been living with relatives until recently. They never said anything about an eating disorder."

"She left for her appointment just before noon, so breakfast Saturday?" Sofia suggested and then turned as Leonardo interrupted her.

"Ria – um – Evie... She came into the kitchen on Saturday morning. Matilda was in one of her moods and started going on about Friday night. Evie turned around and left without eating anything."

"Then Friday afternoon at the staff gathering?"

"No," Matilda said uncomfortably. "She didn't eat anything Friday afternoon. I saw Marco swap plates with her, so that it looked as if she had eaten what was in front of her."

"Don't look at me!" Marco cried defensively. "She said she wasn't hungry."

"Anything at all on Friday?" Nancy asked.

"She slept-in on Friday morning, so there was no time for breakfast," Matilda admitted. "I was in a hurry and I wouldn't wait."

"And she was busy working on the new menus from the time she arrived at the restaurant," Sofia added.

"Thursday afternoon or evening then?"

Marco looked sheepishly at the floor. "Thursday we had pizza. Mama Rosa kept filling her plate. Evie had half a piece, and I ate all the rest."

Nancy frowned at each one in turn, before going to relay the information to the doctor.

How embarrassing for a family that celebrated food to fail to notice when one of their own stopped eating?

ৡ ✪ লঙ

Sebastian swore and sat down, thinking about the implications of this revelation. Evie hadn't had anything to eat for three days. That explained the fainting spell they'd just witnessed. Would it also explain her collapse at *Romano*?

"Why would she stop eating?" Mama Rosa exclaimed.

"I can answer that!" Marco piped up, and in a perfect imitation of his grandmother, he said: "You're too thin, Maria Evangelina. How do you ever expect to get a husband? A good husband needs curves to hold on to."

Mama Rosa looked shocked. "That is just what your Nonna used to say to me and my sister Maria! All the time we were growing up, she was on at us about what we needed to do to get ourselves a husband. I promised I wouldn't do that to my daughters."

"Maria didn't live here," Matilda reminded her. "She was thin when she came."

"No," replied her grandmother with great remorse. "We sent her to live with Nonna and my sister Maria."

"I don't understand," Matilda continued. "If Nonna was always telling you to eat so you could get a 'good husband', why was Ria so thin?"

Sebastian laughed at the irony. Perhaps by not eating, Evie had been sabotaging her chances of getting a 'good husband'. Had she decided she wanted to marry him because he would be a bad one? Then another more encouraging possibility came to him. Perhaps she recognised his attraction despite her elaborate efforts at making herself unappealing.

"Nonna was lost without my Papa, and never recovered after his death," Mama Rosa continued sadly. "My sister was taking care of Nonna even then. No-one expected our Mama to live another forty years after Papa. We stopped going home to visit because Nonna didn't remember who I was, and my sister said it disrupted her routine too much. It was to my sister we sent our little Maria Evangelina."

Her family seemed as surprised to witness Mama Rosa's sorrow as Sebastian was. Mama Rosa turned to her husband. "Papa is so much better at explaining than I am."

"I had better start at the beginning," Benito said. "A long time ago, in a little village in the province of Calabria, back in Italy, there were two sisters, twins born only minutes apart. But though they were similar at birth, as they grew they became as different in temperament as day and night. Rosa was gentle and welcoming like a fully blooming summer rose. The other sister Maria was proud and aloof like an exotic orchid.

"In the same village, there were two boys, childhood friends who fell in love with the sisters. They were all very young, making promises to marry one day. Their children should be raised together, cousins to benefit from strong family bonds of love and security.

"Life was hard, and it seemed best the boys emigrate to Australia to make a better future for everyone. The two young men made their way by boat and were to send for their sweethearts when they had made their fortunes.

"Not long after they departed, a scandal arose at home. The girls' father, a wealthy and well-connected man, was accused of an affair with another man's wife. To avoid retribution, he uprooted his family, following his daughters' fiancés to Australia. The young men were at first delighted their sweethearts were with them so soon, but their father demanded large dowry payments because he was a proud and wealthy man.

"One of the young men found employment in an Italian restaurant and prospered. He saved every dollar to meet the bride price, and quickly earned the hand of his beloved Rosa. Benito and Rosa were happily married. They established themselves comfortably in their new homeland.

"The other young man, Paulo, was equally industrious, but he took the path of a manual trade. When he visited his future bride, he came with work-worn hands and grease-stained fingernails. He found Maria more distant with each passing week until she refused to see him at all. She insisted she would not marry him unless he came to her as the owner of his own business, and with deeds to a big house. He realised it would take him many years to meet her demanding requirements. With a heavy heart, Paulo broke off the engagement and moved away.

"From time to time, letters were sent between the two young men. One day a letter arrived, bringing news of Paulo's impending marriage to an Australian girl. She was already pregnant with their first child. Maria was furious at the news and cursed their union. A few months later, news came that his bride had died in childbirth. Paulo would have to raise his son on his own. Maria laughed and declared God had given her justice for his betrayal.

"Perhaps things would have gone differently for Maria. She may have found another husband, but then her father had another affair. His new mistress was the daughter of an important family. Her father would not give up his lover this time.

"Maria held the young girl responsible. She accused her of seducing and stealing away her Papa. Maria told anyone who would listen about this girl's selfish ambition. Maria and her parents became ostracised. The Italian community sided with the girl's mortified family. Maria's father's health deteriorated and he died suddenly. His wife and unmarried daughter were left with barely enough resources to survive.

"For the rest of her life, the girls' Mama – your Nonna – mourned for the man she had loved. She had followed her husband across the world to this strange and unfamiliar land. Her mind retreated to the familiar memories of her youth. Maria settled into her role as carer. She wore her maidenhood as bitter testimony that all men were faithless.

The women who pursued them should be despised. It was a sorry welcome any young woman would find at her door."

Silence fell.

"What happened to Paulo, the friend who would have married Maria?" Marco eventually asked.

"That story must wait for another time," Sebastian said abruptly.

The nurse appeared in the open doorway. "The doctor says you can return, but she's to remain calm."

ଓ ☼ ଓ

Evie waited nervously for their return. After the doctor left, Nancy had persuaded her to shower. Now she wore the beautiful red nightdress and rose-patterned robe. This robe covered her exposed shoulders but revealed a hint of pale skin above the bodice. Now Evie feared this had been a mistake. The luxurious fabric felt strange against her skin. Her long hair was still loose, arranged to fall around her shoulders. Evie wondered what Sebastian would think of her displayed in his finery.

Knowledge –
A Promise for
Understanding

ᚹ ☼ ᚻ

1 Peter 3:13-15a
Now who will harm you, if you become imitators of that which is
good? But even if you suffer for righteousness, you are blessed.
"Don't fear what they fear, nor be troubled. Sanctify your hearts."

ᚹ ☼ ᚻ

Sebastian took a position against the end wall, not trusting himself to come any nearer. He struggled with the recent revelations. His anger burned towards Evie's family for neglecting her. So annoyed was he at her foolishness in starving herself, he wanted to shake Evie. But he was even more furious with himself for contributing to her troubles. He doubted the wisdom of his presence here.

He was equally confused about what she was wearing. He had imagined how she would look in the red nightdress – indeed he was not disappointed! But he had not expected her to accept his gift. He thought Evie would have changed into the sensible nightdress Sofia had delivered.

Sebastian marvelled at how attractive she had become. The shimmering colours accentuated her paleness and complemented her dark hair. Her fragility intensified now her thinness couldn't be concealed. His determination to protect her strengthened.

ᘓ ✹ ᘒ

Evie waited as everyone resumed the same seats. Nancy procured extra chairs for Leonardo and Marco, which were placed near Sebastian. There was an awkward silence.

Finally, her father spoke. "The doctor said you have an eating disorder. Why did you keep that from us?"

"Until the doctor mentioned it today, I didn't know."

"You didn't know you were ill?" Mama cried.

Evie hesitated. How much did she want to reveal to her family?

Lord, I don't want to sound as if I'm bitter about the past. You know I'm struggling with my emotions. I know that forgiveness requires more than words. I have to make an active choice to let it all go. I am learning that even the memories which torment me are serving a purpose.

Always be ready to give a gentle answer...

"I was told my symptoms were natural consequences of my guilt and shame."

"What doctor would tell a young girl that?" Mama Rosa demanded.

"I didn't see a doctor."

"What?"

"Until today I haven't spoken to a doctor since I lived in Melbourne with you."

"How can you not have seen a doctor in twenty years?" Benito asked with growing concern.

"Zietta Maria was waiting for God's will to unfold."

"What did she mean by 'God's will'?" Matilda demanded.

"She said I was still alive so God hadn't finished with me."
Her quiet response drew shocked gasps.

Benito spoke for them all. "How ill did you become?"

Evie had been looking down and now lifted sorrowful eyes. "I thought I was dying."

"But you didn't," Sofia snapped.

"No, but I was so afraid of dying. Zietta Maria sent me to confession every day. Father Finnegan gave me Scriptures to memorise as penance. One of the first ones was about Jesus being the Bread of Life. I didn't realise until much later this was his antidote for the curses spoken over me. All the negative words were poisoning my soul."

"How can you sit there and say these things so quietly?" Matilda asked. "Didn't you care what happened to you? Don't you care now? I would have complained until someone listened to me. I would never let anyone treat me like that."

"Perhaps I care too much?" Evie countered quietly.

"You speak of your illness as if it was a long time ago, yet you've been starving yourself now," Mama Rosa said. "I don't understand."

"I didn't know I was starving myself. I just wanted to make as little fuss as possible. I had forgotten how emotionally challenging mealtimes could be. I'm so very sorry I've caused so much trouble."

ဆု☼ﬞCଔ

"Stop saying you're sorry for everything!" Sebastian barked, his growing frustration pushing him away from the wall. He stopped at the foot of her bed. "I can't stay here and listen to you apologise to everyone for the way you were treated. When you get out of the hospital you'll be coming to live with me. That's the only way I can be sure you get proper care."

"You can't take her away from her family!" Sofia shrieked.

"She was with you for three weeks, and nobody noticed she needed help!"

"That's unfair!"

"Unfair?" Sebastian laughed sarcastically. "I've been waiting for someone to say they're sorry for what happened to her. Instead, Evie's the one apologising!"

There was an awkward silence. He refocused his attention. "Evie, I'm leaving before I say something I regret. I won't be able to come and see you until after work tomorrow, but I'll be phoning to check how you are."

Striding to the door, Sebastian turned and looked at Sofia. "Pack Evie's bags and send them to the workshop with Leonardo in the morning. I don't want there to be any doubt where she'll be living from now on."

"You have no right—" Sofia began, but he silenced her.

"Don't speak to me about right, after what *you* did to her."

He slammed the door without waiting for Sofia's reply.

"What did he mean?" Marco asked. "What did Mama do?"

ဢ ☼ 03

Into the awkward silence that followed, Evie quietly spoke. "I think there has been enough talk about the past."

"I agree," said Leonardo, walking to where his hero had stood. "But there are still some things that need to be said. Evie, I want to say sorry for ignoring your unhappiness. I was more concerned about how you were upsetting Matilda and wanted life to go back to the way it was. And I'm worried about what is going on between you and the Boss, which is none of my business. So I'm sorry for that as well."

Before Evie could respond, Matilda was also standing. "I want to say sorry too. I haven't been very nice to you, and the more you tried to make peace with me the angrier I got. It might be too late now, but I'm hoping we can start again."

Marco was looking from one sibling to another and jumped hurriedly to his feet. "I'm sorry I ate all your food," he exclaimed earnestly, and there was a ripple of awkward laughter.

"That's okay, Marco. I took it as a great kindness. You intended no harm."

"I'm sorry too," Mama began with tears streaming down her face. Papa reached out and put his arm around her shoulders. "I should have realised my sister wouldn't take proper care of you. I should have insisted you come home. I abandoned my little girl when she needed me most, and I beg your forgiveness."

"Mama!" Evie tearfully reached out to her mother.

"I too need to apologise," Papa began. "Firstly, to my little Maria Evangelina for not recognising the truth. For acting out of pride and hastily judging you. I must also apologise to the woman Ria, the changeling daughter who came back to us. I tried to fit you back into the family as if nothing had happened. Then I sent you to your peril with Romano. I should have realised you were vulnerable. Finally, my dear Evie, I must apologise for taking so long to remember my responsibility to keep you safe. I should have defended your honour. I pray it isn't too late for us to make amends and welcome you back to your family."

"Oh, Papa!" Evie exclaimed, and he joined her and Mama in their tearful embrace.

Marco was standing at the foot of the bed, looking from one relative to the other. He must have realised the only person remaining silent was his mother, and he turned towards her. Evie wasn't sure how to read the expression on her face, but Sofia was crying silent tears.

"Maria," Sofia began as she stood up and walked to the edge of the bed. Evie smiled sadly at her sister's refusal to accept her changed identity and reached out to take her sister's hand. "There's no need to say anything," Evie whispered. "Forgiveness works both ways. I forgave you a long time ago."

"But you don't know what I did! I lied to Papa. I was happy when he sent you away. I didn't want you to be with Nicholas. Then afterwards, when I could have made it right, I kept quiet. If it hadn't been for me, none of this would have happened."

"The past is dead and buried," Evie said quietly. "This was dealt with long ago. I cried too many tears, made too many confessions. I could only receive forgiveness from God because I gave up all the things I held against you. I have released everyone else who played a part in my downfall. It still feels like a disaster, but I know God is doing something amazing.

"I am here in Melbourne because I believe God called me to return. I know His plan is still unfolding. Forgiveness comes with great power. It opens up the opportunity for new beginnings and amazing futures."

"You deserve an amazing future, Evie Fontana," Sofia exclaimed tearfully. The two sisters hugged.

Evie's heart was overflowing with gratitude. Finally, she was reconciled with her family. She could feel God's presence as waves of peace washed over her. Surely everything was going to be alright now...

"Are you really going to live with Romano?" Marco asked. She laughed as his siblings chastised him for his inappropriate timing.

"There is always someone who looks ahead to the next problem," she said pulling a wry face, and then she smiled at him. "There will be plenty of time to worry about that tomorrow."

Lovely -
A Cherished Promise

꙰ ☼ ꙰

1 Peter 3:15b-17
Always be ready to give an answer to everyone who asks you to
give a reason for your hope, with humility and fear, having a good
conscience; that, while you are spoken against, those who curse you
will be disappointed. For it is better, if it is God's will, that you
suffer for doing well than for doing evil.

꙰ ☼ ꙰

Evie awoke to find herself alone. She must have fallen asleep, and her family had gone home. Her phone lay beside the roses. Carefully, Evie reached for it. She deliberated over whether she should contact Sebastian. The screen told her it was only eight pm. Carefully she typed a message, reading and re-reading it before she pressed the send button.

Hi Sebastian.
Thanks for coming today.
I'm especially thankful for what you said
as you were leaving.
Your words unlocked an avalanche of apologies.
It is good to have everything out in the open.
Evie.

Her phone pinged.

Good.

She waited to see if anything else would follow but there was silence. Finally, she sent a second message.

I hope I'm not disturbing you.
Can we talk?

Again she waited. Just when she decided Sebastian wasn't going to reply, the phone in her hand buzzed. Startled, Evie dropped it over the edge of the bed. By the time the nurse retrieved the phone, she had missed Sebastian's call. Immediately she pressed the recall button, only to reach his message service. Annoyed at her clumsiness, Evie forced herself to wait. Her impatience grew. She sent another message, which read:

Dropped phone. Please call back?

When his incoming call finally came, she talked eagerly with him. She began with a retelling of the conversations after he left. He asked what she had eaten for dinner. He seemed satisfied a nutritionist was scheduled to visit her to talk about avoiding a relapse. There was a lull in the conversation when she could think of nothing else to tell him. "What were you doing when I messaged you?" she asked.

"Sitting here drinking beer, and thinking about you," Sebastian replied. Unsure how to respond, Evie waited, hoping he would continue. "Meeting you has done something to my head," he informed her. "I can usually have three or four beers, and never think anything of it, but today

I can't bring myself to finish one. In fact, it has grown too warm to drink, and I'm going to tip it out."

"Is this something I should say sorry for?" she murmured, and he laughed.

"Only if you can explain how you've become my conscience. I keep remembering the way you looked at me when I offered you a beer and the conversation that followed. If I'd known what was going to happen next, I would have stopped drinking right then and saved us both a lot of pain."

"Thinking about what could have been won't help," she replied.

"Your pastor said the same thing. He said the only way I'd be free from this guilt would be if I surrendered everything that happened to God. He said I should ask God for His forgiveness."

"Do you think you can do that?"

"I don't know. You and I have a lot more in common than I thought. You struggle to put off all that condemnation, while I'm dealing with my aunt's ideas about justice and punishment. I believe God is waiting to punish me, and I can't see how anything has changed, especially as I harmed one of His own."

"But God doesn't hold you responsible."

"You can't know that."

"He was there in the room with us when you thought I was dead. He was waiting for you to ask Him for help."

"What?"

"God was right there waiting for you to call out to Him. He knew if you could do that, the door to forgiveness would swing open for you. He had a plan, and whether we understood or not we each contributed to what happened.

There were choices you had to make and choices I had to make."

"What choices did you have to make?"

"I had to decide whether I could be obedient to God and come back. I had the option of telling God I couldn't face this world of pain anymore. His love for you was so strong and powerful I never doubted that coming back was the right thing to do."

"So God made this happen?"

"He didn't *make* it happen. Our human nature and our poor choices did that. God *allowed* this to happen. There's a big difference. He knows what will bring the best outcome for us."

ଫ ☼ ଓ

(Monday 3rd July)

Overtaken by weariness, Evie was thankful to return to her room on Monday afternoon. She had been subjected to a barrage of tests and scans. Whispered consultations brought her assurances someone would talk to her later. Yet she had no satisfactory answer to her question about when she could leave. Now she sat in a wheelchair watching her few possessions being assembled.

"The main tests showed nothing requiring twenty-four-hour supervision. You are transferring to a new ward."

Quickly, Evie sent messages to Sebastian and to her family. She was greatly relieved she would no longer be hooked up to the electronic monitors and confined to bed.

Lord, I'm very tired but thankful You helped me endure this day. Please continue to bring healing to my body and peace to my mind. You know I'm impatient about staying here, but also more than a little anxious about what comes next. Thank You for promising to look after all the details. Please teach me how to trust You in the midst of so much uncertainty. I know You have a perfect plan and I want to wait for You to reveal it.

One of the fruits of the Spirit is patience. Rest in me, and all you need will be provided.

"Let's get you moving," the nurse said, piling her belongings onto her lap. Evie struggled to hold the vase of roses. As they arrived at the elevator, the doors whooshed open and there stood Sebastian.

"Good," said the nurse. "You can push Evie, and I will take those roses before she drops them. Follow me."

Taking command of the wheelchair, Sebastian delivered her to the new room. It was furnished in an identical style. Only the view from the window had changed.

"Back into bed," a new nurse said briskly, turning back the sheets on the bed. Evie had already passed over her possessions, and the red roses were in their customary place. The single white rose was pushed from prominence and seemed forlorn.

෨ ✿ ෭

Sebastian lifted her out of the chair, while she was staring at the roses. He held Evie close to his chest, reminded again of her lightness. "I could get used to this," he confessed, before lowering her onto the bed. The new nurse was quick to cover her up with the sheets, reminding Evie she was not allowed out of bed without assistance. The nurse seemed reluctant to leave her alone with Sebastian. He waited until the door closed.

"I dreamt you came to my room last night," he said quietly, lightly caressing her face. He watched closely for a reaction before stepping away. "You put your arms around me and asked me to hold you, but I knew it was a test. I sent you away. I understand now I have to prove God has chosen me for you. To do that I must wait."

Wide eyes followed him as he confidently drew a chair closer to the bed before reaching for her hand. He marvelled at how tiny it seemed in comparison to his own. Placing a small gift in her hand, he closed her fingers over it. He kissed her hand gently before allowing her to examine his gift. Resting on her palm was a cross pendant set with small rubies. She fastened the fine gold chain around her neck. The pendant focused his attention on her pale skin. It lay above the rose neckline of her red nightdress.

"Thank you," she whispered. "It's lovely. You don't have to bring me presents. You've already done more than enough."

"This present is for me. Wear it to remind me of the promise I've made to God."

Thoughtfully, she looked at it again. "What promise have you made?"

"I've promised to wait for you to decide where we're going with this relationship."

ಬ ✿ ಐ

"We're in a relationship?" she asked, her heart beating more rapidly as she waited for his answer.

He leaned closer and looked directly into her eyes. "Friend or enemy, I don't know which, but my life has changed forever because of you. Not since I first saw you has anything been the same. You annoy me, worry me, distract me, argue with me, challenge me... and *tempt* me. I don't know *why* you have this power over me, and perhaps you will break my heart, but I have to take that risk."

The arrival of her evening meal saved her from making a reply. Sebastian lifted the lid, and she self-consciously started eating. Tonight's offering was roast chicken and vegetables, with ice cream and jelly for dessert. She found it difficult to swallow because he was watching her so intently.

He must have realised why she was struggling. He turned to retrieve something from the floor beside him. Taking a silver notebook computer from a black bag, he plugged the charger into the socket beside her bed. She continued eating, as he set up the screen beside her plate.

He activated a video. At first, she saw only an empty room furnished with black couches. A metal table suggested this was where she had reawakened on Saturday. As she watched, the room filled with men who took up different positions on the couches and around the room. The room was larger than she remembered. There must have been forty people present. They were all wearing uniforms emblazoned with the *Romano* logo. Either black overalls, or jeans with red polo shirts. She recognised Dave and some others from the dinner. Standing in the far corner were the young apprentices. Evie recognised Leonardo and Matilda's boyfriend. Evie wondered what her nephew and niece had told people. She looked at Sebastian for an explanation, but he pointed at her meal.

Obediently, she resumed eating. With her eyes fixed on the small screen, it was easier to forget that Sebastian was studying her.

"I've called this meeting," he said in the video," Because there are a few things I need to tell everyone. Please hold any questions until the end. This meeting won't take long. I'm recording everything, so Freddie at the servo knows what's happened."

There were nods and informal comments from the gathering.

"Some of the facts can be confirmed by Dave and Leonardo, and you can ask them later. Firstly, the girl in the office is another temp from the Caprice Agency. On Saturday I found a permanent office manager, but she couldn't start today.

"The new manager's name is Evie. Some of you met her on Friday evening, at the *Ristorante di Fontana*. There she was called Maria Evangelina or Ria, and she is Leonardo's long-lost aunt. She came here for an interview on Saturday.

"That's the good news. The next is not. Evie is in the hospital with a fractured skull. There was an accident, and I believed she was dead. The police agreed with me, and I thought I was going back to prison. Dave can tell you when he arrived I was halfway through emptying the drinks fridge, resigned to my fate."

On the video, there were exclamations of outrage and shock. Sebastian held up his hand to silence them.

"The short explanation is: we argued. I forgot the dogs were loose in the workshop, and in their excitement, they knocked her down. Evie assured me she was okay but she wasn't. Then she died."

The audience went still. They were staring at their Boss. Dave moved from his seat to stand beside him.

"But she didn't stay dead," Dave reminded him.

"No, she didn't stay dead. All the time the police were here, she said she was standing right next to me. She was praying for me because she could see how upset I was. Evie said God's love was so strong in this place she knew right away what choice God was putting before her. She said there is greater rejoicing in heaven for one lost soul saved than for ninety-nine saints. So when I asked God for a second chance, she willingly came back to me."

"She chose to come back to you?" Dave exclaimed.

"She said heaven is always in her future, so it wasn't a hard decision. Except she didn't expect the pain to be so intense. It turned out she also needed saving, from the lies of the past, and now God has put a choice before me in return."

"What kind of choice?" Dave asked, stepping even closer and glaring at Sebastian.

"Evie will live here; she needs twenty-four-hour supervision. I plan to marry her."

"Why would you want to marry her?"

"She was more than a little crazy when I first saw her in the hospital," he conceded. "She said she wanted to get married. What was I supposed to say?"

"You could have said no!"

"Instead I said yes, but not without making sure she understands what being married to me will mean."

Leonardo's sudden laughter rang out in the ensuing silence. Sebastian shot him a warning look. Sebastian dismissed everyone, but the video continued recording after they left.

Dave remained. He hadn't finished with his questions. "You said she made you angry? What are you going to do next time you argue?"

"Every time I look at her I'm reminded not to lose control of my anger. My pride was wounded because I thought she had rejected me without giving me a chance, and that won't be a problem now. She's already chosen me, and that changed me inside. I don't think I will ever be the same again."

"What if she wants to leave when she's better?"

"It will hurt. But it won't change the fact that while she was between death and life, she cared enough to choose me. Aunt Constance convinced me no woman worth having would ever see anything good in me. Evie has proven her wrong."

Reaching across to turn off the computer, Sebastian waited for her to respond. Evie acknowledged her compassion for this man. What was she to do with his continuing sense of obligation towards her? He had said his anger had been a response to being rejected by her, and she was in awe of this new power he said she had over him.

Lord, please help me choose my words carefully. Only you can bring the two of us into a safe place where Your love can bind us or release us, according to Your perfect will.

My love brings you healing and restoration, rest in my presence and trust me.

"You said you weren't sure whether I was your friend or your enemy?" she asked tentatively. "If those are the choices then we should be friends."

Reaching out to take her hand, he smiled. "We both know I want much more than friendship, but if that's what you're offering, I accept."

Mission -
A Promise for Guidance

ಬಿ ✿ ಅ

Isaiah 30:21
When you turn to the left, and when you turn to the right, your ears
will hear a voice behind you saying, "This is the way. Walk in it."

ಬಿ ✿ ಅ

The decision to discharge her from the hospital on Friday morning came unexpectedly. Evie faced a difficult choice. She could leave the hospital in her nightdress, or wear Sebastian's revealing clothes. The hospital had already confirmed he was on his way. But he had not replied to her text messages asking him to bring her something to wear. All her possessions were at his flat. Her concern about how his employees would receive her appearance was growing.

Lord. I don't want to start my new life like this, angry and annoyed with him. Why am I so worried about what other people think of me? For most of my life, everyone presumed even worse. Please help me to focus on the important things, and help me deal with my pride and selfishness.

Remember I have made you the way you are, and learn to live the life I have prepared for you. These little anxieties are unimportant and have already been defeated. Learn to rest in my provision.

As she put on each item of new clothing, she had to pray off old condemnation. She began with the lacy underwear. These flimsy garments revealed more than they concealed. As promised, the skinny black pants did cling like 'a second skin'. But the tartan miniskirt was more concealing than she first thought. Her reflection in the bathroom mirror did not seem as scandalous as she feared. The T-shirt's scooped neckline was very low. Her jewelled pendant looked like it was floating on a sea of bare skin. Evie prayed Sebastian would remember his promise.

Stepping from the bathroom, Evie found a young nurse packing her possessions. The roses had been removed from the vase and were now wrapped and lying on the trolley-table. The nurse turned to look at her and smiled.

"You look lovely in that outfit," she said approvingly. "Would you like me to help you with your hair?"

When the nurse finished the braid, Evie was thankful for her kindness. She sat on a padded chair and attempted to put on her boots. The unfamiliar footwear proved stiffly resistant. Her trembling fingers had trouble with the laces. She didn't notice Sebastian standing in the open doorway watching her.

"Let me help you with those," he declared, and she gave a startled cry. He was already down on one knee, and he laughed and put his arm out to catch her. "Whoa! Are you always this jumpy when someone offers to help you with your boots? I hope you will be calmer when we get home and I help you out of them again."

Evie tactfully held her tongue. The thought of him helping her 'out of' her boots raised concerns about what was to come.

"Stand up and let me look at you," he commanded after the boots were laced to his satisfaction. "Turn around. I can't see why these clothes are so unsuitable. But as you were so insistent with your texts, here is a jacket to wear over them. Tomorrow I will buy you some new clothes. I couldn't find anything in your suitcase I wanted to see you wearing. In fact, I was tempted to throw everything away, but then I remembered that was the first thing your aunt did. The decisions about what you bring forward from your old life should be all yours."

Evie took the knee-length black jacket he held out to her, and hastily put it on. It was one of the few items of clothing she had purchased recently. It was a surprise to realise it went well with the black pants.

"Thanks," she said gratefully, adjusting the belt.

"Are you ready to go?" he asked and turned to where the nurse was waiting with the wheelchair.

"I can walk," Evie protested, but they both silenced her.

"Hospital policy," the nurse began.

"Hospital policy," Sebastian repeated sternly, depositing Evie in the chair. "I'd carry you all the way, but departing patients have to be wheeled to the exit."

She discovered he had already completed the paperwork. All that remained was her signature on a document confirming she was leaving in his care. This time, she was the one holding the roses. The nurse walked alongside, carrying her possessions.

They paused to collect her pain medication and repeat prescriptions. There were too many, and medical appointment reminders for next week. The nurse accompanied them to the main entrance. Again, Sebastian lifted Evie from the chair. Her bag was placed in her arms, and he turned towards the space reserved for patient pickup. She gasped.

His Maserati sports car was red and shiny in the morning sun. The black leather canopy was closed, a concession to the bitter wind. Pedestrians were pausing to admire the gleaming paintwork and the immaculate interior. Evie had to concede everything about Sebastian Romano attracted attention. She experienced an unusual sense of pride to be with him. Now if she could only get him to stop treating her like an invalid!

"I can walk on my own," she reminded him, and he laughed.

"Of course you can, but this is much more fun," and he playfully crushed her close to him. He lowered her carefully to her feet beside the sports car.

After securing Evie in the passenger seat, he eased himself behind the steering wheel. Sebastian drove with extreme confidence. Evie tried to stop thinking about his speed. Instead, her thoughts turned to their destination.

"Are you sure about this? I'm not an easy housemate, as Matilda can attest. I spend a lot of time praying for real and imagined problems, talking to myself and getting in everyone's way. I'm annoying and clumsy. I hate housework and I can't cook." Evie paused to breathe, and he interrupted her.

"I'm not expecting you to do housework or cook for me. I have a cleaner who comes once a week. The same firm looks after Reception and the staff room at *Romano*. And your Mama Rosa is going to feed us. Leonardo has been bringing food with him, and the freezer is full.

"I don't mind if you get in my way, because I enjoy looking at you, now you're wearing more acceptable clothes. As for praying, once you realise I'm your biggest problem, things will be much simpler for you. You should be worrying instead about how you'll put up with me."

Evie could think of no response, and they continued in silence. When they arrived, Sebastian activated the side roller door to the black *Romano* building, driving his Maserati inside. He walked around to open her door. Evie placed both feet on the polished concrete. She glanced around anxiously, to see if anyone was watching. Her heart was racing, and she felt flushed and lightheaded. Without thought, she reached out to him, and Sebastian caught her before she fell. Her embarrassment escalated as he continued holding her close to him. He lifted her chin to look into her eyes before releasing her. Evie brushed her hands over her long jacket and smiled awkwardly.

"Hey, Evie!" Leonardo called to her as he hurried over. "You certainly know how to make an entrance!"

She took a couple of uneasy steps, endeavouring to smile.

"Leonardo, bring Evie's things up to the flat," Sebastian growled. Suddenly he lifted her into his arms again. The belted jacket fell open. Now instead of covering her legs, it drew attention to them. The other men working nearby had stopped to look at her, and she could feel their gaze upon her. She turned her face towards his chest, away from watching eyes.

Ascending the nearest stairs, Leonardo was a few paces ahead of them. He hurriedly opened the door to the flat, and then Sebastian carried Evie over the threshold. Continuing on through the archway, he laid her down on the black couch. She closed her eyes and sighed. The dizziness dissipated as suddenly as it had begun. When she opened her eyes he was kneeling with concern beside her. Smiling hesitantly, Evie reached out her hand to touch his arm.

"Please don't worry about this dizziness. It comes and goes. I think I need to sleep now," Evie assured him, closing her eyes again. "Put my phone beside me, and I'll call you if I need anything."

ॐ ☼ ☾

Sebastian returned to find her still sleeping. He was reluctant to wake her, but the hospital had insisted he establish regular meal times. There were also pills she was supposed to take.

"Hey, Evie," he said, patting her hand. "Wake up."

"Hey," she said sleepily. "How long was I asleep?"

"An hour. You have to eat something to go with these tablets. I can't cook either, but I'm an expert at reheating things."

Cautiously, Evie sat up, taking the tablets and a glass of water from him. She swallowed carefully. The bitter aftertaste of the medication needed more water to wash it away.

"Could I have more water please?" she asked.

ॐ ☼ ☾

Watching him rush to accommodate her request increased her sense of helplessness. A tear escaped her eye. She hoped he wouldn't notice, but when she wouldn't look at him directly, he turned her face towards him. More tears escaped, and he brushed them away with his hand.

"Please don't cry. Eat something, and then I will show you to your room. There you can sleep the rest of the day away." He sat patiently beside her as she ate. Several times, he prompted her to eat more until she pushed the half-empty plate into his hand.

"I can't. Please don't try to make me eat anymore."

He looked at the concern on her face and put the plate on

the coffee table. Taking her hand, he led her through to the bedroom wing. Pausing before the first room, he reached out as if to grasp the door handle. "This is my room," he said, before leading her further along the passageway to a second door. "And this is yours."

Opening the door, he stepped aside, allowing her to go in alone. Taking a few steps forward, Evie entered the large white room. There was plush grey carpet underfoot. Against the opposite wall was a carved wooden king-sized bed. A set of bedside tables with white lamps stood on either side. To the right of the door was a large matching dressing table. Several rows of small square windows topped the wall above the bed. A large skylight filled the room with light. A red two-seater couch and matching armchair were on the other side of the dressing table. Through an open door, she discovered a white bathroom. Built-in wardrobes filled the fourth wall. On the bed was a floral patterned quilt in red, white and grey, with coordinated cushions and a blanket on the couch.

Evie was speechless at the grandeur of the room. Cautiously she opened the robe doors. There she found her meagre belongings. Next, she went through to the bathroom. Peeping through another door she found an unfurnished room. When she returned she sat on the edge of the couch and looked at the bed.

"You said this was my room? It's much larger than I was expecting."

"The room or the bed?" he asked in amusement.

"Both," she said, acknowledging his suggestive remark with a hesitant smile. He had invested more meaning in her simple statement. He was still outside her room looking in from the hallway which reassured her he would honour his promise.

"Will you be okay on your own?" he asked. After she nodded, he turned away.

She listened to his retreating footsteps. Finally, a distant door closed and she knew she was alone. Remaining seated, Evie prayed about Sebastian's generosity. After thanking God for His protection, she shut the bedroom door. She only unlaced her new boots and removed her belted jacket. Lying down on top of the quilt, she remained fully clothed in case he returned to check on her. The afternoon passed as she slept. When she awoke she felt refreshed, the lethargy of the preceding days a fading memory.

Carefully sitting up, she was relieved the dizziness was gone. Her head still ached, and she was thirsty. Shyly, she walked across the carpet to the door and went towards the kitchen. Her glass was neatly rinsed and sitting beside the sink. Refilling her glass with water, she drank deeply. As she turned from the sink, she discovered her phone on the kitchen bench.

Curious about how much time had passed she picked it up, to find a simple text message from Sebastian.

Awake yet?

The message was sent hours ago, for it was now 4:30 pm. Sebastian's workday would soon be over. Unsure how she should spend the remaining time,
Evie sent a reply to his text.

Can I come down to the workshop?

A few moments later her phone rang. "Wear your boots and helmet," he said, startling her with his brevity.
"Are you joking or serious?"
"Serious."

"Are the dogs loose?"

"Yes, but I can send them out."

"Don't, because I want to see them. It wasn't their fault, and I need to overcome my fear."

Retracing her steps, Evie searched for the helmet and put it on after battling with the straps. Her reflection in the mirror – darkened bruise and white dressing – reiterated his caution. This time, putting on the boots was easier to manage. When she reached for the long jacket, she paused, looking intently at her reflection again. The slender dark-haired woman who gazed back at her wore the clothes well. The skirt was not too brief nor the top too figure-hugging or revealing to be rejected as excessively provocative. Remembering how someone whistled at the sight of her legs, she realized it wasn't the clothes, but the body underneath she needed to accept.

Sebastian had made it clear he didn't want her hiding who she was anymore. Perhaps this was an opportunity to find out whether she could live with that. Evie left the jacket behind. She slipped her phone into the front pocket of her skirt and stepped out of the flat.

Descending the staircase slowly, she came to the small divided landing. Turning towards the working men, Evie continued until she could sit down near the bottom. There she planted her feet firmly on the floor.

Lord, help me not to be afraid. If I'm to live here, I have to put my fears to rest. Help me to remember what I've learnt, and keep me safe when Tiny and Fifi come running to greet me.

Taking a deep breath she gave a long sharp whistle.

131

Ever vigilant, Sebastian looked around the workshop as she appeared on the landing. More than one pair of eyes watched her careful descent. At her whistle, everyone stopped working, waiting to see what would happen next. Evie seemed so fragile and delicate as she sat on the stairs. Leonardo wanted to go to her, but Sebastian held him back.

"She has to do this on her own."

• ✿ •

Moments later, she heard the 'click click' of hurrying canine paws. Tiny and Fifi appeared from among the maze and approached Evie. "Stop!" she called out and signalled with her hand, hoping she looked more confident than she felt. Both dogs instantly obeyed her. "Stay!"

Tiny stood closest, his head to one side and his ears pricked high on his head. "Here Tiny!" she called again, and the dog moved towards her outstretched arm. He sniffed her hand and accepted a scratch and a pat. "Good dog," she continued. "You remember me?"

Tiny barked as if in reply, and at his response, Fifi surged forward. "Wait!" Evie commanded, and Fifi stopped before Evie called her again. Rewarding the second dog with a pat, Evie hugged both of them. She endured some uncomfortable licks as they reacquainted themselves. They were curious about the strange adornment on her head. When she sensed they were about to start more vigorous play, Evie spoke again. "Away!" she said, signalling like Sebastian had done when he sent the dogs off on that fateful day.

Tiny barked again, and both dogs ran away only to reappear a few minutes later. They waited to see what New Friend would do next. Evie was considering her options when she heard the sound of someone clapping. Looking up, she saw Sebastian coming towards her.

"Well done!" he said. "When did you learn to do that?"

"I haven't spent all my time in hospital sleeping," she responded with a bright smile. Her face glowed with gratitude because she had pleased him. "The computer you left with me was most helpful. I wasn't sure if I was confident enough to give it a try."

"Tiny and Fifi were impressed."

It wasn't the dogs she had wanted to impress. As they were talking, Sebastian steered her towards Leonardo, the dogs following behind.

"Nice helmet," Leonardo laughed. "But bright pink is all wrong with your outfit."

Evie put her hands on her hips and turned to Sebastian. "How long do I have to wear this ridiculous helmet?" she demanded, her cheeks flushing with embarrassment at Leonardo's teasing. Immediately she regretted the sharpness in her voice. The doctors had said the extreme mood swings should soon settle, but she was so easily upset! Frustration turned too quickly to remorse, which made her sound even angrier.

"For as long as I tell you to," Sebastian said bluntly.

He picked her up and perched her high on a metal shelf. He shook his head. "My workshop, my rules. Is that clear?"

"Obviously," she snapped. "Now get me down from here. You've made your point." Her legs couldn't reach the ground, and she mustn't risk an undignified tumble.

"Boss, I don't think that's a good idea," Leonardo spoke cautiously.

"Why not?" Sebastian asked. "When Dave's daughter comes to visit, she loves to sit up there."

"Evie's not a five-year-old."

"Then she should stop acting like one."

Leonardo looked nervous. He took a few cautious steps towards Evie. Sebastian frowned and waved her nephew aside before lifting Evie down and carefully setting her on her feet. Without apologising, Sebastian turned his back on Evie and went back to work. Evie folded her arms across her chest, fuming over what had happened. He thought *she* was behaving like a five-year-old! He asked her nephew questions about the oil leak the young apprentice was trying to rectify. Leonardo glanced at Evie, and she moved to stand beside him, peering over his shoulder. Immediately she realised Leonardo had missed the simple cause. She pointed into the engine cavity.

"Have you checked the oil pan bolts?" Evie asked Leonardo.

Sebastian responded in surprise. "You said you didn't know anything about cars."

"Dog commands weren't the only thing I researched. Leonardo should use a torque wrench. Consulting the manufacturer's specifications will determine how to correctly tighten those bolts."

Leonardo followed her advice.

"That is the second surprise this afternoon. What else did you research?" Sebastian asked with growing interest. She looked at him for a moment, and then remembered the sports car adorned T-shirt she was wearing.

"Your dream car is a 1962 Maserati 3500 Vignale Spyder. There were only two hundred and forty-two made—"

His eyes widened, and he interrupted her speech. "I was wrong to treat you like a child. If I keep you out of the way, you won't learn anything about how to be part of my team. But I'm not going to get any work done with you distracting me. Go and annoy someone else."

"Anyone in particular you want me to annoy, Boss?" she asked. He grimaced at her sarcasm.

"Dave's working over near the roller doors. Go and annoy him. He needs convincing you're here to stay."

Before the heat of her determination faded, Evie set off across the workshop looking for Dave. She was surprised at the intensity of her emotions. First he treated her like a child, then he said she was annoying him. What was she doing wrong?

A gentle answer turns away wrath.

That comes from Proverbs, Lord?

Evie stopped, forgetting where she was. She reached into her pocket and took out her phone. Finding the Bible app, she typed 'a gentle answer' into the search bar. The first result looked promising. Clicking on the link she read the text on the screen.

"Proverbs chapter 15, 'A gentle answer turns away wrath, but a harsh word stirs up anger. The tongue of the wise commends knowledge, but the mouths of fools gush out folly... A fool despises his father's correction, but he who heeds reproof shows prudence... There is stern discipline for one who forsakes the way; whoever hates reproof shall die'."

When her eyes came to the final verse, her heart confirmed what God wanted to say.

Lord, I'm sorry. Sebastian's right that I don't know how to keep myself safe. I don't understand why I'm upset. Please forgive me and help me to do better. Help me to follow his advice with Dave and achieve whatever it is You need me to do to make things right. Thanks for not letting me keep going on the wrong path.

With a softer heart, Evie continued to where Dave was working.

ꕥ

He had seen her coming. When she stopped beside him, Dave wiped his oily hands on a rag, waiting for her to speak.

"Hi," she began hesitantly. "Sebastian sent me to talk to you."

Dave was surprised at the relaxed way she used that name. Usually, his friend discouraged such familiarity.

Evie continued speaking. "He said I should go and annoy someone else."

"And he picked me?" Dave looked across towards his oldest friend. What did Seb hope to achieve with this latest move? Was this for her benefit or an attempt to change Dave's mind about her?

"I've just finished here, and am taking the docket to the office, so you can tag along." Turning to the apprentice beside him, Dave gave instructions for the end-of-day clean up. Then he beckoned her to follow him towards the office.

Slowing his pace, Dave ensured Evie kept up. Despite his irritation, he had some sympathy for her situation. When they reached the door, Dave signalled for the dogs, who were shadowing her every move, to go away. The agency girl was terrified of them. After submitting the paperwork, Dave continued to the break room. He went over to the drinks fridge and took out a beer for himself and a soft drink for her.

"Wait here while I clean up and change out of my work gear," Dave advised her, taking his beer with him, and leaving her alone.

ꕥ

She could hear Dave moving around in the next room. The opening and closing of a metal locker brought fleeting memories of a previous visit. Was it only a week ago her world had turned upside down?

Evie walked around the room until she was standing where she had been in the vision. The couch where her lifeless body had lain was to her right. There were six couches. Two metal tables broke up space in the centre of the rectangle. On the other side of the room were tables and chairs, with a large television screen on one wall. Cautiously she sat down facing the door through which Dave had disappeared.

This door was one of three, located behind the couch she had awoken on last week. Sebastian must have carried her here from the shower, through the locker room. She had just walked through the door behind her, so the remaining door was the one the police had used. She guessed this led out to Reception. Lost in thought, Evie relived the memory of standing apart from her body. Then she lost herself to the memory of meeting the One who inhabited the light. Only then had her fear fled.

ଛ ✡ ଓ

Dave watched from the doorway. Her eyes were fixed on the couch, the unopened soft drink still in her hands. This reminded him of his own response to Seb's shocking revelation she was dead.

"What was it like to be dead?" Dave asked.

Evie was startled by his voice and almost dropped the bottle. Dave walked over, twisted the top off and placed the drink on the table in front of her. Sitting across from her, he waited for a reply.

"I didn't know I was dead until I heard Sebastian say he had killed me. I thought the memories would come back, but the last thing I remember is him picking me up after I fell in the workshop."

"You heard him say he'd killed you?"

"I was standing right there," Evie pointed, "and I could see my body lying on the couch, but at first I didn't know it was me. Then Sebastian spoke, and I wondered how this could be? Until that moment I thought I was dreaming. It was terrifying at first – galaxies of swirling rainbow light followed by an explosion of stars. Then roaring waves of pain obliterated everything. When the stars and the pain ended, as suddenly as they began, I was in a river wild and dark. It seemed like I floated forever before a distant light appeared. The light came closer and brightened until there was nothing in the universe except the light."

Her eyes were ablaze with the memory. Watching her face transform, Dave allowed some of his doubt to slip away. There was something miraculous in the change he was witnessing. He began to understand why his friend had fallen under her spell. The smile that lit her face was enchanting.

"At the centre of the light was a person, and I knew Him even though I'd never seen Him before. His name is Jesus, and He is my Saviour Redeemer. I put my faith in Him a long time ago, and He proved Himself to be true. He was there with me when death came. I asked if I was in Heaven and he told me I was to stand with Him to watch and pray while a battle was waged over Sebastian's soul.

"Then I found myself in this room, surrounded by light and unafraid, though the things I heard and saw were terrifying. I saw you arrive with the police and listened to Sebastian take full responsibility for my death. I couldn't believe he would throw his life away without trying to defend himself. That was so unfair! Jesus knew all that and more, and He already had a plan to save Sebastian. The love that filled this place was electrifying. Then I realised Jesus had a part for me to play if I would choose to obey.

"The moment I realised what was happening seems more like a dream than anything else. Again there was an explosion, and the pain was back, worse than before. I find myself wondering, now I know coming back is so painful and difficult, would I have the strength to make that choice again?"

Evie fell silent.

"What are you doing here?" Dave asked, leaning forward and watching her closely to gauge the truthfulness of her answer.

"Here as in 'alive' or here as in letting Sebastian take care of me?"

"Here as in with Seb."

"I don't know," she replied, and Dave saw the joy disappear from her face. She looked troubled now. "I thought I'd never forget the peace and joy I experienced just before I came back. I was so sure of God's love that I thought nothing would ever trouble me again."

Evie picked up the soft drink and looked at it for a moment, before placing it back on the table.

"Do you love him?" Dave asked.

"Love him? How am I supposed to answer that question? What if I don't know how to love him? A week ago I didn't know Sebastian existed. He was just someone Papa introduced me to, and it feels as if I know him even less now. Sebastian keeps surprising me by doing the unexpected. I don't know how to respond to his attention. Should I thank him for taking care of me or tell him he has done more than enough, and ask him to release me? Nothing is certain anymore."

"Why should he release you? Release you from what?"

"I've allowed Sebastian to take me away from my family, but I don't know what will happen when he tires of me," she cried. "Here I sit in this ridiculous helmet, wearing fewer clothes than I should because he told me to. Talking to you, even though I know you want me gone. I was so sure I knew who I was and what God required of me, but I see the world through different eyes now. I don't know if I like what I see. Sebastian means more to me than anyone I've ever known. What if he doesn't care for me at all, and is just doing all this because he feels sorry for me?"

"There's no doubt he cares," Dave said, "or you wouldn't be here. You can take him at his word. If he says he loves you, then he loves you."

"But he hasn't said he loves me."

"You stole his heart even before he left the restaurant. That's the only explanation for him inviting you here alone. But I think he would have let you come and go without you ever knowing his real intentions. He thought he was immune to love. If you'd proven true to your reputation, if you had taken his attempts to dissuade you from staying at face value, then I think he'd have let you go. But it is too late to talk about that now. You're his first love, but you'll also be his last. Sebastian won't forgive himself for putting his trust in you, nor recover from your betrayal when you leave."

ဝ ✿ ༕

"If he loves me, why would I leave?" Evie asked, unsettled by Dave's assessment of the situation. What was she to make of this information? She had been thinking of asking Sebastian to release her from his feelings of obligation. Now she was horrified he might send her away.

"You told him you wanted him to marry you, but your heart is cold towards him. He'll wait for you forever, content with the occasional smile and kind word. How long before you realise other men find you attractive, and you turn to them for attention?"

Evie was shocked and jumped to her feet. "I'd never do that!"

"If that's true, then everyone here will take care of you because of your loyalty to him. But if you're lying, then no-one here will be your friend."

An unexpected chorus of agreement arose. Other employees had entered quietly as the workday ended. More than a dozen men had gathered in the background without interrupting their intense conversation. A wave of dizziness overcame Evie, and she swayed before dropping back onto the couch.

"Are you okay?" Dave asked.

"Just dizzy," she whispered. "It comes and goes. Please don't tell Sebastian!"

"Don't tell me what?" Sebastian said from the doorway where he had also been listening. Before he could reach her, she blacked out completely. When she awoke, she was lying on the couch. She insisted on sitting up. Sebastian sat beside her, with his arm around her shoulders. Dave passed him the drink she had yet to start, and she took a careful sip.

"Now tell me," Sebastian growled, "whether I was wrong in making you wear that 'ridiculous' helmet?" He tapped the top of the shell lightly with his knuckles and then undid the straps to remove it from her head. "Now I'm here, you can take it off. I want some answers. That is the second dizzy spell I've seen. It isn't a good sign. Did the hospital know this was happening, or did you pretend everything was fine so they'd let you leave?"

Evie turned her attention to the soft drink to avoid answering his question.

Unexpectedly, Dave came to her rescue by passing his friend a bottle of beer and asking, "How long were you listening?"

Sebastian looked from Dave to Evie. "Long enough to hear you ask whether she intended to stay. It would be a very courageous man, or a foolish one, who would try and take her from me."

"But if she decides she can't love you?" Dave persisted. "What will you do if she asks to leave?"

"Would you leave, Evie?" Sebastian asked her. "All you have to do is ask, and I'll let you go." To match his words, he took his arm away and put distance between them.

"I'll only go if you send me away," she replied sadly, not daring to look up as she opened her heart to him. She feared her unshed tears would betray her. Dave had said Sebastian loved her, and such hope had sprung into life at those words. "You know I've made a promise to you. I've placed my future in your hands. Haven't my actions proven my intent to honour that promise?

"Why do you talk about someone taking me from you when you hold me so lightly? Do I matter so little you would release me from my promise so easily?"

"I said I'd let you go," he said sternly, drawing her close. "I never said I'd send you away. I have promised to take care of you, and you can rely on that. If you don't trust my word, consider Dave's wisdom, because he knows me better than anyone else. He said you're my first and only love."

Novelty –
A Promise Renewed

෨ ☼ ෫

Isaiah 43:18-19
Don't remember the former things, and don't consider
the things of old. Behold, I am doing a new thing.
It springs out now. Don't you know it?
I will even make a way in the wilderness, and rivers in the desert.

෨ ☼ ෫

Her first evening with Sebastian was uneventful, and sleep came effortlessly. Evie might have slept longer, but he had programmed a personalised ringtone on her phone. His 9:30 am call startled her awake.

"Breakfast in bed?" his voice asked boldly, followed immediately by laughter at her protest. Moments later, she found him serving bacon and eggs in the kitchen. In her haste, she had thrown the floral robe over the red nightdress and hurried out with her feet still bare. From his smile, she decided he was pleased to see her still wearing his gifts.

Relieved, she sat down to the smaller plate of food. With Sebastian more interested in his huge breakfast, Evie cautiously ate. The simple food was delicious and soon her plate was empty. He smiled at her as she set aside her fork, obviously viewing this as a major victory.

After breakfast, Evie was tormented over what to wear. A battle raged in her heart. Why was she donning lacy underwear instead of her more practical garments? Had she changed so much in the past week? She reminded herself of the importance of making honourable choices. Finally, she emerged from her bedroom wearing her grey check skirt with the hemline below her knees. This skirt had been her favourite – second-hand but of good quality to give her serviceable wear. But she was wearing the black T-shirt he had given her. She could find nothing else that complemented the pendant he had given her.

"Where are my shoes?" she asked.

"Everything you were wearing that day, including your shoes, was ruined so I threw them away."

"They were the only shoes I had," Evie cried, and immediately realised her mistake. "I can't wear boots all the time," she added as his face clouded over. How ungrateful she must sound!

"If I'd known they were your only shoes, I'd have tried to save them. Wear the boots and I'll buy you a new pair of shoes."

Returning in the boots, Evie had another problem she was unable to solve. Her handbag had gone the way of the missing shoes. She had found her bank card and the little money that had been in her old purse in a drawer beside her bed.

"I don't have a pocket," she said apologetically. "Could you take care of my phone and money for me?"

"The skirt I bought you has a pocket," he reminded her, as he tucked her possessions into his black leather jacket. "Why aren't you wearing that?"

"I only have the black pants to wear underneath your tartan skirt, and I struggle to get in and out of them. I thought I should wear something easier to manage in the change room."

"Remind me again why I didn't throw away your old clothes," he muttered as they made their way from the flat. He insisted on keeping his arm around her waist as they crossed the workshop. The dogs were locked in their yard. He freed them when Evie was safely outside.

This was her first visit to the neighbouring shopping centre. Accompanying Sebastian filled her with trepidation. He had expensive taste and strong opinions. She prayed about her anxieties and fears.

Lord, everything about this shopping trip makes me worry. I don't want to argue with him, but You have seen the choices that he made about what he wants me to wear. I need You to help me to stand up for myself, and not to give in because I want to please him.

Breathe in My peace, My child. Your restlessness will wear you out. Know that I have already provided all you need. This man will take care of you because you are My child. I have given him great wealth so you do not have to worry about these little things. Let him learn what it is to be loved by the way you respond to his generosity with humility and grace.

Determined to be obedient to God, Evie remained silent when Sebastian said he was paying for her new black shoes. She tried to conceal her alarm at the cost. While she explained to the assistant that she intended to wear the shoes immediately, he stepped away. When he returned, he surprised Evie with another two pairs, one pair bright red and the other blue. Before she could say anything, he was selecting a black handbag with red trim from the shelf behind the counter. Next, he pointed to a red purse from another display. The smiling sales assistant added these to his tally.

From the shoe shop, they slowly made their way past brightly lit shops without speaking. As they walked through the crowd with his arm around her waist, Evie felt self-conscious. Passersby turned to look at him as they went past, and some even deliberately stepped aside to let him pass. His confidence increased her awe of him.

The next shop Sebastian entered had blue jeans on display in the open doorway. "When was the last time you wore jeans?" he asked, and without waiting for an answer turned to the shop assistant who hurried towards them.

"Evie doesn't know what size she needs, so choose what you think might fit and show us to the change room."

Evie hesitated. He whispered a reminder about having already seen more of her than she was going to reveal now. Unless she needed help, he promised to remain outside the small cubicle. He passed a pair of jeans to her over the door and she hurriedly tried them on.

She thought the first pair would suffice, but Sebastian asked her to come out so both he and the young male shop assistant could make sure she was right. He repeated the process with other pairs until she was confused about what they had selected.

Seated outside the shop she looked in the shopping bags.

"Why do I need eight pairs of jeans?" she asked, counting four blue pairs, three black and a red pair.

"You need heavy duty clothes for the workshop, and you need variety. I can throw these in the machine with my own without having to worry about ruining them."

"But they must have cost—"

He interrupted her by pointing to the bright red 'Sale' signs hanging in the shop window. "Everything was on sale."

Taking the bags from her, Sebastian again put his arm around her waist. He steered her through the crowd, delivering her to another store with 'Sale' signs. Evie hesitated when she saw the illuminated name above the door. This fashionable boutique belonged to an international designer label. She looked closely at the mannequins in the window and wondered what Sebastian had in mind.

"Colour," he said when the trendy young sales assistant approached them. "And something that doesn't remind me of my old maiden aunt."

This time Evie entered a spacious curtained change room. The young woman passed her different dresses, skirts and tops. The assistant gave her expert opinion about whether the style suited her. A second assistant ran to and fro with more garments. Evie was only paraded before Sebastian when the first assistant was satisfied. In this way, they selected five brightly coloured casual dresses with hemlines above the knee, six fitted shirts, three colourful tops and four skirts, including one which fell all the way to the floor and accentuated her slender figure.

Thinking she was finished, Evie was alarmed when the second assistant returned with a sensuous black lace dress.

"Every woman needs a little black dress," the first assistant told her with a knowing smile. The two assistants were enthusiastic with their praise. They turned Evie around so she could see how the stretchy lace fabric clung to her every curve. The sleeveless dress had a very brief skirt with a scalloped hem. The neckline was demure at the front, but the back was scooped low to reveal bare skin to below her waist. The colour drained from Evie's face. Then she felt immense relief when the second assistant spoke. "He doesn't want you to model this dress for him. Save it for a special occasion."

Suddenly Evie was impatient to be out of the shop. The implications of how he might respond when he saw her in that black dress added to Evie's confusion about their relationship. She couldn't deny her intense response to the appreciative way he had been looking at her. The dawning revelation she was physically attracted to him threw her into greater turmoil. This thought pursued her and now she found it difficult to put aside.

Evie rested at a small table in one of the busy cafés while he went to the counter to order their lunch. The opportunity to sit still was welcome. Shopping with Sebastian was an intensely exhausting experience.

"What are you thinking about?" he asked. He must have been sitting opposite her unnoticed for several minutes. His simple comment brought colour to her cheeks. He reached across the table for her hand and all her calm resolve fled.

Glancing down at their joined hands, she answered truthfully, "I was thinking about you."

"Good thoughts, I hope? Haven't I been kind and generous towards you?"

"You've been more than kind. Your generosity astounds me," she assured him quickly, looking up to find he was teasing her again. Laughter lit up his face and the way he was gazing at her caused her heart to beat even faster.

Evie was thankful when the waitress appeared with their meals.

"I can't believe you've never had a chicken burger." He showed her how to hold the massive bun in both hands. Mayonnaise ran down her chin and onto her hands with her first bite, and he used a serviette to wipe it away. She had only eaten a quarter by the time he finished his larger meal. He surprised her by reaching across the table to steal one of the potato wedges from her plate.

"Hey!" she exclaimed, and he grinned at her, taking another one.

"Don't tell me you intend to eat all that," he chided her. "While you were sleeping, I was working out in the gym. Now I'm ravenous. Give me what you don't want, and drink your milkshake."

Responding to his teasing by taking another mouthful of food, Evie chewed thoughtfully. She continued eating for several minutes while he stole her food. When she conceded she was full, they swapped plates. This reminded her of the way her nephew Marco had covered for her, and she felt confused. "I thought you were trying to make me eat more?"

He responded by shrugging his massive shoulders before placing the milkshake before her. They were interrupted by his phone. Putting down the remnants of her burger, he arose. He walked a short distance away while she sipped on her milkshake. When he returned a few minutes later, he hurriedly finished the food. Wiping his hands on another serviette he apologised to her.

"I have to go. Dave needs help with his wife's car. I said I'd meet him in ten minutes. Stay here and finish that milkshake. Then go upstairs to find the lingerie shop where I bought your nightdresses. I'm sure you don't want me to make underwear choices for you. If you see anything else in other shops, don't hesitate to buy it. Call me when you're ready to be collected."

Without waiting for a reply, he reached for his wallet. Refusing to listen to her protests, he presented her with a large amount of cash. After watching her stow the money securely in her purse, he handed her the lunchtime medication. When she had swallowed it, he checked she had her phone in her new handbag. Gathering all her shopping bags together, he left her.

The woman who had phoned him brought her coffee to the next table. Jenny Prescott was one of the more experienced agents at *Maximum Security*. She studied her assignment carefully. Evie seemed oblivious to her surroundings, stunned and confused by Romano's sudden abandonment. Jenny watched Evie close her eyes, and when she opened them again she seemed more confident. For the remainder of the afternoon, Jenny would shadow Evie's every move.

ଅୁ ☼ ୪

Sipping the milkshake slowly, Evie waited for her courage to awaken. Her purse had never contained so much money. It had been a long time since she purchased something for herself that didn't come from a discount store or a charity shop. The temptation to find a discount store was strong. She knew he would be expecting shopping bags from the exclusive boutique he had selected. Would it be wise for her first solo opportunity to go against his wishes?

Making her way towards the escalators, Evie loitered before each storefront. The money in her purse demanded her attention. She wandered in and out of shops, looking at the brightly coloured textiles. Examining the delicate fabrics awakened a sense of freedom. Could she really purchase anything she wanted? Evie selected a plain top with a similar neckline to the black T-shirt she was wearing. She studied her reflection in the change room mirror, before carrying the bright orange garment to the counter. Her heart beat rapidly. Evie counted out notes to pay for a garment that wasn't on special and no-one else had selected for her. Emboldened by this small victory, Evie went upstairs and began to look for the lingerie shop.

Again she wandered in and out of the shops until she discovered a small jewellery store. Her hand went to the necklace around her neck. Might she find a suitable gift for Sebastian? If her pendant reminded him of his promise, perhaps she could give him something that reminded her not to give in to temptation? She checked her bank account to see how much of her own money she had to spend. It was not very much, but she hoped it would be enough. When the young man behind the counter asked, she said she wanted to purchase an inexpensive friendship token for a male friend.

The sales assistant drew her attention to a tray of stainless steel pendants on chunky chains. She chose a stylized cross that reminded her of one of Sebastian's tattoo designs. With her heart beating more rapidly, Evie took her bank card from her purse and paid for her purchase. She had less than ten dollars in her account now, but her conscience told her it was a good choice. The wrapped gift fitted easily into her handbag.

A few minutes later she located the lingerie shop. Here her courage evaporated. The intimate apparel displayed immediately inside the door was both provocative and expensive. She fought the urge to flee.

"Can I help you?" asked a blonde woman, who physically resembled her sister Sofia, both in confidence and style.

Having stammered a reply she could not remember afterwards, Evie found herself in a fitting room. The woman turned towards Evie with a tape measure. "I already know my sizes," Evie protested then reluctantly complied with the request to undress. The woman hesitated, recognising the underwear Evie was wearing. She looked at Evie's bruises and bandage, before describing Sebastian perfectly. Evie felt uncomfortable as she listened. Apparently, his arrival in their shop had been memorable. He had caused great speculation about the recipient of his gifts.

After assessing how well the garments she was wearing fitted, the woman conceded the sizes he had selected for her, based on some old tags, had been correct.

"Your friend isn't with you today?"

"He thought I'd be too embarrassed," Evie confessed awkwardly. "I've never worn anything like this before."

"You wear it well, and you have nothing to be embarrassed about. You have a well-proportioned figure, although you've lost too much weight recently. Of course, that's understandable following your accident. Now, what can I tempt you with today?"

Responding to the woman's kindness, Evie told her she was open to suggestions. There followed an intensely intimate session where she was assisted into and out of an assortment of garments. The woman showed her how to make the necessary adjustments to get the best fit, and helped her discover styles that favoured her figure. Evie settled on two designs and was directed to the racks so she could choose the colours she wanted. When she approached the counter with her selection, the woman was waiting with another garment laid out for her consideration.

"While your friend was here last week, he considered buying this."

Evie took up a fold of delicate white fabric and then traced the lacy pattern on the low cut bodice. How would her family have responded if he'd offered her this skimpy negligee a week ago?

"This is something we recommend for the first night." The woman watched Evie closely.

Frozen at the counter, Evie blinked and took a deep breath. Colour drained from her face. The familiar dizzy sensation pushed at the edges of her consciousness. She had little time to make this decision if she wanted to avoid another humiliating fainting spell. Grasping the counter, she hastily added the white negligee to her purchases. Paying with his money, she made her escape.

Immediately opposite the shop was a water feature surrounded by bench seats. Evie hastened to sit down. Closing her eyes, her awareness of the surroundings diminished. She focused on breathing slowly while waiting for the rising darkness to retreat.

ℬ ☼ ℭ

Unnoticed, Jenny followed Evie from the shop. When Evie collapsed, the security officer phoned Sebastian. As they talked, Jenny saw someone approaching her charge. Evie had her eyes closed. Jenny calculated how long it would take to cross the distance, and swore eloquently. She was too far away.

ℬ ☼ ℭ

"Are you okay?" an unfamiliar voice asked, and Evie felt someone sit beside her. The stranger stroked her arm. Her eyes flew open to discover an untidy man beside her. He leaned closer and she was frightened by his sinister smile. "Are you on your own?" he asked, placing his arm around her. "A pretty woman like you shouldn't be on your own."

"Hey Evie," a voice shouted, and Evie looked up to see a woman rushing towards her. The menacing man stiffened. Evie jumped up, stumbling towards her unknown rescuer. Jenny caught her. "Sorry I'm late," Jenny continued, looking towards the man. "We have to hurry. Our friend is waiting."

Jenny hastily drew Evie away, taking the shopping bags to make it easier for her to move. Neither of them looked back at the man. Out of sight from the water feature, Jenny steered Evie into a café, shoving her onto a padded bench near a wall. With her eyes closed, Evie struggled to remain conscious.

"Water!" Jenny cried. "Evie, stay with me. Don't black out now. You're safe, and Romano is on his way."

He's coming, Evie thought as darkness claimed her.

She awoke prone on the bench seat in the café surrounded by a crowd of onlookers. The proprietor wanted to phone for an ambulance, but Jenny said this wasn't necessary. When Sebastian arrived a few minutes later, Jenny had Evie leaning against the wall. Jenny held the glass of water so Evie could drink. At his entrance, the onlookers pulled back. They were unsure whether the drama was over or if more trouble had arrived.

CHAPTER 15
(Saturday 8th July)

Obedience –
A Promise Followed

Psalm 139:7
Where could I go from Your Spirit?
Or where could I flee from Your presence?

Sebastian was confused by conflicting emotions. What was he to do with Evie? Why was she angry at him, and how was he to explain himself without giving away too much of his past? In the old days, he would have gone after the unknown attacker and made sure he never threatened Evie again. But six years ago, Piper Maxwell had made Sebastian promise that he would no longer mete out his own justice and retribution. Until now, none of his enemies had tempted him to break this commitment.

"You hired someone to follow me?" Evie asked again.

They were alone in his flat, sitting uncomfortably together on the black couch. Jenny had introduced herself and walked with them from the shopping centre. Sebastian had wanted to carry Evie but she insisted on walking beside Jenny, vehemently resisting his offer of support. Only when they reached the *Romano* building did Jenny leave.

Once inside the door, Evie admitted she needed help. Sebastian carried her upstairs. Dave was in the workshop beside his wife's car. He made his presence known, but her response was less than cordial.

Refusing to be taken to her bedroom, Evie sat on the couch waiting for an explanation.

"I wanted to make sure you were safe."

"Then you shouldn't have left me alone."

"I didn't leave you alone. Jenny was there."

"Jenny isn't the one I'm 'in a relationship' with. Don't you trust me?"

"No," he said, and his honesty hurt her. "You haven't been truthful about these dizzy spells. If I'd been with you, would you have warned me or suddenly collapsed?"

Stubbornly Evie refused to admit she had been at fault.

"So you had me followed because you were worried I was going to faint again? That doesn't make any sense."

"I can't be with you all the time. It isn't that I don't want to be, but if I'm always there you're going to feel like my prisoner. I wanted you to have a sense of freedom and independence without any risk you would come to harm."

"That worked out well, didn't it?" she retorted, and he flinched at the savagery of her words. "Who was that man and what did he want?"

"What do you think he wanted?" Sebastian growled.

There was a look in his eyes that frightened her. Then he blinked and it was gone.

"You were vulnerable and alone," he continued. "Piper, my security consultant, is checking the cameras in the area to see if he can track him. There's a rumour of a bag snatching gang working the centre, but there's not enough information to identify anyone. It looks like this man was attempting to abduct you. If Jenny hadn't been there…"

His passionate explanation broke through her annoyance. His concern was obvious.

"I'm sorry I didn't tell you I was feeling dizzy," she conceded. "I've been trying to convince you I'm well, so you don't feel burdened by my helplessness."

"You're no burden," he assured her. "I'd sacrifice everything I have for your safety. I'm sorry I didn't tell you the truth. Will you forgive me?"

"Promise me you won't keep any more secrets from me!"

"Finally we agree on something," he grumbled. "I'll make that promise if you promise not to hide things from me. Are we agreed?"

"Agreed," she replied cautiously. "Would it be okay if I rested now?"

⟨ ✦ ⟩

Reluctantly, he let her leave him. While she slept in the privacy of her room, Sebastian returned to help Dave complete the work on his wife's car. They had agreed to undertake a full service, including brake pad replacement. His friend discovered he was in no mood for conversation. The pair worked efficiently for the next hour. They were reassembling all the components when Evie appeared above them.

"Do I have permission to come down, Boss?" Evie asked and began her careful descent. She was wearing a pair of tight blue jeans with the black T-shirt, as well as both the helmet and boots.

Dave glanced up. He turned to Sebastian and said, "Now that is a surprise! On Friday night, no-one would have guessed she looked like that under those horrible clothes. I can see why you don't want her out of your sight."

Sebastian nodded his agreement and focused on the nuts he was tightening. Without looking up, he waited until she came to stand beside him, before asking, "Did you have a good rest?"

"Yes, thank you," she replied cheerfully. "I had the most wonderful dream, and I didn't want to wake up."

"What were you dreaming about?" he asked cautiously, still focusing his attention on the tight space where he was working.

"I was dreaming you were lying next to me. When I woke up and you weren't there, I was very disappointed."

At her confession, the wrench to which he was applying pressure slipped. Sebastian swore as he tore the skin on the back of his hand. He stood up and reached for a clean rag, wrapping it around his hand tightly to stem the flow.

"You're bleeding!" Evie exclaimed, stepping closer to take his hand in her own.

"You'll get grease on your new clothes," he growled, trying to put more distance between them. Did she realise what she had just implied?

"I have more," she retaliated. "You said my new clothes could be tossed in the machine, so it doesn't matter if they get dirty."

Surprised by her audacity, he threw his arms around Evie and held her close to him.

When she didn't resist, he leaned down and kissed her more passionately than he intended.

"I love you, Evie Fontana," he said softly.

"And I love you, Sebastian Romano," she replied and leaned into his embrace, kissing him again.

"I can finish here on my own," Dave said from the other side of the car, "if you want to take Evie upstairs."

Evie blushed, and Sebastian kissed her again lightly before releasing her. He turned to Dave. "What kind of friend are you to put ideas into my head? Evie wants to wait until our wedding night, and I have a promise to keep."

Turning back to Evie, he teased her. "Unless you've changed your mind now you've confessed your love for me?"

Evie smiled in reply. Reaching into her jeans pocket she took out the stainless steel pendant and chain. He watched as she held them out to him. "I bought this with my own money," she began. "This is a token of the promise that I make to you. This will remind me I've promised to help you wait until we're married."

He leaned down so she could place the chain around his neck, and looked at her anew. What did this mean? Was she telling him she wanted him and the waiting would be hard for her too? Like a newly lit fire came the realisation she might struggle with the same desire tonight. He prayed to God for strength.

"Hey Dave, your youngest brother recently married. How long does it take to get a marriage licence?"

"I think it takes a month, but first you have to find someone who will agree to perform the ceremony. The two of you have only known each other for a week. Unless Evie is already pregnant, you might have trouble finding someone to agree."

"You're not pregnant, are you Evie?" Sebastian asked with a grin, holding her close. "No? Then we will have to ask God to help us find someone who understands my impatience."

"My Mama will want more than a month to prepare for a wedding," Evie cautioned him.

"We can talk to Mama Rosa and Benito tomorrow. We're having lunch with your family, but we don't have to be there till 1 pm. That will give us time to go to your church service in the morning. We can ask Pastor Edwards if he'll agree to marry us."

Her face showed her surprise. Was she reconsidering her decision already? He decided to press on.

"Dave, would you be my best man?"

"You ask me even though I'm trying to discourage you?" his friend responded cautiously.

Sebastian persisted. "You're my oldest friend. You've steered me true these past few years. You were the sound voice of wisdom when I struggled with Aunt Constance's criticism. Your support kept me strong. It was you I called when I thought I'd killed Evie. There is no-one else I want with me when I marry her. Your doubts about how fast this is happening will help me keep everything in perspective. I know I can trust you to tell me the truth."

꙳ ✿ ꙳

Wiping his hands on a rag before answering, Dave looked across his wife's car. He remembered a conversation from this morning. His wife Marilyn thought Dave should be encouraging Seb's relationship with Evie. Marilyn was hopeful his old friend had found true love. Instead, Dave's focus was the potential for heartbreak and disappointment. Marilyn had been praying for Seb. She thought the miracle Dave had witnessed last Saturday was a sure sign Evie was part of God's answer.

"As long as you know I'm still the voice of caution," Dave informed him, "I'd be honoured to be your best man. Marilyn has been asking when she can meet Evie. Do you want to come to a barbecue this afternoon? Evie can meet the kids and Marilyn can tell you what she thinks of your wedding plans."

೮ ✿ ೮೩

Sebastian looked at Evie and thought of the long hours they would be alone together if he declined the invitation. His emotions were still volatile, and it would be a struggle to push temptation from his mind. Perhaps this was how God answered prayer? He remembered Dave's wife once telling him she was praying for him. It would be good for Evie to have a female friend from among his circle to help her with any lingering doubts about him. He suddenly realised he should have recruited Marilyn to help him this morning, instead of having Evie followed.

"A barbecue would be great." Releasing Evie, Sebastian turned back to the car and resumed the final work. "Let's get this job done, and you can go home and help Marilyn get ready."

೮ ✿ ೮೩

Curious about the direction this conversation had turned, Evie realised she had heard little mention of Dave's wife. She had wondered if Sebastian held the wives and girlfriends of his employees at a distance. Now she realised Dave's wife Marilyn counted herself as one of his friends.

"Dave, how long have you and Marilyn been married?" she asked quietly.

Dave considered how to answer while he continued working. "My eldest boy is seventeen. He was born nine months after the wedding, so we have been married eighteen years this October. We were engaged for two years. Marilyn was still living with her parents and they were very strict. It worked out for the best that we had to wait until after the wedding. Marilyn fell pregnant on our honeymoon. I don't think our relationship would have survived if I'd pressured her and she found herself pregnant before the wedding.

161

Marilyn has similar beliefs to you, Evie, and her honour was very important to her."

"Did you find waiting difficult?" she asked.

"We had little opportunity to be alone. It wasn't the same as the kind of pressure you're going to face living together. That is one of the reasons I told Sebastian you shouldn't move in here. The temptations the two of you will face could destroy your relationship before you have time to decide if this is what you really want."

Dave asked a particularly challenging question. "Have either of you considered what will happen if Evie falls pregnant? Are you ready to bring children into the world when you're still learning how to get along with each other? Raising children puts immense pressure on a relationship, and I'd hate to see either of you raising a child on your own. Sebastian's life is a testimony to how disastrous that can be."

"But we won't be on our own," Sebastian insisted. "Evie has her family to support her, and I have you and the others. Both of us are survivors, and that makes us strong. My dad was on his own in a new country when my mother died. He had no support except for Aunt Constance. All the good things about my character come from the love Dad invested in me. I can assure Evie any child of mine would have the best of everything."

Both men looked to Evie for her response.

"Sebastian, you know I'm already thirty-five. I don't know yet if it's even possible for me to have children. But if God were to bless us with children, I know He would also give us all we needed to take care of them."

᯾ ✪ ᴄ᷂

Sebastian looked back towards Dave in triumph, convinced her answer was a wise one. He added children to the growing list of things to pray about. This list continued to amaze him as his once predictable life disappeared. If he had ignored his curiosity in the beginning would he have ever reconsidered giving her a chance? The consequences of meeting this woman were so unexpected. His life was so much richer and full of promise now.

Patience –

A Sustaining Promise

ɞ ☼ 03

Philippians 4:8
Whatever things are true, whatever is honourable, whatever is just,
whatever is pure, whatever is lovely, whatever is good;
if there is any virtue and if there is any praise,
think about these things.

ɞ ☼ 03

"Are you ready yet?" Sebastian called impatiently, his voice muffled by her closed door.

While the men had finished working on Marilyn's car, Evie had gone upstairs to prepare for her outing. She had trouble deciding what she would wear, before settling on the orange top she had chosen for herself. Matching it with the long skirt he had purchased, she teamed it with the red shoes. Now she was standing in front of the bathroom mirror debating whether to put her up hair or leave it down. "I need a few more minutes!" she called.

Hurriedly, she grabbed an elastic band and pulled most of her hair up in a high ponytail. She hadn't worn this style since she had been at school, but there was no time to do anything more sophisticated now. Taking her brush, she pulled the remaining hair sideways to conceal the white dressing on her forehead and tucked the long ends behind her ear. Looking at her reflection, she felt a pang of regret. All those years ago her aunt had confiscated her pierced earrings, and the memory still hurt. At least having no makeup to apply would save her time. Her only adornment was the pendant Sebastian had given her. Smiling at her reflection to remind herself all would be well, Evie took a deep breath. Collecting her phone she opened the door.

℘ ☼ ℃

Sebastian studied her paleness and asked himself if the excitement of the day was already too much for her. The way she had pulled up her hair made her seem so young and vulnerable, and he wanted to protect her. "I can phone and tell them we aren't coming," he suggested.

"Please don't do that," she assured him. "I'm looking forward to meeting Marilyn. I want to make a good impression."

Confident she had nothing to worry about, Sebastian led her downstairs. His Maserati zoomed through the Saturday afternoon traffic, heading away from the city. Sebastian navigated the suburban streets, having visited this family home many times. He hoped this visit would alleviate Dave's doubts.

℘ ☼ ℃

They turned into the driveway of a large two-storey brick house set in a well-manicured garden. Rosebushes lined the path from the driveway to the main entrance to the house. The closest one had only creamy buds but drew her attention. Evie remembered the white rose Sebastian had placed in her hand at the hospital.

Why am I remembering that white rose, Lord? Is this something important, or am I looking for a distraction? I'm feeling anxious about meeting Dave's wife. Help me to say and do the right things because I want her to like me.

The sports car hadn't stopped before the front door of the house burst open. Two children came running down the rose-lined path towards them.

"Uncle Seb!" the little five-year-old girl shouted. Her brown hair was held neatly by an Alice band and she was wearing a pretty pink dress. As soon as Sebastian stepped from the car, this child threw herself at him, and he embraced her then he tossed her high in the air. She screamed in delight as he caught her before lowering her back to the ground.

"Lilly," he laughed, "you're growing too fast. It takes more strength to lift you each time I see you."

The little girl danced around him with delight. Sebastian turned to greet the other child, a boy of about eight who was eagerly looking at the sports car. "You finished it! Can I sit in the driver's seat?"

Sebastian stepped aside to allow the brown-haired boy to clamber in. He adjusted the seat so the child could reach the steering wheel. Only then did the boy notice Evie still seated in the car. "Hi. I'm Rory." He held out his small hand solemnly for her to shake. "Has Uncle Seb let you drive yet? I bet this car's really fast!"

Shaking the offered hand, Evie marvelled at the easy way these children greeted Sebastian. The earlier conversation about the possibility of pregnancy took on a greater significance. Now she understood his insistence that he would add children to his prayer list.

"Hi Rory, I'm Evie. I only get to be a passenger, but you're right. This car is very fast."

"Are you two going to sit in the car and talk all day?" Sebastian asked, opening Evie's door and leaning down to look in at them. "I'm getting hungry, and we'd better go inside before I starve."

"Oh, Uncle Seb," Lilly cried, "you're always hungry!"

The little girl waited until he helped Evie out of the car. When she saw Evie holding his hand, Lilly seized his other one. The three of them walked up the path together with Rory running ahead of them.

"Uncle Seb's here and he's brought a girlfriend!"

"I've never been called anyone's girlfriend before," Evie confessed when they reached the front door.

"Girlfriend, lover, wife. I'm sure you can get used to all those names," he laughed as he put his arm around her waist to lead her inside. He leaned over and kissed her.

"Oooh!" Lilly squealed. "Now he's kissing her! Are you getting married? Can I be the flower girl?"

Thankfully, Dave and his wife Marilyn came to their rescue.

"Lilly, leave Uncle Seb alone. Go and wash your hands for dinner. Rory, you can go too," Dave commanded.

"Oh, Dad!" Lilly protested but followed her brother up the passage.

"Hello, Evie. I'm Marilyn." The smiling woman was an older version of Lilly. "I hope the children haven't embarrassed you? We didn't tell them you were coming, and they aren't used to sharing Seb with anyone."

Immediately Evie felt welcome. She talked freely with Marilyn as they walked in the garden. Dave and Sebastian were on the paved patio in the backyard cooking on the barbeque. Lilly and Rory played chasings.

"I'm so pleased Seb brought you to meet me," Marilyn said. "I've been praying he would find someone, and you've made it hard for him to forget you. Dave said you two are talking about getting married."

"Dave told Sebastian it's too soon," Evie confessed, and she felt something shift in her spirit. This woman was someone she could trust. "Everything has happened so quickly. A week ago I didn't even know Sebastian, and now I'm sharing a flat with him. I've never been in a relationship before, and I don't know what to expect. There are times when he touches me, and I want to push him away and say I'm not ready for this. But there are moments when I want to do anything he asks to have him hold me a little longer."

"Falling in love is complicated," Marilyn told her. "Dave and I only discovered how complex being in a relationship was after the wedding. I don't think the amount of time before the wedding counts. But it is important you are both prepared to consider what is necessary to make the other person happy afterwards."

They walked among the rosebushes. Marilyn stopped beside the white rosebush Evie had noticed before. Marilyn examined the new buds closely. "I thought I'd lost this bush. It's precious to me. It came from my grandmother's garden. The original bush provided the roses for my wedding bouquet. I want it growing in my garden as a reminder of the promises I made to God all those years ago."

Looking at the bush with renewed interest, Evie remembered her vision and the questions she had about the symbolism of a white rose. To hear her new friend talk about the flowers being a reminder of a marriage promise caused her heart to skip a beat. Should she tell Marilyn about this? Just as she was about to speak, Lilly and Rory ran up to say it was time to eat.

The delicious feast surprised her. It differed from her schoolday memories of blackened sausages in soggy white bread. Evie ate more than she expected – little chicken things and unfamiliar food on wooden sticks. She was too embarrassed to ask what it was, but now she was satisfyingly full. The adults lingered at the table, debating whether to stay outside or move before it became too cool.

ೞ ☼ ೪

At the other end of the table, Alex the eldest son was playing a game on his hand-held console. At seventeen, he was pretending he wasn't listening, but he was in awe of Evie. He had watched the way Uncle Seb held Evie and noted his care over her during the meal. This beautiful stranger had captured Uncle Seb's heart.

"Would it be okay if we prayed with you about getting married?" his mother asked Evie and Uncle Seb. Alex looked up in surprise. He didn't know how either his Dad or Uncle Seb would respond to this request. Until last week, his Dad hadn't shown any interest in God, and they'd never prayed with Uncle Seb before. Something had happened. It must be because of Evie's accident.

Glancing at Evie, Uncle Seb agreed.

Alex's mother suggested all four of them hold hands. Then she asked Alex if he would like to join them.

Alex moved to sit between Evie and his mother. Evie's hand was trembling. He closed his eyes. His mother began to pray. Alex waited for God to give him something specific to say when it was his turn. The teenager felt shy in this new situation. Almost immediately, he saw an image of a single white rose in Evie's hand and heard a voice saying "one for each night".

A shout from the garden interrupted his thoughts. Rory came running onto the patio carrying a small wicker basket. His sister chased after him.

"Lilly's been picking flowers again!" Rory yelled, throwing a small pair of scissors onto the table with a clatter.

The girl snatched the basket from his hands. Alex's Dad began speaking severely to Lilly, but she burst into tears.

"God told me to," she sobbed, dumping the contents of her basket on the table. "He said Uncle Seb needed them."

"Why would Uncle Seb need flowers?" Alex's Dad asked as his Mum's eyes grew wide with recognition. On the table were the precious buds from her white rosebush. Uncle Seb was staring at the flowers in bewilderment.

Then Evie reached out her hand. "Marilyn, I'm so sorry. I don't know how Lilly knew. God told me to watch for a white rose as a sign of His promise," she whispered.

"You have to count them. Put them into groups of seven so you can count in weeks," Alex said suddenly and started to help her. "God said there would be one for each night."

"God said?" his father asked incredulously.

"I was praying about what to say. I saw Evie holding a white rose and then I heard a voice say 'one for each night'."

"Ah!" exclaimed Uncle Seb and everyone looked at him. "I asked God a question, and this is His answer. I told Him I wanted a clear sign in front of witnesses so I couldn't argue with Him afterwards."

Everyone cleared space on the table and watched as Evie sorted the buds into groups. There were forty-eight rosebuds on the table, and then Alex spotted one fallen on the ground. He picked it up and was about to add it to the final group, making the total forty-nine. He knew God's perfect number was seven, so it made sense there would be seven groups of seven. His Dad reached across the table and stopped him.

"What was the question?" his father asked Uncle Seb with a frown. Unexpectedly it seemed as if he might be adding a confirming voice.

"I asked God how many nights I must wait for Evie."

Alex's father took the bud from him and, with an interesting smile, dropped it into Uncle Seb's hand. "This is for last night."

Uncle Seb stared at the rosebud.

Alex's mother wiped tears from her eyes and reached out to fold Uncle Seb's hand around the small flower. "You were both waiting for a sign. Evie expected a white rose, and you asked a specific question that needed a numerical answer. These buds come from my wedding bouquet rosebush. Lilly has ambitions to be a flower girl at your wedding, and Alex heard God say the buds represent nights. God has given you the date for your wedding."

Alex's father spoke again. "The wedding is in seven weeks, on the last Friday in August. You already have a dinner scheduled at *Ristorante di Fontana*. I don't think you can get a more specific answer."

Qualified -
A Promise Claimed

୧୦ ☼ ୧୫

John 14:1-2
"Let not your heart be troubled. You believe in God, believe also in
me. In my father's house are many mansions. If it weren't so, I
would have told you. I go to prepare a place for you."

୧୦ ☼ ୧୫

"Good morning," Sebastian said with a smile as he stood outside Evie's open door. He handed her a bowl containing two dried rosebuds. It had been Marilyn's idea for them to take the rosebuds home. She had provided him with instructions for oven-drying the fragile blooms. This task had made it bearable for Sebastian to kiss an exhausted Evie goodnight. While she slept, he had worked into the early morning hours. He was unsure he understood what was happening. His usual pragmatism was being replaced with sentimentality. The remaining buds were in a similar bowl in his room, and he would bring Evie one each morning.

୧୦ ☼ ୧୫

Kissing him quickly, Evie carried the bowl to the bedside table. She placed it beside the vase of roses he had given her in hospital. Those blooms were starting to wilt, but she hoped they would last a few days longer. She paused to reflect on the promises they had made and marvelled at how her life had transformed.

Over breakfast, they talked about the coming day. This morning would be the first time they attended church together. Evie was uncertain how his presence might change her experience. In the past, visiting God's house had strengthened her to face life's difficulties. Now her biggest challenge was the man who sat beside her. Would she find his presence distracting?

Sebastian intended to confirm their wedding date with Pastor Edwards. This thought intruded into her every prayer. After church, they were expected at the restaurant for Sunday lunch where Sebastian would tell her family. She was uncertain how her relatives would respond.

So many things, Lord, are pulling at my heart. My mind can't settle one way or another. This restlessness is worrying me. Please still my troubled mind and restore my sense of peace.

Be anxious for nothing...

Evie was surprised to discover her new church was near Sebastian's home. The bus she'd used previously had taken a circuitous route. Unfortunately, they still arrived with only minutes to spare. She felt light-headed, and her face was flushed. They hurriedly sat on the end of a row close to the back. Immediately Evie closed her eyes and prayed for calmness. When the first song began, she was unable to stand for more than a few seconds. The dizziness dropped her heavily back into her chair. Sebastian leaned towards her, focused on her quiet struggle not to give in to tears. One of the stewards behind them noticed what was happening and came to kneel beside them in the aisle.

"Is everything okay? Can I pray with you?"

With tears streaming down her face, Evie nodded, reaching out to take hold of Sebastian's hand. The steward held their joined hands and prayed quietly.

"Father, we have come into Your house today to bring You praise and worship. Consider the weakness and distress of Your daughter and grant her Your peace and wholeness. Heal her body and release her mind from all that is draining her of Your joy."

The steward paused. Into that moment, Evie heard Sebastian speak. His voice was so quiet she had to focus all her attention to capture his words.

"God, I don't know why You'd listen to me, but I'm asking again. Evie isn't well. Please help her."

"When two or three pray in agreement, God promises to give them His answer," the steward said. "Our prayers have been heard, sealed by the faith He has placed in our hearts."

With a smile, the steward stood up and began to leave, but then turned to speak again. "At the end of the service, you should both go forward for prayer. God has more to say to you today."

Evie smiled her thanks and felt much calmer, the dreadful darkness receding. A second song was beginning. Evie stood up and began to sing along with the unfamiliar words.

⁘ ☼ ⁖

Sebastian watched her closely, and at first, he was oblivious to the music around him. There was something special about the atmosphere in this place. The same power which had tossed him away from her when she returned from death hovered in this place. He glanced around him. Others in the small crowd of about sixty people looked as if they too could sense this presence.

Unexpectedly, he realised he was following along with the words. He was not ready to sing, but he was experiencing something he could not define. What did it mean to invite the King of Heaven to come down?

There were other songs, but this one stayed with him afterwards. When the singing was over, Pastor Edwards stood up and began to speak.

"Today God has directed me to the Old Testament story of Jacob from the book of Genesis. Let me set the scene: Jacob has run away in fear of his life. His brother Esau wants to kill him. Jacob has tricked him out of both his inheritance and his father Isaac's blessing. While on his way to his mother Rebecca's family, Jacob has an encounter with God. The Lord promises to go with him and take care of him. Starting from Chapter twenty-nine, we read how Jacob first met and fell in love with his cousin Rachel. As the story unfolds, we find his uncle determined to trick and deceive him at every turn. Jacob agrees to work for seven years to marry Rachel. Let us look now at verse twenty."

The words appeared on the big screen behind the Pastor.

"Genesis 29:20. 'Jacob served seven years for Rachel. They seemed but a few days because of his love for her'."

"Have you ever wanted something so badly you were prepared to work seven years to get it? Perhaps you've saved for a deposit on a house, or worked on a renovation project? How far into the process were you before you began to wonder if you'd ever make it to the end? Sometimes I can't even wait long enough for the internet to finish loading a page. When I'm waiting for the pizza I've ordered I can become very impatient. Jacob was a man used to taking shortcuts to get what he wanted. Yet, here we read those seven years were 'only a few days to him because of his love for her'."

"What does this ancient story have to do with us today? What can we learn from this? Time has a mysterious quality. Sometimes it seems to race ahead, and yet it can also slow down almost to the point of stopping. Without fail, the minutes, hours and days keep adding up. They can be measured and counted. In the New Testament, we have another story about waiting. Turn with me to Matthew chapter twenty-five."

Evie had insisted Sebastian bring his father's Bible with him. Now she helped him find the passage, even though the text appeared again on the big screen. She whispered that it was always good to read the words for himself. He could mark the place in case he wanted to go back and read it again. The heading said "The Parable of the Ten Virgins" and that grabbed his attention.

"'Then the Kingdom of Heaven will be like ten virgins, who took their lamps, and went to meet the bridegroom. Five of them were foolish, and five were wise. Those foolish virgins took no oil with them, but the wise took extra oil with their lamps. Now while the bridegroom delayed, they all slept'.

"Some translations say bridesmaids instead of virgins. These women are waiting for the bridegroom, who represents Jesus Christ our Lord. All ten went out with eager expectation to welcome Him. The night lengthened, and the lamps burned low until all the maidens had fallen asleep.

"It has been two thousand years since Jesus died and rose again, promising He would come again. Like the bridesmaids, the first Christians prepared their hearts for His arrival. Yet He has tarried for so long there are some who doubt He will ever come. Today we're looking at the implications for those of us who still believe – contemporary Christians who are still waiting for the bridegroom to come. Let's continue reading.

"'At midnight came a cry: 'The bridegroom is coming! Come to meet him!' Then all the virgins arose, and trimmed their lamps. The foolish ones said to the wise, 'Give us some of your oil, for our lamps are going out.' But the wise answered, 'What if there isn't enough for us and you? Go and buy for yourselves.' While they were away, the bridegroom came. Those who were ready went in with him to the feast, and the door was shut'."

Sebastian reflected on his own experience. Those long hours with the woman he desired so close, yet her door firmly shut. How terrible for those bridesmaids who were shut out. He was lost in thought but came alert with a jolt. The Bible in his hands was now open to Revelation, and Evie was pointing to the relevant verses.

"Chapter 3, from verse 7. 'He who is holy, he who is true, he who holds the key of David, he who opens and no-one can shut, and who shuts and no-one opens, says these things: I know your works (behold, I have set before you an open door, which no-one can shut), that you have little power, and kept my word and didn't deny my name'."

These words hit him with the same power he had felt before, and he marvelled he was not thrown from his seat. He clenched the open book in his hands. God knew his deeds, and yet still offered him an open door. One no-one could close? He only realised he was crying when Evie leaned towards him.

Reminded –
A Promise Confirmed

 how ☼ ʬ

Philippians 4:11b-13
I have learned to be content. I have been humbled, and I have
enjoyed abundance. In all things I have learned the secret both
when I am full and when I am hungry. I can do all things through
Christ, who strengthens me.

how ☼ ʬ

Were it not for Sebastian's skilful driving they would be late for lunch. After the service, they had both gone forward for prayer. When it was their turn to consult the pastor he already had his planner ready. The wedding date was confirmed. The same steward had joined the elders and Pastor Edwards to pray for them. Many words of encouragement were spoken over them.

Sebastian noticed an immediate change in Evie. Now she was the one reaching out to him, drawing him close to her side. Yet the softening of her resistance did not awaken the recriminations that tormented him in the sleepless watches of the night. He no longer feared he would lose control or use his superior strength to force her to comply with his wishes. Now that he understood she was unreservedly promised to him, his love for her would make it possible to wait. Sebastian laughed at the reminder that Jacob from the Bible had waited seven years.

"What are you laughing about?" she asked him as they walked towards the restaurant. He lifted her off the ground, kissing her before replying.

"I was thanking God he didn't ask me to wait seven years for you. Seven weeks I can manage. Seven years would be a completely different challenge."

Ž☿c.

Blushing, Evie grinned in reply. Together they turned towards the side entrance to the restaurant. His Maserati was parked beside her sister's car so she knew they were the last to arrive. She glanced down at her new dress, taking a moment to smooth the hem before leading him inside.

Her family sat around the table in the dining room. Evie paused in the doorway feeling unexpectedly shy. What would they think of the changes, both in her appearance and seeing her so in love with Sebastian? Without realising, she squeezed his hand, causing him to stand closer to her. Marco saw her first, and his mouth fell open in amazement. The others turned to look at them, and then her mother rushed over. Sebastian tactfully stepped aside.

"Maria Evangelina!" Mama Rosa cried, alternately hugging her close and then moving her back so she could marvel at the change in her daughter's appearance. "You look wonderful!"

Benito approached Sebastian cautiously. Leonardo had been carrying messages between them since the hospital confrontation. After a moment's hesitation, Benito embraced Sebastian as he had always done.

"We need to talk," Sebastian conceded, "but there will be time later."

Benito nodded and led him to a place at the table, not beside but opposite Evie. Sebastian baulked as if he might protest, but then sat down. Sofia turned and welcomed Evie beside her. Benito sat in his usual place at the head of the rectangular table. At the other end, Mama Rosa reached out to Sebastian and Evie, holding their hands during the blessing.

Hearing Benito include a welcome to Sebastian in his blessing was a positive sign for Evie. She longed for her family to accept him on a permanent basis. She smiled across the table at him. She gestured towards the white roses that were part of the decorations between them.

Sofia leaned towards her. "Are you well? It has only been a few days since you left the hospital. Leonardo said you're experiencing dizzy spells."

Evie glanced towards Leonardo. What else had he said? Cautiously she replied to her sister. "Sebastian is concerned about my dizziness, but we were prayed for at church this morning. I'm hoping that will make a big difference."

She sensed the emotional ripple her words provoked but it was Marco who asked the question.

"You said *we* were prayed for?" Marco asked. "You took Romano to *church*?"

Evie laughed. "Actually, Sebastian had to take me because I can't go anywhere on my own. I wasn't going to miss another Sunday service!"

"Why can't you go anywhere on your own?" Sofia demanded. She made no attempt to conceal her concerns about her sister living with 'this man'.

"She fainted at the shopping centre," Sebastian said into the silence when Evie hesitated in answering.

"You fainted at the shopping centre!" Sofia exclaimed.

"Mmmm," Evie replied, tempted to kick him under the table. "There was too much excitement on my first day."

"What kind of excitement?" Marco wanted to know.

"If you'd seen all the clothes he wanted me to try on," she began, grinning at Sebastian and daring him to contradict her.

"You should have seen the fuss she made about spending my money," he retaliated. "Aunt Constance told me the only women I could attract would want to spend my millions. She obviously never met anyone like Evie. She found one dress and thought that was enough."

"It's a very nice dress," Evie pouted, standing up and showing off the one she was wearing. Her family stared at her.

Benito was walking around the table filling wine glasses. When he reached Evie's seat, Sebastian leaned across the table to place his hand over her glass. "No wine for Evie," he advised sternly, placing her lunchtime medication on the table as a reminder. There was an awkward pause, during which Leonardo left the table to get her a soft drink. There was no doubt Sebastian took his role as her protector very seriously.

At the end of the bountiful feast, when even Sebastian was protesting he could not eat another mouthful, it was time to listen to one of Benito's stories. Marco reminded him there was an unfinished story from last Sunday.

"You were telling us about two friends who were in love with two sisters, but you never told us what happened in the end."

Evie watched her father look towards her mother, who nodded her approval. "A long time ago in the Old Country, there were two sisters, born minutes apart, but they were as different from each other as summer is to winter."

"We already know that bit," Marco protested, and his mother reminded him to be patient, or there would be no story at all.

"The sisters were loved by two friends, and they made promises to remain true to each other. They planned to get married, and their children would grow up together. One sister Rosa was warm and comforting, promising to follow her Benito to the ends of the earth if she must. The other sister Maria grew hostile and cold, keeping her young man Paulo at a distance. She vowed to make him wait until he had earned his fortune and could provide her with all she wanted. Benito and Rosa's story you know very well, but the other couple, Maria and Paulo – you don't know their story at all."

Glancing at her mother, Evie realised she was hearing a new story. Until she had gone to live with Zietta Maria she had known very little about her vindictive relative. It was a surprise to discover her mother's sister was already very resentful and cold at the start of her story. With interest, she turned her attention back to Papa.

"The two young men, Benito and Paulo set off across the ocean to the faraway land of Australia. Benito went to a distant relative, where he worked in their Italian restaurant in Sydney. Paulo travelled with him, determined he would find some way to make his fortune. Benito prospered in the familiar environment, the food of his heritage a permanent reminder of home. He dreamt of opening his own restaurant and wrote home to Rosa asking her to learn her family's recipes. Meanwhile, Paulo apprenticed himself to an auto-mechanic. He proved himself a diligent worker, eager to learn and not afraid of getting his hands dirty. The two were confident with their plans and expected they would soon be able to send for their brides.

"It was then calamity struck. The girls' father fled to Australia with his family to escape a shameful scandal. He arrived in Sydney with high expectations he would again make a name for himself. For this reason, he demanded a handsome dowry from each of the young men. Benito's savings had grown steadily because he was living with relatives and all his meals were free. It took him less time to raise the dowry price. His friend Paulo told him not to wait, and soon Benito and Rosa were married. Rosa went to work at the same restaurant, and they prospered.

"Paulo found his Maria even more distant in the new land. She remembered the high standing her family once enjoyed. She looked at Paulo's work-stained hands with disdain. When he assured her he had reached the dowry price, she dismissed him. She insisted she would not agree to marry unless he established himself as the owner of his own business. She would not lower herself to marry a tradesman. She added a requirement that he place in her hands the deeds to a big house.

"Broken-hearted, Paulo sought advice from his old friend Benito. Finding no consolation in his counsel, Paulo broke off the engagement with Maria. To make the estrangement complete, he moved to Queensland. He had heard there were many opportunities there to make a fresh start. At first, regular letters to Benito and Rosa told a divided tale of opportunity and heartache.

"Eventually, Paulo wrote about meeting an Australian girl, already pregnant with his child. They were going to be married as soon as possible. When Rosa unwittingly revealed the news to her sister, Maria flew into a fierce rage. She cursed the man who had abandoned her and vented her anger towards anyone who crossed her path. She bullied Rosa into giving her Paulo's address and wrote a scathing letter to him. In response, he made a vow never to allow this woman to hurt him again.

"Benito and Rosa were unable to attend the wedding. They planned to visit after the baby was born, but the expected letter never came. Through their relatives, they discovered Paulo's wife had died in childbirth. Paulo's unmarried sister was dispatched from their home village to care for the child. The letter Benito and Rosa wrote expressing their sorrow was returned unopened.

"Years passed with no further news. Maria became more stubborn and proud. Her anger at Paulo transformed into mistrust and hatred towards men. She made life difficult for Rosa because of her successful marriage. When her beloved father took himself a young mistress, Maria saw this as a deeper betrayal. Now her anger burned like a destroying fire.

"Rosa's situation became unbearable when Maria discovered her sister was pregnant. This forced Benito to move his family to Melbourne, where their first daughter was born. Three years later a second daughter arrived. Benito and Rosa felt their life was complete.

"From time to time, they thought about their childhood friend Paulo. They didn't know, until much later, that Maria had continued sending her poison letters. This forced him to change his name, making it impossible for her to find him. Only when Paulo walked back into Benito and Rosa's lives did they discover he had been living but half an hour away for eighteen years."

The listeners around the table grew quiet.

"Why didn't he come and see them sooner?" Marco asked.

"While Benito and Rosa's story was one of happiness, Paulo's story was one of broken dreams and loneliness. His sister never stopped reminding him of the mistakes he'd made. Paulo had worked hard to make a success of his life, becoming very wealthy. In his final days, he was content to have reconnected with his old friends."

"His 'final days'?"

"Alas, he was already very ill, but he told no-one. We saw him but a few times before he was gone from our lives forever."

"But you said he had a child, the one who is our cousin?"

"Ah!" Benito sighed. "Paulo had a son, and he did his best to raise him. But the long hours he worked meant the boy spent too much time with the unmarried sister who resented him. That sister had always admired Maria. She continued to remind Paulo he should have stayed true to his childhood promise. She accused him of throwing away his future for an Australian girl who had no morals. Paulo never argued with her. He was thankful she was too ashamed of her association with the boy to contact Maria. He did not need two women filling his life with the same poison."

"And what happened to the son?" Marco asked again.

ॐ ☼ ଔ

Sebastian had listened silently to the story. Until that moment, he had never had a full explanation. His father had isolated himself from his past. Now he understood why his aunt had been resentful. The father he knew had answered to Paul and taken his mother's surname. He looked across the table at Evie. It was a shock to realise the same Maria who had made her life a misery had first turned her hatred towards his Dad. He saw by her tears she had already guessed the truth.

Benito was looking at him. One by one the others followed Benito's gaze, and slowly the truth dawned on them.

"Romano?" Sofia gasped.

Sebastian nodded to her, and then answered Marco's original question. "That son isn't your cousin, Marco," Sebastian said solemnly. "But soon he will become your uncle. This is how the story continues: Paulo's son grew up angry and alone until one day he met Benito and Rosa's youngest daughter. It was not a happy meeting, for she was too broken by her encounter with the first Maria. The end of the story is yet to be lived, and each of us will get to play a part."

"Well said," Benito conceded, standing as a signal. "Romano and I need to have a private conversation, so please excuse us."

ℬ✡ℭ

While they were away, everyone cleared the table. Despite her mother's protests, Evie insisted on helping. "I'm not an invalid," she said. There was so much more she wanted to say, but she would have to wait until Papa and Sebastian came back. At first, raised voices rang out in the main dining room. Now it was quiet. There was nothing to indicate how the interview was going.

Lord, please guide this conversation. There has already been too much heartache and sorrow in our shared family story. I want the future to shine with Your blessings.

When the men returned, they appeared to be on good terms. Sebastian smiled at her but stayed by her father's side.

"We heard shouting," Sofia spoke first, and everyone waited expectantly.

"There were some little details we disagreed upon. Sebastian has asked for permission to marry our Maria Evangelina. I have given my blessing."

Everyone started to speak at once, and Benito held up his hands to quieten them so he could continue.

"Sebastian has booked the restaurant for their Betrothal Celebration in seven weeks' time. I tried to tell him seven weeks would not be long enough, but he put up a very persuasive argument. He doesn't want to wait nor risk a long engagement."

"Betrothal Celebration?" Evie whispered across the room to Sebastian. He shrugged and said no more.

"Why doesn't he want a long engagement?" Sofia asked suspiciously. "Does he think my sister will change her mind?"

Benito looked at Sebastian with some discomfort, and the younger man replied. "I gave your father a difficult choice. He could have the wedding date of his choosing, and risk having his youngest daughter walk down the aisle heavily pregnant. Or he could agree to the date we have already decided upon and have a white wedding."

"Are you pregnant?" Marco asked with wide eyes, and everyone turned towards Evie.

Red with embarrassment, Evie frowned at the mischief in Sebastian's eyes. "Of course not!" she self-righteously protested. A little of the old Ria surfacing in her outrage that he would put her in this situation. "I've only known Sebastian for a week, and even then I was safely guarded in hospital. He has promised he will wait until after the wedding because he knows how important my virtue is to me."

"But I'll wait not one hour past the day you have promised yourself to me," Sebastian teased her. "So if your father had persuaded me to postpone the wedding I would still expect you in my bed."

"The other thing we disagreed upon..." Benito interjected – he wanted to move this conversation to a safer topic – "...was who would pay for the wedding, and what dowry I would require."

"Dowry?" Sofia exclaimed. "I've had two weddings and you never asked for a dowry for me."

"Of course I told him that in this modern country there was no need for a dowry. He wants to fulfil the old family agreement his father made so many years ago. I said I wouldn't take his money, but there is no arguing with Romano. So instead, I've agreed he can take over payment for all the flowers we use in the restaurant. In that way, there will be a lasting reminder he has fulfilled his covenant. The only provision is to always have white roses."

"As for the wedding, I insisted that we must pay for the wedding dress and the food. He can pay for anything else."

"When is the Betrothal Celebration?" Mama Rosa asked. Evie realised her mother was already planning the menu and adding names to the guest list.

঒ ☼ 03

"The last Friday in August," Benito replied, "the night already set aside for the *Romano* monthly dinner. He said seven is his lucky number." What would Rosa say when she learned the wedding would happen at the same time?

The younger man had not been happy about keeping his intentions secret. Benito insisted Evie be allowed the opportunity to change her mind. If she had any doubts she could ask for a longer engagement. It was then Sebastian told him his patience was limited. He would take her as his lover whether there was an official ceremony or not. That had been the start of the shouting.

Benito had been forced to admit his pride was still a force of influence. It had caused him to cast his youngest daughter out without hesitation all those years ago. Sebastian had offered to pray with him so he would know he was forgiven. This was a humbling experience. It provided an opportunity for Benito to realise there was more to this future son-in-law than he could have imagined.

Sustained -
An Enduring Promise

ଉ ☼ ଓ

Proverbs 16:1-3
The plans of the heart belong to each one, but the final answer is
from God. All the ways of humanity are clean in each one's eyes;
but the Lord weighs their motives. Commit your deeds to the Lord,
and all your plans will succeed.

ଉ ☼ ଓ

With ease and grace, Evie climbed the metal staircase to the upper storeroom. Sebastian had agreed to her plan to hire someone part-time to cover Reception. Avril, the single mother Evie had chosen, was grateful for the regular work and flexible hours. The late start and 2 pm finish made it possible for Avril to collect her two children from school.

Avril's presence provided Evie with the much-needed freedom to work on the storeroom inventory. She had impressed Sebastian with the customised database she had created. Evie also needed time to plan for her impending wedding. She met regularly with Dave's wife Marilyn. They had become such good friends Evie asked Marilyn to be her Matron of Honour. Evie could not ask Sofia, as her sister was still vehemently opposed to the wedding.

The sisters had talked about Sofia's disastrous marriage to Nicholas. Together they had cried over the heartache that man had caused them. Evie was unexpectedly thankful she had been sent away. Her exile had denied Nicholas the opportunity to violate her. Life would be completely different now if she had been his first victim. Yet this added sorrow to her regret, because if she had spoken up her sister may have been spared.

Sofia disagreed. She insisted nothing Evie could have said would have dissuaded her from making the wrong choices. Instead, Sofia was thankful she had saved her sister. Sofia's first husband had proven himself to be as evil and vicious as he had promised Evie he would be.

ଈୠ ☼ ଓଷ

Sebastian watched Evie ascend the stairs much faster than he liked. He stood in the workshop thinking about the changes her presence had brought to his life. The diminishing rosebuds in the bowl beside his bed were a daily reminder that time was passing. From Genesis 29:20, about how Jacob's wait for Rachel had seemed only a few days, he had claimed a promise that he would find the strength to remain true. He still found the nights longer and filled with more temptation than he would allow her to know. He wondered if she knew the sight of her was enough to drive him crazy with desire?

It had been two weeks since the doctor had cleared her of any complications from her accident. She had chided Sebastian for his over-protective attitude. She thought he'd asked too many questions, but he'd not risk losing her again.

Her pain had dissipated in the second week, and she was medication free. The red scar on her forehead was starting to diminish. Evie had cut her hair to provide a fringe of concealment. Sebastian was pleased she hadn't shortened the rest of her dark hair. He still trembled inside at the memory of the first time he saw it unbound.

He was thankful the doctor who stitched her wound had been skilful. He reached up and touched the thick ragged scar on his own forehead. He had other scars hidden among his tattoos. This visible one was a constant reminder of the role violence played in his past. There had been many vicious battles before he gained the respect which kept him safe. As a naive teenager in an adult prison, he was easy prey. With his fists and his feet, he had proven his fellow prisoners wrong. His hard-fought victories had lengthened his sentence and added to his father's sorrow. He had done what was necessary to survive. If he had his time again, nothing would change.

His violent prison reputation kept his business protected from petty criminals. It brought him a truce with the criminal elite. He would not threaten their control provided they left him in peace. These things he kept to himself, believing there was no need for Evie to know this unsavoury reality.

"Are you going to do any work today?" Dave asked him. "I know you can't keep your eyes off her. But it would make your nights easier to bear if you kept busy. You need to occupy your mind with something other than your desire for her during the day."

Sebastian laughed at the frank advice. After punching Dave lightly for his bluntness, he resumed his slow patrol of the workshop. It had been interrupted when she appeared.

He no longer needed to watch the door for her coming, nor did she have to send him a message. Those faithful dogs always alerted him. They seemed to understand the need for gentleness. The dizziness never returned after that Sunday prayer. Reluctantly he allowed her to dispense with the helmet. He believed his precautions ensured her safety within his domain.

Whenever she entered the workshop, the dogs materialised beside her in seconds. They barked until she gave them the treats they knew she would have in her pockets. When they were satisfied with her generous attention, they left her in peace. They disappeared back to whatever activity had occupied them.

Such was the routine of their days. Sebastian worked with his hands, while his heart waited for her to make another appearance. Evie came and went, smiling and teasing him with gentle kisses and embraces, then returning to work of her own. Today had been like any other, and he was satisfied there was nothing more he could do to make her safe.

Three hours later, Sebastian became uneasy and stopped work. What was the reason for this growing sense of alarm? He trusted his instincts. Scanning the workshop revealed nothing to justify his concern. Turning his thoughts to the last time he had seen Evie, he was sure everything had been as it should be. She had joined him at lunchtime, content he was allowing her to run errands and play a part in the daily routine. Everyone had welcomed her into the break room. Now he looked at the time and realised Avril had left, so Evie would be alone in the office.

The main entrance buzzer sounded. Moments later the dogs suddenly appeared, barking at the door leading to the office. There was urgency in the way they threw themselves at the door. They were demanding Evie open it to them immediately. Tossing aside his tools, Sebastian started to run in their direction. Activating his phone to access the security camera feed, he saw a stranger standing in reception.

The other men looked up from their work. Sebastian signalled to Dave and Leonardo who were working together. Immediately, they ran in the same direction.

🕉 ✿ ☙

Evie didn't immediately turn from the open filing cabinet when she heard the buzzer sound. "I'll be with you in a moment," she called out. She finished filing the documents before she gave the visitor her full attention.

On the other side of the counter stood a middle-aged man, tall and thin with brown hair and a short beard. He had an air of arrogance that added something to his smile which made her uneasy. His eyes were slowly looking her over, and she noticed him check to see if she wore a wedding ring. He leaned on the counter, and having read the name tag she wore pinned to her chest, he spoke. Hearing his voice, her mind screamed in recognition. Years of practice had glued a professional smile on her face, and he seemed to have no idea she knew who he was. If he had been looking at her face, he might have known, but his attention was focused elsewhere.

Nicholas. Lord, help me!

"Hello, Evie," he said, and she froze at the counter, her own hand just a few centimetres from his. Hastily she pulled her fingers back and took a step away.

"What are you doing here, Nicholas?" she heard herself ask, at the same time hearing the dogs clamouring outside the door. What would happen if she let them in?

He looked at her in surprise, studying the dark hair and eyes, before recognition came to him. "Maria!" he exclaimed, and then he smiled suggestively. "So the little sister has returned. We'll have to get reacquainted..."

Suddenly the door flew open and the two dogs stood on either side of her. They snarled, and Nicholas took a cautious step backwards. Sebastian looked from her to the stranger at the counter, and she reached out for him. Placing him behind her, she pressed her body against him. Sebastian wrapped his strong arms around her.

"Sebastian, this is Nicholas," Evie said sounding calmer than she felt. "Nicholas, this is my fiancé, Sebastian

Romano." Sebastian grew tense and she wrapped her own arms over his to stop him from letting her go. She didn't want Sebastian to lose control of his temper, because she feared what he would do to her old enemy.

Nicholas looked at the way Sebastian was holding her and laughed. "So, little Maria, you're as cunning as your sister in getting what you want. I hope she's worth it," he said suggestively to Sebastian who responded angrily.

"You're not welcome here!" Both dogs barked in agreement. Evie held onto his hands as if her life depended on it. A single gesture from their master was all they required to deal with this foe.

"I've come to see Leonardo," Nicholas sneered in reply. "I have a right to see my son, and you can't stop me."

"You gave up your rights a long time ago," Leonardo said. He stepped unexpectedly into the room to stand beside Sebastian, who reached out to him. Leonardo was shaking with resentment, shocked to learn this man was his father.

"Leonardo?" Nicholas said in surprise, apparently taking in the way Sebastian was offering protection to his son. "Every son needs to know his father, and it's time we got to know each other."

"Where were you when I needed you before?" Leonardo cried. "Papa Benito was the one who looked after Mama and me when you left us. I don't need you now!"

"I'm still your father!" Nicholas protested, his own anger starting to show.

"The Boss is more a father to me than you!" Leonardo shouted. "Get out of here! I never want to see you again!"

Tearing himself from Sebastian's grasp, Leonardo ran out. Dave stood silently nearby. Sebastian nodded, and Evie watched Dave turn and follow Leonardo. She was more confident Sebastian had control of the situation.

"Evie!" Sebastian commanded. "Call security, and then if he is still here, phone the police." Evie staggered from his arms to sit behind the wooden desk. Her trembling hands reached for the telephone. Both numbers were automatically programmed into the console. He had made her practice how to use them. As she pressed the first button, her eyes widened as Sebastian took a step closer to the counter.

Oh, God! Don't let Sebastian kill Nicholas!

ༀ☼ༀ

Nicholas realised he'd made a mistake, angering this giant. Romano could reach out his massive hands to destroy him. Before he came in search of his son, Nicholas had done his research. He was well acquainted with Romano's violent reputation. He didn't doubt any threats would be carried out, without hesitation.

Amid his growing fear, anger stirred. His sources had failed to tell him Sofia's sister was here. Judging by her fiancé's hostility, she had told Romano about their thwarted encounter so many years ago. He had compounded the problem by addressing her so freely.

"He's still my son," Nicholas said begrudgingly. "When he's calmed down he'll realise his mistake. Here's my number so he can get in touch with me."

Carefully placing a card with his contact details on the counter, Nicholas backed to the door.

ༀ☼ༀ

Sebastian watched him go, then reached down to press the button under the counter. The front door locked and all the external roller doors began to close. He listened as the alarm sounded in the workshop. A full lockdown procedure was in place. The building would now transform into a reinforced fortress.

197

His phone buzzed with an alert from the private security firm, which he ignored. He already knew they were on their way. Evie had pressed the call button. The response to threat had been well planned. The camera's live feed would have revealed the nature of the emergency. He stood at the counter, looking down at the offensive card, wanting to rip it to shreds, but it was not his decision to make.

"How did Nicholas find us?" Evie whispered as she hurried from behind the desk and threw herself tearfully into his arms.

"I don't know," Sebastian told her, promising himself he would find out. He would not tell Evie of the extra protection to be put in place, both for her here and for her family. His instincts, finely honed by the hard years in prison, warned him he needed to prepare. Nicholas would be certain to try to find another way of reaching them. What did this man want after being silent all these years?

ဢ ✿ ☾

They were still standing there in the office when the security guards arrived. One glance at Romano's hard expression caused Piper Maxwell to hesitate. The owner of *Maximum Security* thought he knew his client well. Piper had extolled Romano's violent prison record to make his enemies reluctant to coerce him into an alliance. But his post-prison years had been relatively innocuous. One look at this angry giant's countenance reminded Piper of his potential to be dangerous. His unspoken response to Evie's brokenness was difficult to ignore.

CHAPTER 20
(FRIDAY 4TH AUGUST)

Tested -
A Promised Refuge

ᘓ ☼ Cష

Proverbs 10:27-29
The fear of the Lord prolongs days, but the years of the wicked shall
be shortened. The prospect of the righteous is joy, but the hope of
the wicked will perish. The way of the Lord is a stronghold to the
upright, but it is a destruction to the workers of iniquity.

ᘓ ☼ Cష

He waited on a bench near the shopping centre entrance closest to the *Romano* building. A battered skateboard lay at his feet, a can of soft drink in his hand. The secret watcher appeared no different to other youths loitering nearby. A master of disguise, today he was wearing torn jeans, T-shirt and a blue hooded jacket pulled up over a blonde wig. The designer sunglasses and his cleanly shaven face made him appear younger. He bore no resemblance to the older man Evie had escaped from several weeks ago. Throughout the shopping centre, his many soldiers were strategically deployed.

When he first encountered Evie, her weakness had made her a perfect target. His soldiers knew she was carrying a lot of cash and had intended to steal her handbag. The plan changed when she collapsed. He had stepped in to take command. Her abduction and ransom promised a greater reward. But as he implemented his scheme, someone had rescued her.

His anger awakened. His watchers had missed the private bodyguard. But he had the woman followed. He discovered his target came and went from the black building across the road. She was the exclusive property of millionaire Sebastian Romano.

The rumours suggested Romano's security procedures were impenetrable. His prison record portrayed Romano as cunning and wily. He repaid insult and offence with disproportionately excessive violence. He showed disregard for consequences. His severe dealings with anyone who tried to control him had extended his prison sentence. For many years, people had unsuccessfully searched for Romano's weakness. The watcher smiled. Here was an opportunity for him to prove to those who had dismissed his offer of allegiance that he was better than them. The key to Romano's undoing had fallen into his new enemy's hands.

He might have been prepared to let this incident go if Romano was not actively hunting him down. It angered him how Romano's interference disrupted his smooth operation. Romano's heavy-handed enquiries had sent ripples through his underworld connections. The watcher had solemnly vowed to have his revenge.

No-one knew the watcher's real identity for he used many names. At the moment he favoured Loki, the legendary brother of Thor from Greek mythology. It pleased him to have a mystery as another layer of protection in his arsenal. Loki's reputation for cunning tricks had allowed him to recruit a small army of minor criminals. He had ambitions to carve out an unrivalled kingdom. He wanted a lifestyle of power and luxury.

The kind of kingdom Romano could have if he had extended his reach beyond the automotive enterprise. His building dominated the streetscape. It would be satisfying to relieve his adversary of his finances and then use them to take control of the neighbourhood. He expected Romano to retreat in defeat from the scene.

He sat reflecting about how key information had fallen into his hands and exalted in his cleverness. If anything went wrong, he had someone set up to take full responsibility for the crime.

ও ☼ ৩

Without concern, Evie made her way to the first café. She exchanged greetings with familiar people behind the counter, collected the orders and turned to leave. Someone bumped into her, and after smiling politely at them, she hurried on her way. Later her arm began to sting and she rearranged her parcels to rub the affected place.

Continuing with her mission, she visited a second café, welcomed again by the staff waiting for her. As she turned to leave, she became aware of a strange sensation. Evie set down her parcels for a few seconds. Effortlessly, she activated a Bluetooth earpiece. Her phone connected with Sebastian immediately.

"Evie? Is everything okay?"

"Sorry to worry you Sebastian, but you said I should call you if anything happened. I think I've been bitten by something and am having a bad reaction. I'm on my way to the traffic lights now, but could you send someone to meet me?"

"Marilyn and the children are here. I'll send them." She heard him calling out before he spoke to her again. "Are you sure you won't wait there until they come?"

"I just want to get back. Stay on the line, so if I decide I need to sit down, I can let you know."

Evie was struggling with a growing fear her illness had returned.

> Lord, I'm feeling frightened. You have promised to walk with me in the Valley of Shadows and told me not to fear any evil. I need Your help.

ꙮ ✪ ꙮ

The pair following Evie hurried forward when she suddenly staggered. One of the women took the parcels from her hands, while the other reached around her to keep her upright. Neither of them said anything as they steered her towards the exit. Evie was unable to speak, and couldn't think what she should do. Loki smiled at how easily she went with them. Any uninformed observers would think nothing of three close friends walking together.

CHAPTER 21
(FRIDAY 4TH AUGUST)

United –
A Promise Declared

ॐ ☼ ೲ

ॐ ☼ ೲ

Alex's mother paused at the traffic lights, distracted by Lilly and Rory's argument. They had been playing Traffic Bingo and Lilly was the unexpected winner. Then Rory spotted a black Holden Commodore parked across the road. This was one of the cars he needed to beat his sister. Alex looked up from his new phone. He wanted to surprise Uncle Seb by capturing Evie on video. The lights changed, and all four stepped off the curb.

"Look, there's Evie!"

Five-year-old Lilly started to run, but her mother caught hold of her. Seventeen-year-old Alex turned the camera towards her. At the same time, the black Commodore pulled out and stopped in the middle of the crossing. The woman in the driver's seat glanced towards them. She had bright blue hair and was wearing reflective silver glasses. They were still a long way from her when she turned her head away from them.

The car was blocking their way. There was a scream, the sound of doors slamming and the Commodore roared away from the scene. Something was very wrong! His mother started to run, dragging both Rory and Lilly along with her.

"Mum! Mum! They've taken Evie!"

ℬ ☼ ℭ

Sebastian watched from the upstairs window. Evie's phone was still active, and he listened in horror to her scream, followed by the slamming of doors. Then a car engine roared. "Give me your phone!" he heard a man's voice shouting, followed by what sounded like a slap. Evie cried out again. A few seconds later there was a loud explosive crackling sound, and the line went dead.

Diving for the stairs, Sebastian shouted for Dave to accompany him. He angrily sent the dogs away when they tried to follow. "Call the police!" he shouted to the others. "Initiate lockdown! Evie's been taken!"

As he left the building, Sebastian could hear the senior employees issuing orders, implementing the emergency plan that Piper had created. What had happened to Evie may serve as a distraction, rendering his building and his loyal employees vulnerable to greater attack. No-one would leave until Piper came to declare that it was safe.

When Sebastian and Dave arrived outside the shopping centre, Marilyn and the children were huddled together on the pavement. In a state of great distress, they were surrounded by curious onlookers. The shopping centre security guards arrived a few minutes later. Word spread through the crowd that someone had been snatched from the footpath.

Silently, Sebastian scanned the gathering crowd for an explanation. People were videoing the scene with their phones. They pressed in close, curious to know what these witnesses had seen. Sebastian took command with unflinching authority. The crowd pulled back in fear as he shepherded Dave and the four witnesses and hustled them back to safety. The shopping centre guards made a big display of preventing anyone from following.

Delivering Dave's family safely inside his fortress, Sebastian sent them to the break room. His mind was full of things he should be doing to get Evie back. But he felt obligated towards Marilyn and the children. Their distress was his fault.

He should have trusted his instincts and kept Evie with him. He had been suspicious when Piper visited this morning. But how could he explain his concern without telling Evie the truth about his many enemies? Piper had warned him to be ready to raise the alert level.

His business was in a prime location and there had been lucrative offers from people who wanted to use the *Romano* workshop as a cover for illegal activities. All his employees were routinely screened for any disloyalty. Piper was adamant that keeping his business secure and fully operational was an essential protection.

Like a general commanding his army, Sebastian checked that the emergency plan was being implemented properly. The 'Closed' sign was in the window. All phone lines were redirected to his phone.

Now Avril was assigned to watch over Marilyn and the children.

The assembled employees waited for him to allocate roles. Until Piper arrived to give permission for anyone to leave, they needed to be kept busy. Some he dispatched to the workshop. Jobs nearing completion could be finished. He asked for a list of the work that would not begin today. The owners would need to be contacted. He sent a group to his flat to reheat food from the freezer to feed everyone. The meals that Evie had been collecting would never be delivered. He asked for blankets and a teddy bear, the present he had stashed ready for Lilly's next birthday. She was in need of it now.

With everyone meaningfully occupied, Sebastian went into the break room. He knew Dave's precious family needed assurance if they were to make a recovery from this trauma. He stopped in the doorway and contemplated the gathering. Apart from Dave's family and Avril, two of his most trusted employees stood watching Evie's nephew Leonardo who was pacing in the corner. Something flew across the room, and Avril hurried to retrieve it. Alex had thrown his phone.

Dave's family were all crammed together on a single couch. Lilly was clinging to her mother, sobbing hysterically with the new teddy bear clutched to her chest. Rory was sitting on Dave's lap, silent and pale, staring into space with wide eyes. Alex sat slumped on the couch beside his father, his anger plain to see. He must be blaming himself because he hadn't been able to save Evie. Dave looked up and Sebastian knew he was questioning Piper's command that everyone remain inside the building during an emergency.

What was keeping Piper? He said he was working in the shopping centre today. The door buzzer sounded. At last. Sebastian went to meet Piper Maxwell, whose security agency had always served him well. "How long until the police get here?" he asked, knowing Piper would already have more information.

"They won't be here for another ten minutes. Your usual enemies aren't responsible – I've had teams on alert, just in case. Nicholas has been openly making threats against you, so it's possible he's involved. The people tracking him were getting close, but he seems to have disappeared again."

Sebastian swore and smashed his fist into the nearby door. The woodwork was demolished, shattering the glass. He was oblivious to the pain and dripping blood. One of the men stepped from the connecting room. Realising what had caused the commotion, he returned with a towel.

"How was this possible? You said Nicholas was a lone wolf, unlikely to cause us any immediate trouble."

"It seems he has been targeted by a woman who is part of a wider network."

"What kind of woman? What network?" Sebastian asked uneasily.

"She calls herself Jezebel. She's the kind of woman who likes to play rough. The perfect bait to trap Nicholas. Someone did their homework. He has been set up to take the blame if this goes wrong. It might be related to the previous attempt to abduct Evie from the shopping centre. That's why I've been across the road today. I'm trying to identify the ringleader. We should soon have all the answers you need."

"What do they want?"

"Expect a large ransom demand, which you're not going to pay."

"Will we get Evie back?"

"Probably. Though the longer she's with Nicholas, the more danger she's in. I think this is about identifying your weaknesses."

"Why now?"

"This unknown ringleader wants revenge. We were able to shut down some of his operations, and he holds you

207

responsible. He must have discovered that you've been holding out on the big operators and thought he could best them at their game. If this new enemy succeeds in bringing you down, that will increase his own notoriety."

"Boss," Avril spoke cautiously, stepping past the shattered door. "You need to see this."

Sebastian took a smartphone from her. Realising what he was watching, he passed the phone to his security consultant. Together they stepped into the break room.

ࠌ☼&#x60B

"Whose phone is this?" Piper demanded.

Marilyn looked up in alarm and then turned to her oldest son. "Alex, did you record what happened?"

Piper reached into his pocket and placed a call. "We have a live video of the main event, and I need those cables. Tell no-one else."

Sebastian grabbed Piper by the arm and drew him aside. "Who did you call? And why did you say 'tell no-one else'?" Sebastian asked.

"Jenny's in the car park, talking to my team of IT specialists on the phone. We have a problem. The shopping centre cameras have been tampered with. Yet the timestamp and security codes are intact. The same goes for all the cameras along Evie's path. A pre-recorded loop shows her walking in and out without anything happening."

The buzzer sounded, and Jenny walked in with a bag of cables. Already familiar with the room, she connected cables to the wall-mounted television. When she held out her hand for the phone, Piper saw that Sebastian recognised her, despite her altered appearance. He turned to Piper, who pre-empted his question.

"Jenny has taken this personally. She's still angry she didn't notice anyone following Evie. We've been working to make it possible for Evie to come and go each day on her own. Until today, everything was fine. We've been using the shopping centre's security camera feed to watch the crowd. I persuaded Centre Management that eradicating this gang was in their best interests. Whenever we identify potential watchers, they disappear. The gang are using multiple disguises. Today we were planning to bring one of them in for questioning."

"Ready, Piper," Jenny called out, and they turned to look at the video playing on the big screen. The first shaky shots were of the traffic lights and passing traffic, before focusing on a parked car. Rory's identification of the make and model rose above the traffic noise. As the car pulled out from the curb, Lilly's shout rang out and the view swivelled again. There was Evie squeezed between two unknown women. The Commodore pulled out and parked on the crossing. It blocked their view. The blue-haired driver looked into the lens.

"It's lucky she didn't realise you were recording," Dave said with concern. "Can we keep this secret?"

Piper nodded, and the video continued. They watched a second blue-haired woman calmly step out of the car and open the rear door. Through the windows of the car, there was a framed shot of Evie stumbling forward. A bearded man in a hooded jacket and sunglasses leapt forward and drew her into the car with him. There was a jumble of action as Evie resisted. The standing woman slammed both doors and walked away as if nothing was happening.

The driver looked in the direction of the camera again. The image was shaky as the car roared off, ultimately revealing the number plate. Something white flew out of the window of the departing car. It smashed on the road before the video ended.

"That white flash was Evie's phone. We already have it," Jenny said. "One tracking device down. Let's hope they don't find the other one."

ༀ ☼ ༃

Now it was Sebastian's turn to look surprised. "What tracking device?"

Piper and Jenny exchanged glances. Sebastian watched them carefully. He thought he could trust Piper but it was obvious the man was keeping secrets from him.

Sebastian insisted he could vouch for the loyalty of the few who were present. Piper nodded, and Jenny explained. "The receiver was set to track her phone. By the time we realised they had thrown it away, the signal from the other transmitter was out of range."

"So if you can find the car, you'll know where she is?"

"We have the number plate now," Piper said.

"Already on it," Jenny reported. "I've accessed the traffic cameras for the next few blocks and they suddenly appear four blocks away, heading in the opposite direction. Someone did a good job covering their tracks. Without this kid's video, we would have no idea what kind of car it was. Witnesses interviewed by centre security have come up with multiple descriptions. One kid on a skateboard said it was some kind of red sports car. That's a direct message for you, Romano.

"They know who you are and what you're worth. Expect your Maserati to be included in the ransom demand. We tried to track down that witness but he gave a false name and address, and without the cameras, we can't track him."

"This is a kidnapping?" Dave asked. "This is about money?"

"Take the video back to when Evie appears. Bring it forward frame by frame," Piper commanded, ignoring the question.

"Stop there." On the screen in front of them, in her struggle, Evie dislodged her assailant's sunglasses. His hood fell back. One by one the watchers turned to look at Leonardo, who Sebastian had forgotten until now. The teenager was staring in horror at the television.

"That's Nicholas! My father took Evie? Nooo!"

Leonardo fell to the floor, his arms wrapped around his head, rocking as he sobbed inconsolably. Sebastian knelt beside him. Outwardly calm, he put his arms around the devastated teenager. They both knew what Nicholas liked to do to women. Leonardo had spoken with Sebastian after overhearing recent conversations between Evie and his mother. In her own graphic retelling of Sofia's story, Evie had held nothing back.

"Evie is going to be fine," Sebastian reassured him with determination. He needed to convince himself too. "God brought her safely back from death. You were here to witness that. God didn't bring her back to us so that anyone could harm her – not even the man who calls himself your father. God has a plan to turn all this around so we win and the enemy loses. All we have to do is wait for Him to give us the answers we need."

"Amen!" Marilyn added, joining the pair on their knees. She was crying, but the light of hope began to shine in her eyes. "God gave Evie the promise of the white rose. Sebastian, you counted the rosebuds and know there is a future that includes Evie. God is called the Promise Keeper, and by His very nature, He cannot break a promise He has made. He made His promise in front of witnesses exactly as you asked Him to. We saw it. Now we are going to stay here as your witnesses while we wait and pray for her return."

The other members of Dave's family came to join them, kneeling on the floor. Leonardo's sobbing fell silent. They huddled together, silently praying for Evie, and for each other. A hush fell over the assembly.

ℬ ✪ ℭ

Unnoticed, Piper and Jenny left the room. Twenty minutes had passed since Evie was taken. Piper was thankful his team had been in the shopping centre, for this bought them precious time.

Verified -
A Refining Promise

ଛୠ ✡ ୪ଓ

1 Peter 1:6b-7 (WEB)
You have been put to grief in various trials, that the proof of your
faith, which is more precious than gold that perishes even though it
was tested by fire, may be found to result in praise, glory and
honour at the revelation of Jesus Christ.

ଛୠ ✡ ୪ଓ

Sebastian was angry that Piper had left and was not responding to his calls. He wanted to talk to the security agent about being part of the search, but without Piper's expert advice he might as well chase the wind. The only information he had received was a series of ambiguous messages sent to his phone by a number that refused to accept a reply.

Progress made

Maintain silence

Stay!

An hour had passed since Evie was abducted. It took all of Sebastian's self-control to maintain his stoic facade. Not even the death of his father had prepared him for the pain he was feeling. His mind could not rest, tormented by reminders of her presence wherever he looked. He wanted to hold her in his arms, and never let her go. Nowhere was it more potent than when he walked into her domain – the office where two detectives now waited by the phone. Sebastian had visited them so frequently there was no need to ask his question. They shook their heads. There was no new information. He left before his hidden desperation revealed its presence.

He turned and scanned the now-empty workshop. His employees had been sent home, and only Dave's family and Leonardo remained. He had taken them upstairs to his flat. As he walked across the workshop, the dogs met him. They silently accompanied him on his inspection. He needed to keep busy, and he prowled his domain like a caged lion. He satisfied himself that all the equipment was correctly stored, and the power was turned off at each station. How many times had he already done this?

Finally, he took out his phone, checking the external security cameras to see how many cars were left to be collected from the car park. He willed the phone to ring. The dogs returned with him to the stairs, where he went up to the flat. In a few minutes, he would repeat the process again. This behaviour had been perfected in prison. It had kept him sane through the long years of vigilance and silence.

℘ ☼ ℃

Evie relived that terrifying moment when she was thrown into the car by an unseen assailant. Nicholas. She recognised him now. He had slapped her when she screamed. Now she drifted in a dreamlike state. Her captors were discussing a drug someone had administered. Perhaps this explained why she struggled to remain present? Nicholas was talking to her, but she mustn't react. Evie silently cried out to God for help as horror flooded her mind. Immediately, familiar darkness consumed her, and her tormentor's coarse threats faded.

Her next period of consciousness came as they dragged her from the elevator to the hotel room. Nicholas threw her onto the bed. Another period of nothingness gripped her. She emerged from it to hear the woman complaining about how unresponsive their prisoner was. Nicholas called the woman Jezebel, and explained in detail what he had planned. Despite salacious taunts from Jezebel, Nicholas wanted to wait. He promised that Evie's torture would be heightened if she was fully aware of what was to come.

Jezebel made suggestions of her own. Together they laughed wickedly at the pleasure they expected to have at Evie's expense. Another wave of dizziness washed over Evie. Jezebel continued to taunt Nicholas for his inaction and his ineptitude. The pair argued viciously, and Evie could hear them wrestling on the other bed. The woman swore, cursed and shrieked at him. When Evie realised this was part of their game she thanked God she was facing the window!

Struggling to block out the sounds of their violence, Evie blacked out again. When she awoke, the room was strangely quiet. Just when she decided she must be alone, she heard movement. Someone leaned over her and grabbed her shoulders. Jezebel shook her violently to see if she was awake. Evie felt strangely calm, and focused on keeping her eyes closed and her breathing steady.

ஐ ☼ ଔ

Glancing at the clock on the console, Piper realised he was no closer to finding Evie.

"Stop the car!" Jenny cried.

Piper stomped on the brake, screeching to a halt in the middle of the street. "What?" Piper demanded.

Behind him traffic beeped impatiently, forcing him to look for somewhere to pull over. His stony countenance masked his emotional turmoil. They were near the city centre, surrounded by multi-storey buildings, each one having an extensive underground car park. There were multiple exits and hundreds of hiding places. Glancing at the clock on the console, Piper saw it was 1 pm. Evie had been taken an hour ago, and he was no closer to finding her.

His team of experts at his security hub had traced the fugitive car to the previous corner, but now the trail was lost. Jenny was following their progress on the high-tech monitor installed on the dashboard. She had never asked how his team could access information so efficiently. The traffic cameras at the next intersection were down. Their quarry was somewhere in the immediate vicinity, but they were unable to pick up Evie's personal tracker. This technical limitation was frustrating and unforgivable.

They drove in and out of car parks, searching for the elusive black Commodore. His concern was steadily growing. He had been too optimistic in his assurances to Romano. He believed his investigative skills were superior to the police. Was it pride that had compelled Piper to leave the scene before the authorities arrived? His actions had concealed the existence of the video recording from the police. Was he justified in his suspicions that the kidnappers had inside information? More and more, the doubts grew, condemning him for errors that could prove fatal.

"Look over there!" Jenny pointed. On a café window across the street, a sign read 'The White Rose'. The café was on the ground floor of a large high-rise hotel.

Piper silently queried her sanity. Did she believe that talk about God and promises? Then he remembered how highly he valued her intuition. She apparently read his doubt and understood his unspoken questions. Shrugging her shoulders, she said, "Do you have any better ideas?"

Turning into the hotel's undercover car park, Piper drove around. To his surprise, he saw the car they were seeking parked opposite the elevator. Together they got out and approached the Commodore. A quick assessment revealed the doors were locked. While Jenny kept watch, Piper deactivated the electronic lock with tools the police needn't know he possessed.

To minimise any forensic trace, Piper pulled on leather gloves. Opening the rear door, he leaned in and removed a blue wig from the floor. It had been discarded after successfully rendering eyewitness accounts unreliable.

Under the wig, he noticed something shiny and extracted a broken chain and pendant. Jenny confirmed his find with a nod. Suddenly, Jenny hissed a warning. A group of people exited the elevator and passed without noticing them. Alone again, Piper and Jenny strolled to the elevator.

"Which floor?" he asked, more inclined to listen to Jenny's hunches now.

"Why don't we go into the café? I've been here before, except it had another name then. The hotel reception is clearly visible from the café. We might get lucky."

Jenny swiftly modified her appearance. She had been in the shopping centre prior to the attack on Evie, and someone might recognise her. Jenny removed her dark-rimmed spectacles and hat, shaking loose her freshly dyed long blonde hair. She undid several buttons on her shirt, took off her jacket and shoved it into her large handbag, and applied a bright red lipstick. These simple changes made a sufficient disguise. Jenny went from nondescript to stunningly noteworthy.

Arm in arm, Piper and Jenny walked from the elevator, across the carpeted foyer, past Reception, to the café entrance. They pretended their surroundings were of no real interest. A balding man sat behind the counter, reading a newspaper. An Asian girl directed them to a table near the window. They made a big fuss about moving their chairs so they could sit side by side. Their table looked directly towards the elevator doors. The door to the stairs was beside it. They also had a good view of the other customers. Jenny flirted with Piper shamelessly while they waited for their order. If anyone asked about them afterwards, they wanted to leave a clear impression. Only two other café tables were occupied.

ಐ ✿ ಚಿ

Failing to get any response, Jezebel dropped Evie back onto the bed. Nicholas suggested they go out for something to eat and come back when she was awake. They tied her hands and feet. Nicholas asked if they should gag Evie in case she screamed when she woke up, but Jezebel laughed derisively.

She assured Nicholas she had been in this hotel many times. No matter how much screaming went on, no-one – except perhaps the victim – had ever complained. The walls and the reinforced concrete floor were designed to keep out the noise of heavy traffic. They muffled other sounds as well. This made it the perfect place for what they had in mind for their afternoon's entertainment.

ಐ ✿ ಚಿ

The door opened and slammed closed. Evie was alone. Too afraid to move in case this was another trick.

Lord, what is going to happen to me? I'm very frightened. Thank You that I can talk to You. I take comfort from Your presence. If it isn't possible for me to be rescued could You please keep me from showing them my fear? Help me endure the pain. I don't understand why this is happening, but I know I can place my life in Your hands. You will sustain me.

Wait patiently. You are about to be rescued. A man will come and you are to stay quiet and do everything that he says.

How will I recognise this man?

He will speak your name.

℃☉ℂ

Their coffee arrived in fine bone china mugs decorated with a white rose pattern, in keeping with the floral decor. Piper and Jenny leaned their heads together, sipping their coffee. They whispered about what they should do next. Suddenly Piper stiffened. "Nicholas just stepped out of the elevator, coming this way. The woman with him isn't happy. Don't look! They're coming in here."

The new arrivals seated themselves directly in front of them. Jenny activated the eavesdropping technology on her phone. The investigators read the text-based translation of the nearby conversation.

The woman was speaking. "...you promised me."

"We have to wait until she wakes up."

"It's been an hour!"

"We have plenty of time. The handover isn't until after dark."

"You hit her too hard."

"We can make our own fun while we wait."

"Why don't we just start with her anyway?"

"I've already told you! I want to taste her tears. I want to see her fear and listen to her pleading."

Piper had seen enough. "You stay here," he whispered and walked out to the reception desk.

The couple didn't give him a second glance. The woman was describing to Nicholas some vile things they could do to Evie while she was still unconscious. Piper resisted the urge to strike her. He had better hurry.

Taking out his leather wallet, Piper removed three $100 notes and laid them one at a time on the counter. The receptionist gave him undivided attention. Piper gestured with his head towards the café.

"I'm a private investigator," Piper began. "I've been paid by that woman's husband to find out if she's having an affair. There's good money in this if you help me."

The manager glanced towards Nicholas and Jezebel as he slid the three notes out of sight. He tapped the counter three times and waited. Piper added three more notes. When Piper extracted the final note, the man said aloud, "Here is your key, sir. I hope you and your wife enjoy your stay."

Waving to Jenny, who hurried to join him, Piper strolled to the elevator. The electronic key tag read 209. With a loud groan, the slow elevator lurched upwards. Jenny confessed she was praying Nicholas didn't take the stairs! Finally arriving, they hastened along the narrow corridor, only to discover the room numbers were jumbled. Inadvertently, they had gone the wrong way. Turning to retrace their steps. Jenny gasped. Nicholas and his companion were stepping out of the elevator.

"Our room is this way," Piper said loudly, walking past to pause further up the passage. Nervous laughter was their alibi for an afternoon assignation. Nicholas looked over at them lewdly before dragging his companion into his room.

When the door closed, Piper and Jenny approached and listened carefully. Jenny confirmed the signal from Evie's hidden device was coming from within. Through the closed door they could hear the sounds of a struggle and excited laughter, then the slamming of an internal door.

Evie lay in the darkened room, tormented by the thought of being rescued. Should she attempt to escape her bonds? She was just starting to move her arms when she heard the door open and slam shut. She recognised their laughter and trembled in fear. How was she to be rescued when her kidnappers were back?

Hearing the familiar sounds of their violent struggle, Evie was startled when another door slammed. There was more screaming, but the sound was muffled. Perhaps they had taken their violence into the bathroom? Should she try to get away while they were preoccupied? She held her breath and prayed for wisdom.

Wonderful – A Promise Defended

❧ ☼ ☙

Proverbs 16:4-6
The Lord has made everything for a purpose - yes, even the wicked.
Everyone who is proud is an abomination to the Lord:
they will not go unpunished.
By mercy and truth iniquity is atoned for.
By the fear of the Lord men depart from evil.

❧ ☼ ☙

Using the electronic key, Piper opened the door. The room was dark, and as his eyes adjusted, he slipped inside. To his left, noises through the closed bathroom door warned him of the danger. He waved Jenny inside, and she stood guard. Should defence become necessary, she extracted another electronic gadget from her voluminous handbag.

Moving into the main room, Piper spied a still figure lying on the furthest of two large beds. She was facing towards the window. "Evie," he whispered as he knelt down in front of her face. To his surprise, she calmly opened her eyes. He signalled for her silence. Her hands and bare feet were tied, and Piper threw her over his shoulder. He stealthily moved towards the elevator, leaving Jenny to close the door and cover their retreat. Instead of waiting for the elevator they moved towards the stairs.

They climbed unseen to the next landing where Piper lowered Evie gently to the floor. Jenny joined them, and together they quickly released her from her bonds. "Can you walk?" Jenny whispered, and Evie nodded as her tears began to flow.

"We're not out of danger yet," Jenny said. "We still have to get you out of the hotel unseen."

Piper decided the safest place for Evie in the immediate future would be in another room. He gestured to Jenny to keep moving upwards, then made two phone calls. He settled on the stairs to wait.

Ten minutes later, hurrying feet heralded the arrival of a male courier he had used before. Piper spoke quietly to the youth, giving him a handful of money. This was stowed speedily into the courier satchel, and Piper was alone again. The young man returned with two more room keys and news about some excitement on the second floor. A hysterical woman claimed her sleeping friend had disappeared. The courier looked at the extra money placed in his hand and asked no questions.

Piper sent Jenny a message and took the elevator to meet them. Quickly he opened the door to Room 716, and the women slipped inside unseen. After drawing the curtains, Piper turned on the lights to evaluate Evie's condition. He was surprised to see her quietly returning his gaze. This spoke of an inner strength he wasn't expecting.

"Thank you," she said. "Does Sebastian know you've found me?"

"Until we find out who else is involved, I can't risk telling him directly. I apologise for neglecting to organise a code."

"Pass me your phone," Evie said quietly. Piper studied her, before deciding to trust her. She typed a brief message, returning it to him for approval. With a confirming nod, he sent the message. His evaluation of this wide-eyed young woman was greatly improving.

"Now he knows," she smiled.

ℰ☉ℭ

Sebastian climbed the stairs to his flat after another frustrating visit to the police detectives waiting in his office for the phone to ring. He had prowled his domain, wanting to rage and vent his anger by destroying something. Instead he'd kept his fists clenched and his voice silent. He cast his restless energy towards God, pleading for news and begging for Evie's safe return. He didn't know if God was listening.

There had been no ransom demand, nor any news from Piper. Sebastian was tempted to tell the detectives about Piper's secret investigation. Sebastian remembered the look in Piper's eyes and held his tongue. Piper was secretive but Romano had to trust his instincts that his friend was Evie's best chance for survival.

As he entered the flat, he knew he was not alone in his vigil. Dave's family and Evie's nephew Leonardo had remained. Leonardo, Rory and Alex were watching a movie in the lounge room, while the adults sat around the kitchen table. Lilly was now fast asleep on Evie's bed, still holding the teddy bear.

Marilyn put a cup of coffee in front of him as he joined them at the table. Her smile wavered as he shook his head, and tears welled up in her eyes. He had no words to offer her comfort. Suddenly his phone vibrated on the tabletop. He stretched out his hand, torn between the need for information, and the fear of what he would learn. The others stared at him. He frowned as he looked at the phone screen, then he leapt up with a grin. He shadow-boxed across the kitchen, before returning to show the message to the others.

225

knock knock 7x7

"This was sent from Piper's phone," he explained. "Evie wrote it. They've found her, but it isn't safe yet. We're the only ones who'd understand the message."

Dave looked from his friend to his wife and saw she was smiling in understanding. "Behold I stand at the door and knock," she said. "It's a verse from Revelation."

Sebastian nodded. "It's also the Ask, Seek, Knock verse I have tattooed on my arm. Evie knocks on the wall between us in the morning so I know when she's awake."

"Reminds me of Rory's knock-knock jokes," Dave said.

Returning to the message, Sebastian typed a single S, sent his reply, then collapsed on the table. His determination that no-one would see him torn apart at her loss had taken all his strength. How fortuitous this message came in the privacy of his flat. Any secret watchers would remain oblivious to his true weakness.

Marilyn spoke comforting words. Her certainty assured him this message was a sign God was at work. Sebastian was thankful no-one mentioned their concerns about what might have befallen Evie. He continued his silent prayers.

𝕊𝕆 ☼ ℭ𝔖

A secret meeting took place in Room 458 between Piper and a powerful man wearing an expensive navy blue suit. This man and his entourage came directly from the car park using the stairs. Two other men wearing black suits were standing outside in the hallway to ensure no interruption. Another pair guarded the stairwell.

"Walls have ears," Piper began. He had not expected this man to be the one to respond to his request. They had once been friends, and he didn't want Jenny to learn more of his secrets. She was eavesdropping from a strategic location.

The man nodded. Piper knew he would also be recording this meeting.

Piper showed the man an image on his phone. He transferred it electronically to the other man's phone.

"We both want the same thing," Piper explained. "A clear message needs to be sent. My client has already regained possession of this stolen package. He wants you to profit by claiming you made the retrieval."

"What's it to us if Sebastian Romano lost and regained his woman?" In this way, he confirmed knowledge about the abduction.

"An unknown individual organised the theft, someone with extensive connections. This intrudes into your territory and undermines your authority. Romano wants this individual brought out into the open and made an example of. He could do this for himself, and no-one would know, but he wants to send a wider message."

The man in the navy suit looked at the falsified image on his phone: Evie bound and gagged.

"How was she retrieved so quickly?"

"Microchip," Piper lied, and the other man shrugged. They both knew there was more to his story.

"Everything necessary will be done."

Pausing on the threshold the man had one more question. "The woman is safe?"

"Very."

The man appeared thoughtful and then smiled. "Good."

This final response confirmed Piper's suspicion, reinforcing the need for caution. His visitor would want to take advantage of the situation.

Patiently, Piper remained in Room 458 until Jenny confirmed his dangerous visitors had left the building. She contacted him again when she had identified the men who waited for Piper's departure. Only then did he open the wardrobe, revealing Evie's current hiding place. He had been truthful when he declared her safe. No-one would expect him to bring her to the meeting. As Evie climbed stiffly out of the confined space, Piper was prepared for the next phase of his plan.

ℰ✿ℭ

Loki was seated at a curbside table outside a popular establishment, savouring strong black coffee. He was congratulating himself on his cleverness when the first text message from an unknown number arrived. The image of the kidnapped woman, bound and gagged, was accompanied by a simple message.

We have what you want. Await instructions.

At first, he thought one of his accomplices had sent the message and made a quick call to Jezebel. She was uncharacteristically hesitant, but he knew how to break through her defensiveness. He was proficient at identifying weakness in others and could easily control her. When he discovered the victim had been taken from their hotel room, he went very quiet.

Jezebel explained how they invented the story about a missing friend as they searched the hotel, but no-one had seen anything. The manager at the reception desk was unhelpful.

Loki responded to her tale by coldly asking her location. Jezebel obeyed quickly, no doubt intending to be gone before he arrived. She was unaware he'd had the Commodore followed. There were already watchers in the street to make sure she didn't double-cross him. Loki had established a temporary headquarters only a few blocks away.

𝕭 ☼ 𝕮𝖘

Studying Evie carefully, Piper compared her present appearance with the photo the police had released at a hastily convened press conference. On his advice, neither Romano nor any of Evie's family had been present to face the media. He asked her to walk across the room and made further recommendations. Jenny had worked skilfully to transform Evie into an elderly grey-haired lady, walking slowly with the aid of a collapsible cane. Piper was thankful his colleague carried many disguises.

"Do you remember what you have to do?" he asked Evie.

She nodded. "Take the elevator down to the foyer. Walk out the front door and turn right. Remain in character and keep going no matter what happens. At the next corner, cross at the lights. Three blocks from here, I turn left and left again. I should then be in familiar territory. When I get to the restaurant, the table is booked for Matherson. Sit with my back to the window, and wait until either you or Jenny comes. Make no attempt to contact my family."

He asked if she was ready. Evie smiled briefly and then lowered her head. She assumed the posture and mannerisms that would get her safely home. After confirming the hallway was clear, Piper sent her alone to the elevator.

𝕭 ☼ 𝕮𝖘

Evie shuffled her way apologetically into the crowded elevator. Jenny entered one floor below but showed no sign of recognition. Arriving in the foyer, Jenny hurried away while Evie hobbled forward to the entrance.

Oh, Lord. I'm so nervous. I'm worried I'll give myself away. Please help me remember everything. Thank You

229

again for rescuing me. Please help Sebastian and my family to be patient. Keep them safe. Keep me safe.

Someone bumped into her as she lingered on the footpath. She inhaled in recognition as Nicholas came angrily out the front entrance. His female companion was right behind him, screaming abuse that made Evie blush under her make-up. Nicholas turned to face his attacker, cursing her vehemently. The woman responded by stopping on the footpath beside Evie. The woman turned angrily towards her.

"What are you looking at!" Recoiling from the woman's raised hand, Evie lowered her eyes and almost stumbled. Thankful for the cane, she froze in terror.

⁝ ☼ ⁞

Loki's hands tensed on the wheel at the prospect of questioning Jezebel in person. To his extreme annoyance, he arrived outside her hotel to witness a public disturbance. There was Jezebel in her distinctive short skirt and high heels, standing on the footpath shouting obscenities at a fleeing Nicholas. By the time Loki parked the car and crossed the road, she was about to strike an old lady who stood transfixed on the pavement.

"What are you doing here?" Jezebel hissed. She struggled as he dragged her across the road and threw her into the back seat of his car. No-one challenged him, and he drove away.

⁝ ☼ ⁞

Evie glanced around. Other passersby were shaking their heads and then everyone moved on as if nothing had happened. One of Jezebel's high-heeled shoes lay abandoned in the middle of the street. Nicholas had stopped to gloat, before continuing in the direction Evie needed to go. His laughter haunted her as she cautiously moved forward, watching him disappear into the underground car park. As she hesitated at the entrance, two men in dark suits crossed her path without pause.

ꕥ

Loki pulled out into the traffic and drove away. After finding all the doors locked, Jezebel climbed awkwardly into the front passenger seat. Eyes averted, she waited for him to speak.

He drove her to a large nature reserve. Following a narrow tree-lined track he reached a remote clearing. He knew there was little risk anyone would see them here.

"Get out!" he shouted, and she hurriedly obeyed. He knew Jezebel, mistress of torture and sadism, was more afraid of him now. Jezebel had promised him her loyalty a long time ago, and he had tested her in many ways.

Her fear of being abandoned had its roots in her childhood. It was only by chance he had discovered her secret. The last time she accompanied Loki to a bush setting, she had clung to his side like a frightened teenager and told him everything. This was precisely what he needed her to do now.

"Give me your phone!" he snarled. Satisfied she hadn't betrayed him, he continued. "How did you lose your prisoner? Start from the beginning."

Jezebel quickly complied, and he listened closely, asking questions to clarify missing details. She held nothing back, explaining how the hostage had reacted badly to the drug and fallen unconscious almost immediately. Nicholas had slapped Evie, and she had remained unresponsive for an hour. They had been careful not to be seen transferring her from the car to the hotel room.

Beginning with an explanation of the argument with Nicholas, Jezebel detailed the intimacy that followed. After binding their unconscious prisoner, they had gone down to the café. There, Jezebel had finally ensured Nicholas' agreement with her plan. They had returned to the room in a heightened state of excitement and been shocked to find the room empty.

Loki pressed her until she confessed. They hadn't checked whether the victim was still there when they returned. He asked her again if she had noticed anyone in the hallway, and she remembered the amorous couple unlocking the door to a nearby room. Satisfied she had told him everything he walked away from her.

"Don't leave me here!" Jezebel pleaded. He shoved her away from him, laughing cruelly at her terror. She chased after his car in desperation, and he knew she would be more careful in the future. Despite his anger, she was useful. He arranged for someone to collect her, then dismissed her from his thoughts.

ಬ ✿ ಛ

The men who found Jezebel crying in the bush were cold and efficient. They stood over her and revealed knowledge of her involvement in the abduction, quoting Nicholas as their source. They had been following her because Nicholas had never met the man who masterminded the plan. It seemed they hadn't realised who had brought her here, and now they wanted information.

Angrily she told them she'd only co-operate if they drove her into the city. Jezebel climbed into the back seat of their car and was relieved when the vehicle began rolling slowly along the track. Both men sat in the front. The passenger watched her in the rear-vision mirror as he asked for confirmation of specific details to prove she was keeping her side of the deal. They knew more than enough about the abduction to convince her Nicholas worked for them. This second betrayal wounded her deeply.

To have two men abandon her in one afternoon was too much. It became easier to reveal secrets. Soon she was telling the men everything they wanted to know about Loki. So great was her relief to be out of the bush, Jezebel revealed more of Loki's secrets than she intended. She was one of the few people he trusted, and her betrayal would be obvious. Her need for revenge came at a great cost. She would have to leave Melbourne as quickly as possible. This would require money, and she knew where she could get some. Loki had money hidden in several locations. She told them about the one closest to the city centre. She knew there were two caches there but she mentioned only one. When she finished talking, the passenger asked her more questions, and then the driver pulled into a parking space on a busy street. The other man stepped out to make a phone call.

Unsure whether this would bring her a good outcome, Jezebel unsuccessfully tried questioning the driver. Upon his return, the other man made her an offer. If she took them to Loki's cache, they would reward her with a plane ticket to the destination of her choice. Thoughtfully considering their offer, Jezebel told them where she would like to go when all this was done. The man smiled and she felt a shiver of fear, but there was no turning back now.

Xenolith –
A Precious Promise

ಠ ✿ ಅ

Psalm 1:1-3
Blessed is one who doesn't walk in the counsel of the wicked, nor sit
in the seat of scoffers; but delights in the Lord. They will be like a
tree planted by streams of water, producing fruit in each season,
their leaf does not wither. Whatever they do shall prosper.

ಠ ✿ ಅ

Onwards, the disguised Evie went slowly, her body developing authentic aches and pains from the hunched posture and shuffling gait. In the gathering gloom, she feared she had lost her way. It had taken her much longer than she expected to arrive at *Ristorante di Fontana*.

The restaurant was already crowded, reminding her it was Friday. She glanced at the ornately carved clock in the window. It was past five o'clock. Slumping onto a chair, she was approached by Danielle, one of the young waitresses. "Do you have a reservation? I'm afraid we're fully booked this evening."

"Reservation?" Evie stammered, lowering her eyes to hide her panic. She had forgotten the name she was to ask for!

"Oh, it was such a long walk," she gasped. "My grandson is meeting me. He wanted me to take a taxi, but I told him I could walk. He made the reservation. Now, what is his name? He's my daughter's son, and I can never remember her married name. Oh, it is terrible to be old and forgetful... I'm sure it starts with an M."

"Matherson?" the helpful waitress asked, looking at the bookings.

"Matherson?" Evie repeated the name, trying it out to see if it was familiar. "Yes, I think it is Matherson." She prayed her old lady act would be sufficient to get her out of trouble if she was mistaken.

"Come this way." Evie slowly shuffled in Danielle's wake to a table in the newer part of the restaurant. She was now under the mezzanine floor where she had met Sebastian that fateful day.

As instructed she chose the chair that placed her back to the front window, but this meant she had no way of knowing if anyone approached her. Her heart leapt every time someone came near. Closing her eyes, she focused on slowly breathing in and out. She wanted it to appear she was dozing. This was not the first time today she had been forced to do this. She hoped she would not have to wait too long. She feared her weariness would betray her and she really would fall asleep.

Evie dozed. She relived again the nightmare of her abduction, but the fear was gone.

She remembered hearing the quiet footsteps that heralded her rescue. Her heart filled with a quiet assurance.

"Evie." She heard Piper softly calling her name.

"Evie!" he said more urgently, and this time Piper touched her arm. With a start, she sat up. Her wide eyes looked up to find Piper waiting for her to acknowledge him.

"Sorry," she whispered, and he silenced her with a stern look.

"Are you ready to go home?" Helping her to stand, he said more loudly. "Come on Grandma. I'd better take you back to your hotel."

He made his apologies to Danielle who hurried over when she saw they were leaving. "My old Gran isn't feeling well." Piper had his arm around her. He was reminding her to stay in character. He took her out the door and along the pavement. A car was waiting for them. Jenny was in the driver's seat.

"All clear," Jenny said. When Evie was buckled into her seat with Piper beside her, Jenny drove out into the traffic. It was peak hour now, and the darkened streets were jammed with cars. Jenny kept glancing in the rear-view mirror, but as they made their way steadily towards their destination, she seemed more confident.

"Why wasn't my father at the restaurant?" Evie asked Piper. "Why weren't any of my family there?"

"We dispatched them to *Romano*, to confuse anyone else looking for you. That is the only reason it was safe to send you there. We needed somewhere you knew how to get to on your own, while we got rid of the people who were trying to follow us."

"Why were people following you?"

"More than one rich reward has been offered for you, including one from the man who came up with this scheme."

"Nicholas?" Evie asked in confusion.

"Nicholas was just a pawn. Someone else made all the arrangements. That woman he was with was the bait that got him hooked. You're a very fortunate lady to have escaped from her clutches."

Evie shuddered. "How did you find me? Do I really have a microchip?"

"That's a good idea," Piper said. "We could set up GPS tracking so we can always find you."

"Stop teasing her," Jenny chided him. "There is no microchip, but we had a tracker put in the boots you were wearing. We had GPS tracking set up on your phone, but Nicholas threw that out of the car."

"Unfortunately the second tracker had a limited range, so it proved useless. It only confirmed what we already knew – that you were in the room with Nicholas."

"So how did you find me?" Evie asked again.

Piper laughed at her persistence and reluctantly told her the truth. "We had a general area to search in and were getting nowhere. Suddenly Jenny insisted we stop because she liked the name above a café door."

"What name?"

"*The White Rose!*" Jenny said triumphantly, watching in the rear-view mirror as Evie's face lit up. Evie laughed and hugged herself with delight. God had pointed her rescuers in her direction.

"I told Jenny we were wasting our time, even after we found the car," Piper confessed. He reached into his pocket and pulled out the pendant she had lost in the initial struggle. "This is yours," he said and held it out to her. Taking it from his hand, Evie's smile grew broader. She had feared Sebastian's gift was lost forever.

"There were hundreds of rooms in that hotel, and we didn't have enough time to search every one of them—"

"So we sat in the café and waited for a miracle," Jenny interjected, and Piper shrugged. "We never expected Nicholas to walk into the café. He was the only one we'd already identified."

"How did you know about Nicholas?"

"Identifying Nicholas was the easy part. Someone managed to take a photo just as he threw you into the car. Working out how he got mixed up in this was harder. We'd been watching him but missed the significance of his new alliance with Jezebel. We still have no clues about the person who controls her. That man is known by many names, and no-one can give us a clear description of him. Jenny's sure he was wearing a disguise when he made contact with you the first time."

Evie gasped at this revelation, suspecting there was a lot more to the story.

"At the moment we're calling him X."

Jenny turned into the private car park where the side roller door to the *Romano* building was opened long enough for them to drive in. As it closed, it shut out the dark world. Evie remembered another promise, one where God said no-one could open a door that He had shut. She fervently prayed this promise was fulfilled in this place.

ಬಿ ✿ ಣ

When his agent called to report that Jezebel had vanished from the nature reserve, Loki was perplexed. A single high-heeled shoe was the only sign she had been there. How could she have disappeared? He looked at her phone on the seat behind him. Did she have a second phone? Had she called someone else to rescue her? Did she have something to do with the victim's disappearance? He dismissed these possibilities. He knew her too well, and the few times she'd lied to him he had recognised her deception. He was certain her outrageous behaviour outside the hotel was authentic. He was confident she had told him everything when questioned, and her terror in the bush had been genuine.

Driving around his familiar territory, Loki told his army to watch for Jezebel. He returned to his city hotel to wait for another message. His watchers at the hotel reported no sign of Evie. The police were still stationed at the *Romano* building, where the victim's family had arrived in great distress. He was assured the police were still actively looking for her.

Puzzling over how the victim had been spirited away roused his temper. Another hour passed. The darkness he had been waiting for brought him no satisfaction. One by one, his network of watchers told him they had nothing to report. He decided to deploy them for another purpose. He gave them directions that would place them at his disposal here in the city.

The next message came an hour after he returned to the hotel. Loki laughed when he saw it:

$10,000

Finding the cash at short notice would be easy, as he had ten times more in his closest hiding place. Why were these unknown people asking for so little when the ransom he was expecting was in the millions? A second message followed immediately, inflating his sense of self-importance.

This is a test. You could be useful to us.

Hastening into the night, Loki went to his hiding place. He extracted sufficient money to meet their demands. There were only two others who knew the location of this secure place, and he was confident no-one had followed him.

Jezebel was surprised when the car drove past the address she gave them and pulled up half a block away. The driver turned off the lights.

"What are you doing?" she asked the front seat passenger, who was clearly in charge.

"Your friend is on his way."

"What?" she exclaimed. The man held up his hand for silence. Prudently she obeyed him. He had given her the flight reservation details, confirmed electronically on his phone. She put her hand in her pocket. The reassuring paper was still there. She smiled in the darkness because she would be present when these men dealt with Loki.

When they allowed Loki to come and go without intercepting him, she puzzled over the game these men were playing.

"You're free to go," the man in the navy blue suit said to her after Loki drove away. Jezebel stepped out into the darkness, grateful to be alive and eager for revenge. Waiting in the shadows until the car departed, she slipped into Loki's building. She was delighted to find the bulk of his cash still hidden under a floorboard. She recovered a small carry bag from a closet. As she filled it with bundles of notes, she laughed because she was only taking what she was owed. She would go by taxi to the other locations and be on the plane to Sydney with enough cash to establish a new identity before Loki even thought to look for her.

She headed out into the night to complete the rest of her plan. Tomorrow she would be gone. Jezebel cursed Loki, vowing she would remember him no more.

₧ ☼ ⑓

The object of her anger was making his own vow. The next instructions from Loki's unknown correspondent confirmed his suspicions – the hostage had been moved to another room in the same hotel. The exchange would take place in the underground car park. Now he had the location, he would deploy his army and be able to retrieve his money after the exchange. He would make his antagonists pay for their disrespect.

One by one his soldiers confirmed their mobilisation. By the time he arrived, there would be more than fifty people ready to fulfil his ambitious plan. He was elated as he drove his car to the designated area and turned off the engine.

The overhead lights in this section of the car park weren't working. Loki scanned the half-light to confirm none of his colleagues was in plain sight. He was early but unconcerned when two dark figures came out of the elevator. They were walking directly towards him. Boldly he stepped forward to meet them.

"You have the money?"

"Where's the woman?"

"Follow us." They were halfway towards the elevator when a speeding car tore into the car park with blinding headlights. He jumped out of the way just in time, landing hard. Heavy footsteps heralded the arrival of more opponents. He was outnumbered. It was time to call in his reinforcements. With a practised whistle he gave the signal for them to attack. The shrill noise echoed around the concrete-lined space, bouncing off pillars, fading into silence. One of the men laughed, and the others joined in.

"No-one is coming to your rescue," a voice said from the darkness. "You helped us by summoning them here. There were still some we hadn't neutralised. Those who wouldn't see reason have been dealt with. Are you conceding defeat?"

Loki arose from the concrete and brushed himself down. He pretended to surrender. Suddenly he threw his bag at one of the men who was blocking his way. He managed to dodge past him, running towards the closest exit. The sound of heavy feet echoed through the car park. Loki was light and agile but his way was blocked. Belatedly, he realised there was no escape.

Yearning –
A Satisfied Promise

ॐ ☼ ☙

Psalm 90:14
Satisfy us in the morning with Your loving kindness,
so that we may rejoice and be glad all our days.

ॐ ☼ ☙

It was two weeks since her abduction. The bruise on her cheek had faded, but Sebastian had not relaxed his vigilance. There had been unwelcome media attention when she had not appeared at the final press conference. Her formal statement had been read, confirming her safe return. She had expressed her gratitude to the searchers with a final request for privacy. Intrusive attempts were made to contact her, and she was kept from public view.

That first evening, after the doctor confirmed she was unharmed, the police and everyone else went home. Sebastian sat with her all night, refusing to be parted from her. She had slept restlessly in his arms in the lounge room while he waited for news of the final outcome. Piper Maxwell came just before dawn. She awoke, but Sebastian had left her then. He went downstairs to spare her unsavoury details.

"I have dangerous enemies," he said soberly.

Evie looked at Piper, thinking of the man from Room 458, and she challenged him. "You have dangerous friends."

Since then, Sebastian had remained overly protective, refusing to allow her to leave the workshop without him. She pleaded with him for more freedom, and he made small concessions. Their shared Friday evening activities were now her choice, provided she accepted the presence of bodyguards.

Last night, two bodyguards waited outside a small restaurant while she talked to Sebastian about their wedding. Concerned about security, he wanted a small private gathering. Her family had made big plans and she didn't want to disappoint them. This wedding was supposed to be a celebration of their love, not a problem for him to minimise and control. He relented, even promising she could go shopping without him. She still needed to find a dress. She could also spend time with her family, provided she took her bodyguards. But only if she dedicated her weekends and evenings to him.

Every morning and evening, Sebastian put himself through strenuous routines in his well-equipped private gym. He said this was necessary to 'work off his frustrations'. His workouts had intensified since her recent adventure. On weekends he now allowed Evie to join him. He had bought her a rowing machine and a recumbent bike, both low to the ground so she couldn't fall.

This morning as she gently pedalled, she examined him closely. Their Saturday outing would include a visit to his tattoo artist. Stripped down to a pair of brief shorts, his tattooed torso was drenched with sweat. She wondered if he had any un-inked skin? He said some of the tattoos concealed scars from his prison experience. There was still so much about Sebastian she didn't know.

A few hours later, Sebastian drove them through an unfamiliar part of the city. Entering an alley adorned with graffiti, they approached a narrow door without a nameplate. They went upstairs to a bright and spacious artist's studio. This was unexpected. The colourful paintings on the walls and incomplete canvases stacked around the room were evidence this space was home to a talented artist.

A teenage girl with brilliant orange hair hurried to meet them. She wore ripped jeans and a green jumper slung low over one shoulder to reveal a colourful tattoo that would have been at home on one of the canvases. Evie stared at the girl's extensive piercings.

"Hey! You must be Romano. I recognise your artwork. My dad didn't tell me you were coming. I'm Zee." The girl turned and led them across the large room into a second studio. There were tattoo designs and photographs covering all the available space. A folding screen partially concealed a bed draped with a white sheet. Zee directed them towards strategically placed chairs. At the sound of their approach, a short thin man with greying hair turned to greet them.

"Hey, Romano!" he said enthusiastically. The pair punched fists and completed a greeting Evie couldn't follow. "Long time, no see! Still working those muscles to the max!"

Sebastian laughed and lightly thumped the other man on the shoulder. He turned to introduce Evie. "Michelangelo, this is Evie. As you can see she's a blank canvas."

Michelangelo walked around her, eyeing her speculatively, and Evie felt underdressed. Acknowledging her discomfort, Michelangelo suggested they sit down, and he turned thoughtfully to Sebastian. Zee brought over a sketchbook and handed it to her father.

"You only booked an hour?"

Sebastian responded by standing and removing his own shirt. "You talked me into leaving space so I could add a name if I ever fell in love. Evie and I are getting married, and I want to add her signature." Michelangelo nodded and signalled to Zee who passed him some sterilising wipes and a stencil pen. After preparing the area, he handed the pen to Evie.

"Write your name here." Michelangelo indicated a red section among the other design elements on Sebastian's chest. Evie blushed as she stepped close to Sebastian. He wrapped his arms around her. With one hand on his chest for balance, she wrote on his bare skin. When finished, she stepped back with relief. Michelangelo looked carefully at her handiwork, making fine adjustments to counter the wavy lines her embarrassment had left.

Zee passed Michelangelo a tattoo machine, and he began to permanently ink her name onto Sebastian's chest. Evie watched with fascination. She was surprised he showed no sign of discomfort because she had read the procedure was painful. While Michelangelo worked, the two men discussed people they had known and happenings since they last met. Evie discovered Sebastian had known Michelangelo in prison. He had helped the artist establish his studio in appreciation for past loyalty. In a few minutes, the process was complete.

Michelangelo looked at Sebastian speculatively. "And the remainder of your time?"

Sebastian pulled a piece of paper from his pocket and handed it to the artist. An unspoken message passed between them that increased her trepidation. "This is an idea I have for Evie. I know what I want but have no experience working with a woman's curves. I have promised to keep my hands to myself, so I haven't been able to practise."

"You have a specific placement in mind?"

"Just as I have her name on my chest, I want her to wear mine."

"I am not getting a tattoo on my chest!" Evie protested and jumped to her feet. Sebastian caught hold of her and gently pulled her back to her seat.

"It will be a discreet little tattoo that curves around the top of your breast," he said soothingly. "No-one but me will know it's there."

"There is nothing discreet about your name! My family will be with me when I get dressed for the wedding. My mother and my sister will see! I am not getting that tattoo before the wedding!"

"After the wedding, then?" he asked her slyly, and she was so surprised at his easy capitulation she nodded. He smiled knowingly and looked at Michelangelo. "Take your time refining my design. I have a couple of other ideas that would benefit from your expertise." He pulled more drawings from his pocket. "So Evie, what are you going to choose instead?" She stared at him, and Sebastian laughed at her. "I've seen the way you study my tattoos. I know you want one."

"Something tiny?" she said cautiously. How had he known she had always wanted a tattoo? "In a place where I don't have to take off my clothes for you to see it?"

She glanced around the room at the designs on display. "A tiny rosebud," she suggested, then noticing the body piercing cabinet she felt unexpectedly braver. "Can I have my ears pierced?"

The eagerness in her voice amused him. While Sebastian and Michelangelo looked at design suggestions, Evie went with Zee to choose her earrings. Thinking ahead to the wedding, she selected a pair of sparkling diamond studs. Zee reached into the cabinet and selected a pair of gold hoops. "No-one has just one pair. I can see you've had piercings before."

"A long time ago," Evie confessed. "I cried when all my jewellery was confiscated." Zee took her to a chair where she looked in a mirror. The teenager marked where the piercings would go. Evie glanced over to where Sebastian and Michelangelo were looking through a design book.

"You can always say no. Dad has to get you to sign a permission form."

"Sebastian is right. When I was younger, I wanted a tattoo. Now I can read his life story in his tattoos. They help me understand who he is. Sometimes I need reminding he loves me. This tattoo will help."

When Zee had finished both sets of piercings, she led Evie back to Sebastian who invited her to choose from two designs. "Which one do you like, and where do you want it to go?" He looked her up and down. Hastily she held out her right arm.

"On the inside of my wrist," she chose quickly. Another surprise awaited her. Instead of Michelangelo, Sebastian took hold of her arm. He prepared her inner wrist for the transfer before Michelangelo handed the machine to him. She pulled her arm away. Michelangelo laughed reassuringly. "You can trust him. Romano taught me all I know. He did his early tattoos himself, and only recruited me when he realised he couldn't complete his masterpiece on his own."

"Of course Michelangelo has the real talent. I just have stubborn determination. He can draw up your designs, but I'm going to be the one who does the work."

Cautiously, Evie relented, and Sebastian expertly applied ink to her inner wrist. She was surprised at the intensity of the pain, but he was patient. He waited each time she thought she could take no more. It was over much sooner than she expected. After the wrap was applied to the inflamed area, Evie went with Zee to look at the paintings in the main studio while Sebastian talked quietly with Michelangelo and then paid generously for his time.

When they returned to the car, Evie looked thoughtfully at her wrist. "I can't believe I did that."

He laughed and agreed with her. "I didn't think you would either. If you had only asked for the piercings, it would have been enough victory for me." Evie stared at him in disbelief, realising he had tricked her into being more courageous. Now she laughed with him.

$$\text{ʚ} \; \text{✧} \; \text{ɞ}$$

(Tuesday 22nd August)

The next week passed in a hectic blur of activity. Evie made several shopping trips with Marilyn, Sofia and Mama Rosa while her bodyguards patiently waited outside. Her companions were in agreement she should wear white. Whether she chose a fairytale ball gown or something much simpler caused greater debate.

Evie examined herself in the mirror, wearing a strapless dress that would have made Sebastian's suggested tattoo clearly visible. She imagined his response if she wore this to the wedding. Stepping from the change room, her companions' shocked facial expressions confirmed this dress was not for her. "If you wear that," Marilyn told her, "Seb will skip the wedding and go straight to the honeymoon."

"And your Papa will have a heart attack!" Mama added.

Finally, she made a choice everyone was happy with, and the dress was safely delivered to the restaurant.

ঙ ☼ ଓ

(Friday 25th August)

On the morning of the wedding, Sebastian knocked on her bedroom door and gave her the final rosebud. He took her in his arms and kissed her passionately. She was breathless and flushed when she pulled away from his embrace. The look on his face warned her intimacy between them might escalate.

"Just a few more hours," she reminded him, pushing him away to close the door so she could continue her preparations. The car taking her to the restaurant would be arriving in thirty minutes, and she wanted to be ready. They would spend the day apart.

When she arrived, she found her parents had prepared a special celebratory meal. Everyone was in high spirits. Sofia was busy organising the reception. The hours passed too quickly. The hairdresser and makeup artist came and went. Evie felt transformed. Guests were arriving for the Betrothal Celebration. Evie waited in the upstairs dining room with Marilyn and Lilly to keep her company. Dave and Sebastian were not expected until ten minutes before the official start.

Matilda had been running up and down the stairs keeping her up to date with all that was happening below. "He's here! He's early!"

Evie jumped up and then sat down again. She still hadn't put on her dress.

"How does he look?"

"Nervous. He keeps tugging at his bowtie and squirming in his tuxedo. If you hadn't told us it was custom made, I'd say it's too small for him. You chose the right accessories. That red disrupts the blackness of his outfit and makes him less intimidating."

"Nothing makes Seb less intimidating," Marilyn said wryly. "Go and get Mama Rosa. Then tell the photographer we're ready for her."

When her female relatives were all present to help her, Evie put on the long white skirt, a billowing rose-patterned lacy layer covering the sensuous under-skirt. Over the top, she wore the white beaded bodice laced tight. Finally, she held out her arms and put on the red outer garment with a scooped neckline designed to display her ruby pendant. The coatdress wrapped around her, fastening with a single button at the shoulder. It cinched at the waist with a sash, falling to the floor to conceal her bridal finery.

Evie's hair was piled high on her head with loose ringlet curls around her ears. Picking up her basket, Lilly bounced with excitement. The bridal bouquet and a white rose coronet were hidden under an abundance of rose petals. "Are you ready?" Mama asked. After each of them had embraced Evie her family slipped away.

"Are you ready?" Marilyn asked again. They prayed together, before sending Lilly down the stairs ahead of them. The little girl was giggling with excitement, for she was the signal for Benito to make a formal welcome. The Betrothal Ceremony was about to begin.

While he was speaking, Evie and Marilyn came down the stairs.

"Dear friends and honoured guests, it is my greatest pleasure on behalf of my wife Rosa and myself to bid you welcome. I would like to present to you my youngest daughter Maria Evangelina."

Evie stepped forward, and her father took her by the hand. She turned to face the crowd, glamorous in red. There were gasps of surprise from those who didn't know of her recent transformation. She smiled and gave a small curtsey.

"Two months ago, I introduced my youngest daughter to Sebastian Romano, the son of an old friend. Our two families have been linked for generations. Sebastian has been like a son to me these past five years."

Sebastian came forward to stand on the other side of Benito who embraced him enthusiastically.

"In keeping with family tradition, I call upon you all to witness the formal betrothal of my daughter to Sebastian. Their promise to each other will bind our families together for another generation. Please raise your glasses to Sebastian and Maria Evangelina."

The guests joined in the toast. When the cheers had died down, Benito stepped back. Sebastian reached out to take Evie's hand. "I thought you would wear white," he said softly, looking directly into her eyes.

"I am," she said with a cheeky smile and he looked at her again. "I thought you were going to kiss me," she said, drawing him closer.

He eagerly took her in his arms and kissed her as if they were alone. The guests cheered until Sebastian reluctantly pulled back so she could breathe. Evie was flushed with excitement and Sebastian grinned. He confidently reached out, undid the sash at her waist, unfastened the single button on her red dress and began to pull the concealing fabric away. Some of the audience cried out in shock at his boldness.

Benito raised his hands to indicate he would speak again. "As you can see, Sebastian is not a man used to waiting. It has been seven weeks since he asked permission to marry my daughter. Seven weeks since she promised herself to him. Sebastian told me he would wait seven weeks and not a moment longer for her to become his bride, so we'd better bring the wedding forward."

Pastor Edwards stepped out from among the crowd, as did Father Finnegan in his formal robes. Someone cheered. Sebastian reluctantly released her and walked across to stand with Dave. Marilyn collected Evie and drew her to the other side. Lilly danced across the room, delivering her flower basket to her mother in a shower of rose petals. The rose coronet was placed on Evie's head. Carefully removing the red coat, Marilyn revealed the wedding dress. Lilly presented her with the white rose bouquet.

The room went quiet. Sebastian and Evie stood facing each other, a metre apart. Her heart was beating rapidly as they waited for the formalities to begin. Father Finnegan addressed Evie. She automatically crossed herself and bobbed in greeting as she had done so many times. He took her by the hand and turned to the assembled guests.

"For twenty years I've watched over this young woman. I have seen her change from a lost and frightened child into a gentle cautious woman. I always believed she deserved more than the loneliness that seemed her destiny. When she met Sebastian Romano, the strength of his character broke through all her defences and set her free to love him. I believe the God of miracles has been at work to bring them to this moment. I pray a blessing on their union."

When he had finished praying, Father Finnegan led her to Sebastian and gave him her hand. The priest went to stand with her parents.

Pastor Edwards began speaking. "Honoured guests, friends and family of Maria Evangelina Fontana and Sebastian Paulo Calabrese Romano, we are gathered here this evening to witness the union in marriage of this man and this woman..."

Zenith –
A Promised Future

ॐ ☼ ೞ

2 Corinthians 3:7
Now the Lord is the Spirit,
and where the Spirit of the Lord is, there is freedom.

ॐ ☼ ೞ

It was the seven-week anniversary of their wedding. A black car pulled into the brightly lit forecourt of *Renaissance*. The exclusive nightclub was situated at the base of *Raphael Towers*. Before the uniformed doorman could move, a tall man in a dark suit sprang out of the front passenger seat and opened the rear door. Sebastian stepped onto the pavement, nodding to his friend Piper Maxwell who had chosen to be the lead agent of their security detail tonight.

Instinctively, Sebastian assessed the location. He scanned the milling crowd near the floodlit entrance, before turning to help Evie from the car. He was puzzled about this destination for their weekly Friday excursion. On the few occasions when they didn't go to her family's restaurant, she planned intimate little dinners in quiet restaurants. Tonight she had chosen one of the most spectacular destinations in the city.

To add to the intrigue, Evie asked him to wear his wedding tuxedo. He found it difficult to comprehend the intense longing he still felt whenever he was near her. This time tomorrow she would have been his lover for more nights than she had kept him waiting. With this realisation, his passion ignited.

As Evie prepared to alight from the car, he looked down at the red high-heeled shoes she was wearing. When had she purchased them and would she be able to walk in them? He admired the way they drew his attention to her slender legs. The white rose detail at the ankles of her fine black stockings reminded him even more of the promised intimacy at the end of the evening.

Taking Sebastian's hand, Evie stepped gracefully from the car. This evening she wore her long red coatdress belted tightly against the cool spring breeze blowing from the river. What might she be wearing underneath it?

Usually, she took delight in having him voice his approval as she dressed, but tonight she was unusually coy. She presented him with a new silk shirt to wear and then went to her old room to dress. She said she didn't want him to be distracted by her preparations. He felt uncomfortably constrained in the tight jacket but was wise enough to know dressing up for these weekly outings was one of her few pleasures. He was thankful she hadn't included a tie. This allowed him to leave the top shirt buttons open. A little discomfort wouldn't hurt him. Every other part of her life was dictated by strict security measures overseen by *Maximum Security*.

This reminded him of the greater respect he now felt towards Piper who was equally committed to Evie's security. Piper was standing on the footpath waiting for them to join him. Taking advantage of valet parking, Patrick Sims, who doubled as their driver, had surrendered the car keys and now stood beside Piper. Together this pair of dark-suited security agents made a formidable team. More than one passerby hesitated and stepped aside so Evie and Sebastian could walk unimpeded towards the revolving doors. They entered the exquisitely decorated foyer.

With a nod, Piper sent Sims up the stairs to the first-floor restaurant. Sims would check arrangements were in place for dinner and send a signal. Evie's eyes were wide with excitement at the unfamiliar sights and sounds. Sebastian could feel her trembling through her coat and held her tightly. He was even more convinced this evening must have some special significance for her. He vowed to rein in his growing impatience.

While she was looking forward to the evening ahead, this place reminded him of the few visits he had made to *Raphael Towers* six years ago. Piper had brought him to meet people who had power and influence in the city. They were the ones who had the capacity to make or break his post-prison plans. Piper wanted them to know the newcomer was no threat, nor was he a pawn with whom to play a wider game. Sebastian looked sideways at Piper who seemed to understand exactly what he was thinking.

Ꮽ ☼ Ꮸ

It was Piper who chose the location. Romano didn't know there was much more at stake here than keeping his pretty wife happy.

Evie had a regular appointment with Piper each week, to discuss her schedule. She impressed him with her obedient compliance, adjusting her lifestyle to patiently accommodate the restrictive requirements. Therefore it was alarming she should diverge from her confirmed schedule this week, making spontaneous decisions with little notice. Jenny's daily reports confirmed Evie's visit to a medical specialist in the city. She had been accompanied by Henderson's wife Marilyn, while her bodyguards remained outside the building.

Following the appointment, Evie immediately asked Piper to change her plans for this evening. She needed somewhere special but very public because she had important news to tell her husband without the risk he would overreact. He was renowned for his stoic public persona.

When Piper pressed her for more information, Evie suggested Romano's immediate response would be to activate a more stringent blanket of restrictions. She feared the loss of the little freedom she had. Her request presented Piper with an unexpected opportunity to bring Evie into a select arena where her presence could be noted.

Unable to get her to reveal her secret, Piper researched her movements. He came up with two scenarios. If his instincts were correct, Evie would become increasingly vulnerable. This made it prudent to remind the recent allies of their continuing protective role.

After her abduction, there had been clandestine meetings with the people who had dealt with Evie's abductors. Piper had appealed to old superstitions about divine providence. He had suggested many blessings would come to anyone who was clearly on Evie's side. Tonight's venue choice was the ultimate reminder. Whichever way the evening went, there would be people watching who would understand the significance and act accordingly to guarantee her safety.

Confirming Piper's suspicions, when Romano helped Evie out of her coat he revealed a stunning black lace dress with a very short skirt and a low-cut back. On anyone else, this would have been a spectacular dress. Piper knew how closely Evie guarded her public modesty. Such an overt display of her feminine charms was doubly significant. Everything about her tonight made a strong statement. Here was a woman who was confident in her ability to hold the affection of her man. Other diners glanced towards them, as Romano turned her around to better admire her outfit before taking her in his massive arms and kissing her.

ଔ ☼ ଔ

Allowing Sebastian just a few minutes of appreciation, Evie pulled away from her husband. She insisted they sit down to look at the menu. He reluctantly agreed. He remembered the day he purchased this dress for her and his advice she should save it for a special occasion. He moved his chair closer so he could keep his arm around her while she read.

"What do you want to eat?" she asked him lightly as if his response to her appearance was of little significance.

"Are you on the menu?"

"Not until much later, so behave."

"You decide." He ran his hand playfully up and down her arm. "I can't concentrate on anything now I've seen what you're wearing. Will you tell me what the special occasion is or do I have to guess?"

"I might tell you later, but only if you're good."

"It's very hard to be good," he laughed, kissing her again. He left her no reason to doubt his sincerity as he caressed her. "Can we skip dinner and go home now?"

Evie playfully slapped his hand. "This is my night, and I want a full dinner and dancing. Then I might let you take me home."

She turned her attention back to the menu, and he listened as she ordered an entree, main course and dessert for both of them. It promised to be a long evening. The drinks waiter came to take their order. She chose his favourite beer and a soft drink for herself. When Sebastian questioned her choice, she warned him she wanted to remain sober lest he persuade her to leave too soon. He laughed for she knew him too well. Realising his zealous approach was probably annoying, he activated his pre-wedding strategy to bring his runaway desire under better control.

While they ate their dinner, a small orchestra played. Some of the other patrons were dancing to the music. Only when Sebastian had finished eating what was left of her dessert, having also eaten much of her main course, did Evie remind him he must dance with her before she confided in him.

The lights in the dining room were turned down low, and the tempo of the music had slowed. Having taken off his jacket hours ago, Sebastian was less formally dressed as he followed her onto the dance floor. They had only danced in public at their wedding, and he felt awkward.

Evie smiled up at Sebastian, inviting him to hold her close. The silk fabric of his shirt made the touch of her gentle hands more sensuous. Together they swayed and he tried to remain focused on the rhythm of the music.

Sebastian's hand wandered to the bare skin on her lower back. How pleasing to have seen a small section of her third tattoo as she'd walked ahead of him. It was still incomplete, and he looked forward to adding more detail during their session tomorrow. He wanted to be reminded of her love for him whenever he looked at her.

The pair had been shuffling for about ten minutes when Evie spoke.

"I've been to see a doctor."

He stopped moving, taking a step back from her. Sebastian was shocked at this revelation, fear welling up in his heart. She placed both hands on his chest, leaned towards him to looking earnestly up at him.

"Marilyn took me to see her doctor because I wasn't sure what I should do. I didn't want you to worry, but for the past week, after you go down to the workshop, I've been throwing up my breakfast. I thought the eating disorder was back. But I was wrong."

Sebastian held her lightly and waited.

"I'm pregnant."

A wave of incredible joy swept over him. He picked her up and spun her enthusiastically around in a circle, before setting her back on her feet. He wrapped his arms around her and kissed her again. Some of the other dancers were watching the unfolding drama with growing curiosity. He looked towards Piper to make sure he was being vigilant.

But she wasn't finished speaking. She pushed him away from her so she could continue. "The doctor said we're having twins."

"Twins? Are you sure? Isn't it too early to tell?"

"I had a special kind of ultrasound yesterday."

"Twins!" he said softly, picking her up and tossing her high in the air. He caught her again as if she were no heavier than their flower girl, Lilly.

Then he realised the risk he had just taken with his unborn children and an urgent need to protect her dampened his mood. As he lowered her to the ground, he placed his hand over her flat abdomen. How long would it be before she showed signs of the growing life within her?

He looked up in alarm. The people around them were applauding and calling out their congratulations. Sebastian dragged her from the dance floor.

Piper was standing beside their table and shook his head when Sebastian declared his intention to leave immediately. Before he could argue, a waiter approached them with a magnum of expensive champagne. "Compliments of the Management," the waiter said, placing the ice bucket on the table. He left as quickly as he came. Sebastian looked from the bucket to Piper and then up to the balcony where he knew 'Management' held court over their establishment. Was this Piper's doing? What game was being played here?

"Did you know?" Sebastian asked with cold steel in his voice. He was offended his wife might reveal her news to her security detail before she told her husband.

"About the baby?" Piper asked with a cool smile, unperturbed by his friend's accusation. Instead, he began opening the champagne. "I guessed. There were only two reasons Evie would visit a gynaecologist and then be referred immediately for an ultrasound. The second reason I didn't want to contemplate."

The champagne cork popped and a surge of bubbles showered Evie and Sebastian.

"Your guess was off the mark," Sebastian retorted. "Not one baby but two."

Pouring the champagne into three glasses Piper raised his glass to make a toast. "Congratulations, Evie. A double blessing to show that fortune favours you."

"Thanks," Evie said with a shy smile. "But the praise belongs to God. He always keeps His promises."

"Two babies?" Piper said again. Sipping his champagne, he looked as if he was already working out new security measures to accommodate this growing family. "Drink. Our host is watching. When people discover Evie is carrying twins..."

ଞ ✿ ଔ

Looking from Piper to Sebastian, Evie brought her champagne glass to her lips. The two men were talking strategies. They seemed to have forgotten her presence. She refilled her companions' glasses. If she was careful, neither of them would realise she was only pretending to drink. The doctor had given her a long list of prohibitions, but Piper had said it was important not to offend the powerful people up on the balcony. Piper said they couldn't leave until the champagne was finished.

Lord, You know I'm thankful You have blessed us, but this will bring change. He's so excited about becoming a father. But I've only just grown used to being the object of his affection, and he loves them so much already.

Evie entertained herself by watching the couples on the dance floor. She tried to decide which couples had been together for a long time and who might be in a new relationship. How ignorant she was about romance! She had intentionally dressed in a provocative way to assure herself impending motherhood increased rather than lessened her value as a woman. Now she would have to guard the hope that her husband's love for her was stronger than his desire to protect his children.

Glancing sideways, Evie found herself torn between the devotion she felt towards Sebastian and increasing melancholy. She refilled the men's glasses again, before realising she urgently needed the restroom. Quickly she stood and signalled to Sims who was standing nearby. Sebastian looked up in alarm, and she reassured him.

ଞ ✿ ଔ

Taken by surprise at her sudden departure, Sebastian watched her walk away. He noted again the fine fabric of her skimpy dress clinging to her hips and the seductive hint of that tattoo. He saw other eyes turning in her direction. As he watched, Sims politely offered Evie his arm, to guide her through the milling crowd near the entrance. Seeing Evie leaning on another man for support brought Sebastian to his feet. Turning to Piper, he discovered his friend's attention drawn to an approaching messenger. Piper delivered an unspoken warning, a reminder that Sebastian's reputation was at stake.

"Come," the man in the suit said, and turned to lead the way upstairs. Sebastian went cold inside. Piper had assured him that the powerful organisation who owned this establishment had agreed to leave him alone in return for uncovering Loki's criminal organisation.

ଓ ☼ ଔ

When Evie returned with Sims from the restroom, there were three women seated at her table. Two were young and exquisitely beautiful, but her attention was captured by the woman who sat between them. There was something familiar about this ancient woman dressed all in black. She reminded Evie of the group of women who sat at the front of the cathedral in Sydney, where she had attended Mass with Nonna and Zietta Maria.

"Maria Evangelina," the matriarch said and gestured for her to sit down. Evie cautiously obeyed, after glancing to Sims for confirmation. She prayed fervently for wisdom.

"I am Doña Gabriella Marcella, and this is my great-granddaughter Gina and my grandson's wife Sara. I have waited a long time for this meeting. You have changed since you were in Sydney."

Sara indicated Evie should pick up her glass of champagne, which was still almost full.

"I knew your grandfather from my childhood – a foolish boy who was the son of my cousin. He brought ruin and shame to his family. Though we cut him off, I still had an interest in how his wife and children fared after his death. Your parents did well to escape Maria's bitter recriminations, but then they sent you to her. Father Finnegan became your advocate, assuring me you had not played the harlot. I acted to secure your future, without alerting Maria to my interest. You proved yourself honest and virtuous. I was satisfied you could restore the family honour. Then you stopped coming to Mass when your Nonna died."

Evie silently acknowledged the reprimand, stunned to learn the reason for her changed fortune in Sydney.

"I kept my interest private, which is why no-one informed me you were here. I would have made sure they understood who you were to me. Romano has done well in securing your affection." Evie shuddered and was thankful he could not hear this older woman's disdain. "I am here to celebrate my daughter-in-law's birthday. Only because my son showed interest in your husband did I recognise you. Congratulations on the blessed news you are with child." The three women each raised a glass and toasted her. She took a tiny sip from her own.

"Thank you. God has indeed been very kind to me. He has given me a new life, a loving and protective husband, and now I'm to be the mother of twins."

Evie watched with interest the glances passing between her guests at this revelation.

"Ah!" the elderly woman declared with satisfaction. "You have indeed been blessed, which brings me to my purpose. Sara has been unable to fall pregnant, despite every effort. I would like you to bestow a blessing on her."

Startled at this unexpected request, Evie glanced sideways at the younger woman. "Why are you asking me this?"

"My son informed me anyone who has turned their hand against you has paid a penalty. Those who have helped you have increased their fortune. My family has been actively aiding your husband in keeping you safe, and now I want a favour in return."

Humbled that God would put her in a position where she could minister His grace into a serious situation, Evie spoke to them about God's compassionate mercy for all who would surrender their ambitions and submit to His authority. After a few minutes, she reached out her hand to the supplicant and prayed aloud the blessing God spoke to her heart.

When she finished, the women thanked her and arose from the table. They left her to wait for Sebastian's return.

ଅଓ☼ଔ

Sebastian watched from the balcony. His stony countenance masked the turmoil in his mind. His beloved was enduring this trial alone! Then he was reminded she was never on her own because God was her true defender and protector. Did Sebastian believe his strategies were the reason she had been delivered from the hands of her enemies? His instincts told him something significant was unfolding before him. Now he prayed she would listen to God and be wise in her response.

Doña Gabriella Marcella returned to the upper level, and everyone deferentially waited. She turned her cunning eyes to Sebastian. "You were wise to claim Maria Evangelina, and God has blessed you. Be confident no-one from this family will raise a hand against you. Your enemies are our enemies. In return for her protection, God will bring peace between your family and mine. This covenant will bring many blessings to us all."

Dismissed, Sebastian forced himself to walk slowly. His eyes were fixed on his wife. Piper talked about the significance of what had just occurred. A covenant of protection guaranteed freedom for Evie and unexpected security for his unborn children. Sebastian was no longer concerned, wanting only to have her in his arms again. But caution warned him he was still being closely observed.

When he arrived back at their table, Piper left him. Sebastian sat down, placing one arm around Evie. He gazed thoughtfully at her for several minutes before emptying the champagne magnum into his glass.

"Do you know who that woman was?" Evie asked, and Sebastian nodded. "She claims to have protected me in Sydney, and she came asking for a favour."

"What kind of favour," he asked cautiously.

"She wanted me to bestow a blessing on her grandson's wife, who has been having trouble conceiving. I tried to tell the old woman that God is responsible for my good fortune, but she wouldn't listen. Then when I told her I was having twins, she offered me and my family a covenant of protection. But you already know that don't you?"

"Piper has spread the rumour that you have miraculous powers," Sebastian told her. Watching her response carefully, he continued.

"Do you remember telling me that I have 'dangerous friends'? I have lain awake at night worrying about what you would say if you knew the truth. Ever since I arrived in Melbourne, I have been under pressure to form a criminal alliance. When I resisted all offers, they turned to threats and intimidation. That's when Piper got involved. He approached me and offered to take over my security arrangements. He mediated a truce, built on an exaggerated account of my violent past."

Evie met his gaze unflinchingly. He continued.

"I never expected to call upon my enemies for help, but Piper insisted the people who abducted you would have to be punished. Otherwise, everyone would know my weakness, and you would be in more danger. I wanted them to pay for your torment, so I went along with his plan. Tonight I found out that Piper has kept me in the dark about what he has been up to. But all his scheming has come to nothing, and delivered you into the greatest danger of all."

"But God is watching over me," Evie insisted. "You don't need to worry about keeping me safe."

"That is what God said. I stood on the balcony while you were with that woman, and God asked me what I thought I could do to protect you. He reminded me that He had been taking care of you despite all my efforts, and that I should leave you safely in His hands. Once I accepted that, it felt as if a great weight had lifted off me."

Evie took a deep breath and responded earnestly. "I've been worried that you might change towards me because I'm pregnant. You pulled me from the dance floor, and I thought my new life was over. Listening to you plan for the future made it seem my only value now was as the mother of your children."

Ashamed his response had inspired this feeling, Sebastian tightened his embrace. He had missed her need for reassurance and considered how to respond.

He finished his drink, then took the glass from her hand and drained it. Having identified the real problem, he knew immediately what should be done. Gently he led her back to the dance floor.

"I thought you wanted to go home and talk with Piper about security," she reminded him, as he wrapped his arms around her.

"There is plenty of time for that," he murmured as his hand brushed against her bare skin. "Now I want to remind you how much I love you until you're the one who is desperate for us to leave." As they settled into a rhythm with the music, he kissed her again and became bolder with his caresses. "Your new life isn't over. It has only just begun."

Character List
Fontana Family (Melbourne)

Maria Evangelina Fontana (35) AKA Ria and Evie -
  Benito & Rosa's youngest daughter
  Sofia's sister
  Leonardo, Matilda and Marco's aunt
Sofia Fontana (38) - Maria's elder sister
Leonardo Fontana - (19) Sofia's eldest son
Matilda Fontana (16) - Sofia's daughter,
Marco Fontana (13) - Sofia's younger son
Benito Fontana, AKA Papa - Maria and Sofia's father
Rosa Fontana, AKA Mama Rosa - Maria & Sofia's mother
Nicholas - Sofia's ex-husband, Leonardo's father
Ristorante di Fontana - Benito & Mama Rosa's restaurant

ഇ ☼ ൠ

Romano Family and Associates

Sebastian Paulo Calabrese Romano (44)
  AKA The Boss, Seb, Romano
  Paul Romano's son
  Constance Romano's nephew
  owner of *Romano* automotive workshop
Paulo Calabrese Romano (dec) - Sebastian's father
Constance Calabrese Romano (dec) - Sebastian's aunt
Dave Henderson - Romano's Business partner
Marilyn Henderson - Dave's wife
Alex Henderson (17) - Dave & Marilyn eldest son
Rory Henderson (8) - Dave & Marilyn younger son
Lilly Henderson (5) - Dave & Marilyn's daughter
Fifi and Tiny - Guard dogs at *Romano*
Jenny Prescott - *Maximum Security* operative
Patrick Sims - *Maximum Security* operative
Piper Maxwell - owner of *Maximum Security*
Michelangelo - Romano's friend, tattoo artist
Zee - Michelangelo's daughter

Sydney Characters

Father Finnegan - Catholic priest, Maria Evangelina's friend
Zietta Maria Gallo - Rosa Fontana's twin sister
Nonna Gallo (dec.) - Rosa Fontana & Zietta Maria's mother
Nero Gallo (dec) - Nonna's husband, Rosa & Maria's father
Mr Williams - Ria's long term employer
Doña Gabriella Marcella Horatio (92) - Ria's Sydney patron

ഌ ☼ ൠ

Additional characters

Caprice Agency - employment agency
Freddie Kidman- *Romano* employee
Avril - *Romano* employee
Danielle - employee at *Ristorante di Fontana*
Officer McCormick- police officer
Officer Ricardo Vitali - police officer
Gaylene - nurse
Nancy - nurse
Pastor John Edwards - Ria's friend
Jezebel - works for Loki
Loki - criminal mastermind
Gina - to Doña Gabriella Marcella's great-granddaughter
Sara - Doña Gabriella Marcella's grand-daughter-in-law

Timeline

June 5   Ria's nephew starts working for Romano

June 12   Ria arrives in Melbourne

June 30   (Chapter 1) Ria and Romano meet

July 1   Ria's job interview

July 2   Ria is in hospital and changes her name to Evie

July 7   Romano takes charge of Evie's situation

July 8   Evie discovers she is being followed

July 9   Evie's family respond to Romano's plans

July 31   An old enemy visits Evie

August 4   Evie is missing

August 25   Evie's Betrothal Celebration

October 13   An announcement over dinner

Acknowledgements

This book could not have been written without the support and encouragement of many people.

Firstly, I am grateful to God for giving me the inspiration, the time and the persistence to bring this story into life.

My writing adventure has not been a solitary one. God provided me with a supportive team - determined to ask the right questions, demand the next instalment and keep me moving forward. Thanks to Gillian Perrett, Naomi McGlone, Glenda Charles, Donna Bullen, Tim Berry, Belinda McGuire and Lisa Haynes for your help with *White Rose of Promise*.

A special thanks to Belinda Pollard, publishing mentor and editor, for taking me under her wing and for the professional advice that has helped make this book better than I could have imagined.

Last but not least, to my patient husband Tony for his constant encouragement and ongoing support.

Chrissy

A Note From the Author

Greetings from Tasmania, Australia.

Thank you for reading my book. I hope you enjoyed it. If you are able, please leave a brief Goodreads or Amazon review, as this will help other readers find my work.

If you would like to receive updates on my progress with other books in the **River Wild Series**, please visit www.chrissygarwood.com and complete the form. Links to social media can be accessed from my webpage.

Publishing a novel was a childhood ambition, one that I set aside a long time ago. Since then, I have added wife and mother, student, childcare educator, visual artist and chaplain to my list of achievements. To help me appreciate the brighter moments, God has guided me through dark days in the wilderness, where my faith has been tested.

I have learned a lot about myself and my ambitions while writing this book. The confidence I have gained as a storyteller has enriched my character. I believe it has made me a humbler disciple of Jesus Christ, a more determined encourager, a better friend.

When I first lost myself to the rediscovered joy of writing, my horizons expanded. My fictional world became populated with characters who whispered their stories to me.
This was how The River Wild series was born.

Chrissy

Book 2 Coming Soon

When Promises Are Broken

A family curse, an evil plot, an unlucky coincidence.
Three destinies entwined.
Sofia sits in angry isolation at the wedding reception,
unspoken secrets and broken promises her only
consolation. No-one will listen, and now it is too late.
Her innocent sister has married a very bad man.
Pastor John Edwards is puzzled by Sofia's animosity.
Her emotional outburst drives him to prayer. When a
sinister stranger warns him to keep his distance, he
wonders if it is already too late.
Valentino makes clear what he wants from Sofia. He is
rich, handsome and available. So why does she
question his motives and reject his advances? He
laughs at her assertion that trouble pursues her, but
then he disappears...

Other books in the series scheduled
for publication in 2020

Book 3: What Price My Freedom?
Book 4: Which Promise This Time?